# THE SHADOW THRONE

THE ASCENDANCE TRILOGY
BOOK THREE

# THE
# SHADOW
# THRONE

## JENNIFER A. NIELSEN

SCHOLASTIC PRESS · NEW YORK

Library of Congress Cataloging-in-Publication Data

Nielsen, Jennifer A.,
The shadow throne / Jennifer A. Nielsen. — First edition.
pages cm. — (The ascendance trilogy : book three)

Summary: Young King Jaron has had nothing but trouble with his advisors and
regents since he ascended the throne of Carthya, and now King Vargan of Avenia
has invaded the land and captured Imogen — and Jaron must find some way to
rescue her and save his kingdom.

ISBN 978-0-545-28417-2 (jacketed hardcover) 1. Kings and rulers — Juvenile
fiction. 2. Rescues — Juvenile fiction. 3. Battles — Juvenile fiction. 4. Adventure
stories. [1. Kings, queens, rulers, etc. — Fiction. 2. Rescues — Fiction. 3. Battles
— Fiction. 4. Adventure and adventurers — Fiction.] I. Title. II. Series: Nielsen,
Jennifer A. Ascendance trilogy ; bk. 3.

PZ7.N5672Sh 2014
813.6 — dc23
2013021841

10 9 8 7 6 5 4 3 2 1          14 15 16 17 18
Printed in the U.S.A.          23

First edition, March 2014
Book design by Christopher Stengel

*To Pat and Barry,*

*whose warm hearts encircle the finest of families,*

*and brought me in with cookies, hugs,*

*and a landing on a cliff.*

# THE
# SHADOW
# THRONE

# · PROLOGUE ·

In my life, I'd had my share of fights, sometimes with fists, sometimes with knives, occasionally with a sword. I'd faced opponents twice my size, twice as mean, and, as a general rule, uglier than I ever hoped to be. But nothing had ever topped the ferocity of the argument now going on in the center of my great hall.

"Bringing you to this castle was the greatest mistake of my life!" I yelled. My fists were curled so tightly into balls that it felt as if my nails might pierce my skin. "And I would order your hanging right now, except that your neck isn't worth the price of the rope!"

The target of my threat was none other than Roden. In the few short months we had known each other, he and I had been through a lot together, including him trying to kill me twice — three times if we counted the broken leg — and me risking my life to convince him to come back to Carthya as the captain of my guard. Obviously, we'd had our share of disagreements. But none were half so loud as this current argument.

"I would gladly die," Roden yelled back, "if the order came from less of a fool for a king!"

Gasps echoed around the hall at the insult. Words like that easily justified my ordering Roden's arrest, but I didn't. There were too many things that still needed to be said, or yelled, if necessary.

"Do you think your position as captain makes us equals?" I asked. "You may command our armies but you do not command me! And I will lead them my own way!"

Roden pointed down at my right leg, which the surgeon had ordered to remain tightly wrapped for at least another few weeks. "You can't lead anything on a broken leg."

"Then maybe you shouldn't have broken it!" I said.

"I should've broken your jaw instead," Roden countered. "Then I wouldn't have to listen to your ridiculous orders!" There were more gasps from the regents in the room and the passing servants, and he appealed to them to continue the argument. "Our soldiers are scattered throughout this country. If Avenia invades from the south, they will crush us."

My high chamberlain, Lord Kerwyn, hurried toward us and in hushed tones said, "My king, could we continue this conversation in the privacy of the throne room? Everyone is listening."

Yes, they were. Not only those who had been in the room when it started, but many others who had heard the yelling and come to see the commotion for themselves. Kerwyn may have felt embarrassed for me, but I had no intention of making this private.

I stepped back from Kerwyn and said, "There's nothing to continue, Lord Kerwyn. The captain of my guard thinks I should have no say in the way my armies are trained."

Kerwyn looked at Roden, clearly appalled by his disrespect, but Roden only tightened the muscles on his face.

"We all bow to the king's will, Captain. So must you." Kerwyn's scolding tone was so sharp, Roden actually flinched.

But before Roden could speak, I said, "No, Kerwyn. I won't have him bow to me and secretly insist he's in the right." Then to Roden, I said, "If you think you can train our men better, then I dare you to do so. Take whomever you wish, train them in whatever way you want. Then we'll compare our two groups. You'll see I'm right."

"Never!" Roden yelled. "I'll begin training in the courtyard at once."

"Not in my courtyard, or even in my city!" I retorted. "If you do this, you will leave Drylliad. Leave with all your arrogance and high hopes, and come back when you finally understand your place."

Kerwyn put his hand on my arm. "Jaron, I beg you to think of what you're saying. You two must make peace. You are still injured, and if war is truly coming, then we need your captain here."

I only brushed off his hand and leaned in to Roden, then hissed, "Get out."

Roden stared back with an anger so fierce, it worried me. Then he announced that within the hour, he would leave, taking forty of the men who had been assigned to him. Despite the things we had said to each other, I hoped he would go with only the best of luck.

I watched him leave, and then stared around at all those who had gathered to watch our exhibition. They were trusted members of the court, servants, and citizens of my country. And quite possibly, at least one of them was here as a spy for our enemies, who would now report that the armies of Carthya were broken and divided.

Ever since the day I returned from the pirates, Carthya had begun making preparations such as had not been seen in a generation. We were storing up food, forging weapons, and building our defenses, but for all that, the thing I needed most would be the hardest to get: time.

As it turned out, we had even less time than I'd expected. Only three short weeks later, the war would begin. . . .

# · ONE ·

I received news of the attack on Libeth at sunset while standing on a wide grassy field near the castle walls. Facing me were Kerwyn, Amarinda, and Mott, but I barely saw them. Libeth was a peaceful town, long insulated from the troubles that had plagued other settlements near Avenia. Its citizens were the families of farmers and traders, and the raid certainly would've come without enough warning for even the strongest to form an adequate defense. I couldn't begin to comprehend the horror of what they'd faced in the night, the destruction left to them now. The thought of it sucked the breath from me.

And, there was more. Imogen had been taken during the attack.

Everyone seemed to be talking at once, none of them realizing that my head was swarming with questions that no one here could answer. Did we know if she was still alive? If so, had she been harmed? What would they do to her if they thought it could hurt me? For that was surely the reason King Vargan had sent his armies after her.

If Imogen was still alive, then Avenia would seek our total surrender in exchange for her return. They would know I couldn't grant that, so I would have to attempt a rescue. She was nothing but bait to them, and I, their prize.

Beyond that, the war I'd been anticipating for several months had finally arrived. But everything I had so carefully planned seemed irrelevant now. So little of this news was what I'd expected. And Kerwyn was steadily making it worse.

"We've also just received word that Gelyn and Mendenwal are advancing from the north and east," he said. "This was a coordinated attack and we are surrounded. Jaron, the war has begun."

They all returned to talking again, but I couldn't hear any of it, or at least, I couldn't separate one word from another. It was impossible to comprehend what they wanted from me.

Amarinda touched my arm. "Jaron, you've gone pale. Say something."

I stared at her without seeing and began back-stepping. "Forgive me," I mumbled. Then I turned and ran, led blindly by some force inside me that had to get away. I needed a place to think, to understand. Somewhere to breathe.

I sprinted toward the castle, only vaguely aware of the sharp pain that still came to my right leg whenever I worked it too hard. The broken bone from Roden remained soft, and yet

I pushed myself faster. If anything, I wanted to feel the pain, to give my panicked emotions somewhere to go.

Servants and soldiers were blurs beside me as I ran. I wasn't sure where I was going, or what I hoped to find there. Only one thought remained locked in my mind, that Imogen had been taken. And they would demand everything for her return.

I soon ended up in the King's Gardens, the one place I could be alone. Hoping to hide myself on a ledge, I tried climbing the vines of the castle wall. Up there I could think. With enough time, I could piece together this disaster into a world that made sense again. But I wasn't even halfway up the lowest wall before the muscles of my weaker right leg failed me and I fell back to the ground. I rolled into a sitting position and leaned against the wall, but made it no farther.

Maybe it had been a mistake to come to the gardens. I'd find no more answers here than anywhere else. As I looked around, the walls loomed over me. It was dizzying, and I couldn't put any single idea in front of the other. Instead, the worries, plans, and choices all swirled around me like smoke, suffocating me just the same.

"Your Majesty, forgive me for invading your privacy."

I stood when I saw that Harlowe had come. After bowing, he walked forward.

"I thought it'd only be Avenia that attacked," I said. "Maybe Gelyn too, but not Mendenwal. And not this way."

"None of us saw that coming."

"There's no reason for Vargan to attack Libeth. Destroying that town gave him nothing." Images of the horrors that must have occurred that night came again to my mind. "Nothing except Imogen."

"I know." Harlowe licked his lips, and then added, "We must have your orders, sire."

"What orders?" I yelled. It was irrational to be angry, especially with him, but I couldn't help it. "I can't fight this! I don't have a plan for anything this big. I couldn't even protect *her*. She should've been safe, away from me." My eyes widened as I gulped in a breath that wouldn't release. "I can't . . . can't —"

Harlowe put an arm on my shoulder and pulled me to him. He'd hugged me this way once before, sensing my fears on the eve of going to the pirates. It was the embrace of a father to a child, and I needed that comfort again.

Despite all my planning, the thought that war was now upon us terrified me. My father had seen a few battles in his youth, before he took the crown. In a small way, I began to understand his dread of conflict. Maybe it wasn't weakness that kept him from standing up to our enemies' demands, as I had always thought. Perhaps it was simply that he'd already paid the price of war.

There would be a price if Carthya fought back this time; there always was. I had a good idea of what it might cost me, but our options were failing. As long as I had enough strength to wield a sword, I would not accept Carthya's defeat.

Harlowe held me until I drew back, with a clearer mind and a resolve that if Carthya was surrounded by enemies and had no chance of victory, then at least we would make a spectacular end of it.

"All right," I said to Harlowe. "I will present my plans in one hour. Gather everyone who needs to be there."

# · TWO ·

Kerwyn sat on my right in the throne room, and Amarinda was on my left. Beside them at the wide table were Harlowe and Mott, and also Tobias, who was supposedly there to help represent the regents. In truth, he had been with me since I had taken the crown, and I wanted his advice. Beyond that, I didn't want anyone else here. Not until we had decided on a firm course of action.

At my request, Kerwyn leaned forward to begin. "Avenia has moved in from the west and will have thousands of men at their call. They will fight hard and without mercy, and because of that, they are the greatest danger to Carthya. Our spies also tell us there is movement from the soldiers of Gelyn. We must stop them from overtaking our northern border. The cavalry of Bymar can help us hold them back."

"*If* Bymar comes," Amarinda said. "My country will answer, but only if we find a way to tell them what's happening here."

"We must also consider Mendenwal," Mott asked. "They have yet to attack, but our spies are certain King Humfrey has ordered his armies into Carthya."

I hadn't expected Mendenwal to be a part of the attack. Of the three countries surrounding us, Mendenwal was the most civilized, least aggressive, and had the longest tradition of diplomatic relations with Carthya. King Humfrey and I had a bit of a history, however — I had cut his thigh years ago after challenging him to a duel. But that was hardly reason to go to war. Besides, he'd deserved it.

Kerwyn was probably taking this news harder than anyone. He and Humfrey had seen a lot together over their years and almost could have been considered friends. Having Avenia as an enemy was bad enough, but Mendenwal worried me as much. Carthya could not withstand the full force of Mendenwal against us, even if they were the only aggressor we faced.

I pressed my lips together and looked at Kerwyn. "Why Mendenwal? Is it because my father lied to them? Or something more?"

"I have sent him letters of apology and explanation," Kerwyn answered. "All have been ignored."

"We can't afford to have them as an enemy. Mendenwal's armies are three times the size of Avenia's."

"But they can be reasoned with," Tobias said. "They're not bloodthirsty like Avenia, or hungry for our gold, like Gelyn."

Perhaps so, but something had drawn them into this war, and I didn't know what. I turned back to Kerwyn. "Can you get King Humfrey to come here?"

"How? If he won't answer my letters —"

"You'll have to travel to Mendenwal and remind him of your friendship." I hated to ask so much. It was a long journey and we seemed to be enemies now. "It'll be risky."

For some reason that prompted a smile from him. "If I've learned anything from you, sire, it's how to take a risk."

"Thank you, Kerwyn." With that settled, I turned to Mott. "You and I must attempt a rescue of Imogen. We'll find the camp near Libeth where they're holding her, then —"

"No."

I did a double take. "What?"

He didn't flinch. "No, Your Majesty. *I* will attempt a rescue. *I* will go there alone, or accompanied by an entire regiment of your soldiers if you prefer. But *you* will not be anywhere near the Avenian camp."

"Yes, I will!" I often wondered if Mott had made it his life's mission to oppose me. If so, he should feel very good about his success. I suspected if I chose something as unimportant as wearing a gray coat for supper rather than a blue one, he'd find a reason to argue about that too.

"They're expecting you to rescue her," he said. "This is a trap."

"Do you think I haven't considered that?"

"I think you've escaped some tight situations in the past and believe you can do it again this time. But it's different now. They know you and they'll prepare for your tricks. If you enter that camp, you will not leave it alive."

I stood, shaking my head ferociously. "If they're watching for me, then you're no safer going in there."

"It's a risk I'm willing to take."

"But I'm not!" I yelled. "You will not fall into a trap meant for me! You will not die for me!" There hadn't been a word from Roden since I'd sent him away three weeks earlier. For all I knew, he was gone. And now, perhaps Imogen too. The thought of something happening to another of my friends terrified me. If he really understood that, then he would stop arguing and let me have my way.

In the face of my frustration, Mott managed to remain calm. He licked his lips and said, "My first duty is to you, Jaron, and I will gladly go in your place. But your first duty is to this country. Not to her."

That only made me angrier. "Do not lecture me about duty! What else have I done in life but my duty? I disappeared in the name of duty and returned for the same reason, and I will fight this war because it is my duty to do so. No matter how I wished to do otherwise, each time duty presented itself, I answered. But not this time. I am coming with you!"

Silence fell in the room. From the corner of my eye, I saw Amarinda lower her head, and I immediately regretted my words. My betrothal to her was a duty as well.

Tobias cleared his throat to get our attention, and then said, "Mott is right. Jaron, you should call Roden to come back. Send him to Libeth instead."

At the mention of Roden's name, everyone grew quiet again. Ever since our argument, I had refused to have any public discussion of Roden. Tonight would be no different.

"Roden can have no part in Imogen's rescue," I said stiffly.

That should have been the end of it, but Tobias pressed further. "Whatever fight the two of you had, he's still the captain of your guard. If we're at war, you've got to call him back."

Thankfully, Mott intervened for me. "If Roden were ready to lead, he would never have left us. Let Jaron be."

I took a deep breath before continuing. "The last question is how to protect the princess. They took Imogen because she was easy prey. We will not risk Amarinda."

Her eyes widened as if she had not considered that she was in personal danger too. She glanced over at Tobias, who gave her a grim smile, then her attention returned to me.

"I want to keep the fighting away from Drylliad," I said. "But if they know you're here, this castle will become their top priority. You must leave to someplace safer."

"She could go to Farthenwood," Tobias suggested. "We could hide her in the secret passages if necessary."

"I'd rather go home to my family in Bymar," Amarinda said. "Someone needs to bring their armies to the border of Gelyn to fight. They will listen to me better than anyone else."

"But you can't get to Bymar without crossing through either Gelyn or Avenia," I said. Neither was a safe route.

Without flinching, she answered, "I must go. The fastest route is through Avenia, where I could get a ship from Isel.

Perhaps with an escort of soldiers, I can sneak through safely."

I smiled back at her. She was braver than I had given her credit for, and she was right: Bymar would answer her call without hesitation.

"Any escort strong enough to protect you is sure to draw attention," Kerwyn warned. "And once you're in Avenia, you'll stand out even further."

"I agree." Mott leaned forward and clasped his hands. "Unfortunately, my lady, you'll be safer with the quietest possible escort."

"Well, that's me." Tobias said it matter-of-factly, as if he had finally accepted what everyone already knew — that he would never be a warrior. Then he added, "Nobody would believe I was all you sent to protect a princess. Jaron, we could use the escape carriage."

Late one night, when we were both too tired for any rational thought, Tobias and I had begun a discussion. It was born out of a joke for how I might one day slip back to Avenia for an afternoon on the beach, and at best was completely ridiculous.

"What's the escape carriage?" Amarinda asked.

"It's designed to look like a church wagon bringing charity for the sick and poor," Tobias said. "It will appear to be carrying only food and supplies, but there's a hidden compartment below it where we can hide, if necessary."

I shook my head. "It was a joke, not an actual plan for escape. It's not safe enough."

"There are higher priorities than safety," Amarinda said.

"Not for you," I said sternly.

"When has your safety ever been a priority in protecting Carthya?" she countered. "Am I fit for nothing but decoration on your arm? We must get word to Bymar, and I am the best one to deliver it."

"You and Tobias? Alone in Avenia?" That was absurd.

"The carriage isn't a joke," Tobias said. "I designed it, and I built it."

I turned to him. "When?"

"While your leg recovered. I wanted to prove it was possible." Tobias leaned forward. "Nobody could look at it from the outside and know it has a false floor. It will protect her. *I* will protect her."

Everything in me fought against their suggestion. But in the end, I knew that our options were narrowing, and none of them were particularly good. If Avenia could get at Imogen, who was supposed to be unconnected to me now, then I didn't dare think of the lengths they'd go to for our future queen. If she could get home to Bymar, she would be safe there, no matter what the outcome of this war.

Reluctantly, I gave my permission and said, "Get it ready for the morning. I want you to bring Fink." Fink was an Avenian boy who returned with me from the pirates. He asked too many questions, paid attention to nothing for more than a few minutes, and seemed intent on crowding multiple sentences into each breath he took. But as far as I was concerned, he was family now, and I had to be sure he was safe as well.

With some apparent reluctance, Tobias agreed, and then I retreated to my seat to address the entire group. "Everything must be done with the greatest of speed. Our armies are strong, but so are theirs. Every day this war goes on, the enemy digs deeper into our lands and terrorizes more of our people. With three countries against us, we cannot outlast them. I want a war measured in weeks, not months."

Heads nodded back at me, though none of them had any more of an idea than I did for how we might accomplish that. I only knew that we had to find a way.

"Is there nothing you want from me?" Harlowe asked. It was the first time he'd spoken in this meeting.

I turned to him, but drew in a slow breath before speaking. "Your assignment may be the most difficult of all. Word must be sent throughout the kingdom, especially to the homes outside the cities. Invite anyone who wishes to come to Drylliad. Here we will offer them sanctuary within the safety of our walls. In exchange, all able-bodied men must prepare to fight in defense of the capital. Those who cannot fight shall help in any other way you ask of them."

Harlowe dipped his head at me, then said, "The regents suggested we offer release to any prisoner willing to fight for Carthya."

"What about Conner?" Even if he were Carthya's last hope, I wouldn't dare put a knife in that man's hand. Bevin Conner would likely protest to his dying day that he was still a patriot, but I'd never be convinced he wouldn't use that knife against our own men, and find a way to justify it in the name of patriotism.

"We wouldn't release him, of course. Especially not now." Harlowe cleared his throat, as if the words about to pass his lips made him uncomfortable. "We just learned he's been sending information beyond our borders, to someone unknown."

My eyes narrowed. "What information?"

"The message we intercepted describes the details of your fight with Captain Roden. There were likely others before it."

"Let it be sent," I said. "And follow it. I want to know who Conner is talking to."

"As you command," Harlowe said. "My king, Drylliad will stand until your safe return."

To which I only lowered my eyes. When I raised them again, Amarinda was staring at me with her brows pressed together in concern. She opened her mouth to say something, but Kerwyn spoke first.

"Your Majesty, I won't bother with protesting about the risks you're taking," he said tiredly. "I know it never does any good. But if you intend to do this, then there is something we must discuss. We'll do everything we can to protect you, but —"

"It's a trap for me, I know."

Kerwyn leaned forward. "After your family's deaths, Carthya nearly fell into civil war. You cannot leave without naming an heir."

Nodding at the princess, I said, "It should be Amarinda, naturally."

But she shook her head. "A Carthyan must be named as successor. Not me."

"That's ridiculous. You might not have been born here, but you're as Carthyan as I am."

"I'm here to seal the treaty between our countries, nothing more," she said softly. "Your people will accept me as the wife of their king, but not as their sole ruler."

"Though you are both young, there is another possibility." Kerwyn's tone was cautious now, careful not to push too hard. "If you were to marry, should anything happen to the king, Amarinda would automatically retain the throne as queen. Nobody could question her rule then."

Amarinda and I looked at each other, startled by a suggestion neither of us had considered and certainly weren't prepared to answer. There had been other royals who had married at even younger ages than we were now, and usually at desperate times like those we now faced. But this was so sudden. I knew I had to say something, and say it quickly. And yet the words were stuck in my throat.

By then I had hesitated too long and Amarinda spoke first. "None of that will be necessary because Jaron will come back from this."

"Maybe I won't." It was foolish to pretend otherwise. And Carthya needed a ruler. "We should marry," I said to Amarinda. "Tonight. To preserve your reign."

# · THREE ·

With my reluctant acceptance of Kerwyn's suggestion, all eyes went to Amarinda. She stared at me in shock, and then said quietly, "The king and I need a few minutes alone."

With respectful bows, the room emptied. I took her hand, but stared at it rather than dare look her in the eye. Things had been so easy for us since I had returned from the pirates. But with the prospect of marriage so suddenly here, all the awkwardness had returned.

"I know this isn't what you want, or the way you want it," I said. "But if we don't do this, you will become obligated to the person I choose as heir to the throne. That's not fair to you, not again."

"But you will return." I shrugged in response and kept my gaze downward. With an unsteady voice, she added, "Jaron, do you expect to die in this war?"

My thumb brushed over hers. Not for the first time, I wondered how her skin could be so soft. Then I said, "With the kind of threat we're facing, I will fight to the death before I surrender. And I don't see a path to victory."

"But you'll find a way. You always do."

"Maybe Carthya will come through this. But mine has never been the kind of life that leads to old age." She squeezed my hand, and I added, "I know the feelings aren't there that we'd want for a marriage. But we should make your title official." I couldn't help but grin. "And if I don't return, there'll be more room on the throne for you."

She wasn't amused. "Stop that! Your death is not a joke to me!" She drew in a deep breath, then continued, "Whatever feelings we share, you are important to me, and to all of Carthya."

I appreciated that, though her words spoke all too clearly of her feelings. She had very carefully said that while we were friends, she did not love me.

Then Amarinda placed her other hand over mine. "Tell me about Roden. I know the fight between you wasn't real."

Amused, I arched an eyebrow. "How did you know?"

"You're only angry with him in public. Mott knows the full story, I assume."

"He does. And I would've told you, except it might have forced you to lie to the regents, and I couldn't ask that."

"Why did you stage that fight?"

"Someone will report it back to Vargan — maybe that's who Conner is communicating with. If I can't make myself look stronger than I am, then I'll do the opposite."

She looked frustrated with that idea, but it had worked for me before, and anyway, the time to debate the wisdom of this plan had passed. She asked, "So where is Roden, really?"

I sighed, relieved to be able to discuss this with her. And yet, speaking the words reminded me of the near impossibility of what I'd asked him to do. "He's up north, on our border with Gelyn," I said. "With forty of our best men, Roden's job is to overtake Gelyn's garrison there, then stop their army from coming through."

"But, they'll never succeed! Give up the border and bring Roden back. He and Mott can go after Imogen."

I frowned. "Why not me? Why is my life more valuable than theirs?"

"The value in your lives is the same, Jaron. But not the value in your roles." Amarinda's grip on my hand tightened. "I think of Imogen as dearly as if she were my own sister, you know that. But if you get anywhere near that camp, you will hand yourself over to them and this war will be lost before it's begun. It must not be you who goes."

Her gaze bored into me until I finally looked away. She was right, and so was Mott — despite my arguing, I knew that. A pit formed in my gut at the thought of not being there to ensure Imogen was safe, but these last few weeks, I had tried to be better at taking counsel from others. It wasn't a natural instinct to me, and the idea of having people in my life whom I could truly trust was something new. But the alternative, of acting entirely on my own judgment, had taught me several painful lessons that I had no interest in repeating. So I looked back at her and nodded. I would not go after Imogen.

Amarinda thanked me, and then smiled. "War is ahead, Jaron, and we know what risks that involves. But we must believe all will end well. Our plans for marriage will remain the same."

I wished I could be as optimistic as her, but the reality of what lay ahead pressed in on me from every side. "No, they won't." I gazed steadily into her eyes, wide with concern. "I release you from the betrothal, Amarinda. You and I will still marry, but only if that's your choice. Not because of any agreement between our two countries or any obligation you were born to fulfill, but if you can love me. However, Kerwyn was right before. Something may go wrong in this war . . . for me."

"Then you must choose the next king." Amarinda was trying to hide the edge in her voice, but it wasn't working. "Am I betrothed to him now, or am I nothing to Carthya?"

Gently, I smiled at her. "You are a princess of this land, and as such, it will be your responsibility to choose the next ruler of Carthya. You can name yourself and rule alone with my official blessing."

"The people won't accept that."

"But Harlowe will, if it's my command, and where he leads the regents will follow. Besides, my lady, the people love you." I sat back in awe of her and then chuckled at my own faults by comparison. "I daresay they'll be relieved once you're in charge."

She weighed that in silence and then asked, "What if I wish to marry?"

"I ask only that you choose a husband from Carthya." My thumb brushed over hers. "Someone who is the proper match for you."

"And if I don't want the crown?" she asked.

"Then you give it to anyone worthy and walk away from the throne forever."

It was as if I had lifted a weight off her shoulders. She straightened her back and nodded. A moment of silence lapsed between us, and if I were someone with any courage I'd have sealed the agreement with a kiss. But I didn't, and I was certain she took note of it too.

We finally stood and I offered to escort her to her apartments. But Mott was waiting at the doorway, his face pinched and grim. His arms were folded and he somehow seemed wider than usual, making it clear I wouldn't get past him. Tobias also lingered nearby, so I asked him to see the princess to her rooms.

Even before they left, I could tell Mott was ready to scold me in the severest tones. I dreaded it, feeling as if Master Graves, my father, and the chapel priests had all combined their energies to prove once and for all how wrong I always was. "We need to talk," he said.

I rolled my eyes. "Don't make this a fight."

"I won't, but you make everything a fight."

Well, that seemed true enough. So I shrugged and let him follow me back into the throne room. When the doors were shut behind us, I turned and started to tell him of the agreement I had just made with Amarinda.

However, he was quick to cut me off. He unfolded his large hand to reveal a crumpled note tucked inside. I was relieved to recognize Roden's stilted handwriting on an open corner of the paper. So at least he was alive, or had been when this note was written.

"When did you get that?" I asked.

"Not ten minutes ago. Roden's messenger said he barely escaped Gelyn alive to deliver this."

"Did you read it?"

"Yes." By Mott's expression, I knew the news wasn't good. "Roden's men successfully snuck inside Gelyn, and engaged the Gelynian army at the garrison along our shared border. Then Roden and his men set up traps that stopped most of the first wave of Gelynian soldiers that tried to come through." Mott's frown deepened. "He sent this note in anticipation of a second wave of soldiers. The rest are on their way."

That could be hundreds of the enemy, or even thousands. "Does he say how many men he still has with him?"

"Eighteen."

Eighteen out of forty. My heart ached at the thought of so much loss. And even though the men who remained would be among the finest warriors Carthya had to offer, the odds against them were terrible. It was likely that by now, none of them were still alive.

Mott handed me the note. "He asks you to bring reinforcements to join him. He believes it's the only way they'll succeed."

I scanned his note for myself. Due to his uneducated background, Roden's spelling and handwriting were poor, but in this case I was grateful for the errors. It proved that this note had come directly from his hand. "The captain asks me to *send* reinforcements, not bring them. You'd rather I go into battle against thousands of Gelynians than to the camp where Imogen is being held?"

"No. I'd rather you hid yourself in a closet until this is over. But I know from experience that even with our best locks, we couldn't keep you there." There was some teasing in his voice, but after a moment's hesitation, Mott became serious again. "They could only have one reason to take Imogen, because they knew you would come for her. Jaron, whatever they have planned, it will be awful. So if it must be one or the other, then, yes, I'd rather you go to Gelyn."

Fortunately, my decision was already made, or else I'd have had to argue, just for the sake of pride. But I only said, "All right, Mott. You win this time, but don't let it become a habit." Then, with my heart pounding, I added, "Promise me that Imogen —"

"I can't promise anything other than to do my best." Nervously, he licked his lips. "And you promise me —"

"I can't do that either." I forced a grim smile to my face. "But one way or another, we will see this war to an end. We must."

## · FOUR ·

The following morning, a regiment of two hundred men left Drylliad for the northern border of Gelyn. I wished I could've sent more, but other men were needed in the south to meet the advancing armies of Mendenwal, and a third contingent was sent to oversee the mighty waters of Falstan Lake, while the rest remained here in defense of the capital. What strength Carthya had was already being divided, and our resources were taxed to their limits. Though I stood tall and proud as I watched them leave, in my heart, I still doubted that we had any chance of survival.

Once they had gone, I joined Tobias, Amarinda, and Fink in the courtyard. My plan was to travel with them to the border of Avenia, to ensure their safety at least that far. Then I would take my horse, Mystic, on to Gelyn from there and hope the devils gave them clearance until the princess was safe in her home country.

The escape carriage was being loaded with clothing, blankets, and food. Tobias cocked his head toward the crates and said, "At least we won't be cold or hungry on this journey."

A mischievous grin tugged at my mouth. "We won't be cold, but I'd advise against eating the food. Today's recipes included an extra ingredient of Ayagall." His groans told me that Tobias knew the plant as well as I did. Ayagall was a weed that grew plentifully near the orphanage where I'd lived, and was the source of many a lively joke when orphanage life grew dull. Even small amounts guaranteed a full day's vomiting. Suddenly, the mystery of why Mrs. Turbeldy hated me so much was solved.

Despite her attempts to remain serious, Amarinda giggled. "Avenia thinks they're battling a king. I doubt they're prepared to fight a boy who thinks childish pranks are practical strategies for war."

"Aren't they?" I said, giving a wink and a smile to Fink, who was already laughing.

Once the carriage was loaded, Amarinda, Fink, Tobias, and I crowded inside. It wouldn't be the most comfortable trip, but if they were stopped at the border, this had to look like a transport wagon, unfit for passengers and certainly unfit for the future queen of the land. Amarinda and I sat beside each other on a small bench at the far end of the carriage, while Fink and Tobias took the floor across from us.

Fink immediately started chatting with Tobias, who told him to hush no less than twenty times before the gates of Drylliad were behind us. I wasn't sure why he bothered. Keeping Fink from asking questions was like holding back the sea. He talked whenever he was nervous, or excited, or bored, or for that matter, awake. Eventually, Tobias gave up pretending to listen and just stared forward. His anxiety was evident in his every expression, every movement, and grew worse with each mile.

I noticed Amarinda smiling back at him, hoping to give him confidence in all that would have to happen over the next several hours. He warmed to that and smiled back. I watched the silent exchange, but noticed his eyes linger on her long after she turned away. Of course they would. Amarinda grew more beautiful by the day. Even a blind man would've noticed it too.

Eventually, Fink ran out of questions and grew as silent as the rest of us. I almost wished he would've continued talking, for the silent carriage felt almost haunted afterward. My mind was no clearer than it had been a day ago, and I was struggling to focus on any one problem facing us without a hundred others begging my attention first. The strain of it made me want to walk or climb or do something other than sit in a crowded carriage as it bumped along a dusty road.

Just to give myself some movement, I stretched out my legs and arms. Sensing my discomfort, Amarinda grabbed my hand and intertwined her fingers with mine. Then she said, "Once the three of us get past the border, it's only a few days to Bymar. If you can hold Gelyn back until then, my people will come to help you."

"I wish you were coming with us, Jaron." Fink looked down, but his head wasn't lowered for long before he looked up again and said, "I heard Kerwyn wanted you and the princess to get married. Why didn't you?"

I wasn't sure who had told him that, but clearly one of the servants attending to that room talked too much. I started to scold him for such a question, but Amarinda laughed and said, "Clearly, you know nothing about a girl's wedding day. If I'm at the altar with Jaron as he rides off to war, what part of his horse do you suppose I'll end up kissing?"

She looked at me and smiled, and I began laughing at the image. Fink joined us too, which only made it seem funnier. But from the corner of my eye, I saw Tobias looking down at his clasped hands, watching his thumbs rotate.

"The escape carriage will work," I assured him. "Cheer up."

His smile back at me was hopeful, but vacant. Something else was bothering him, but obviously nothing that could be shared here.

It wasn't much farther on before our driver called down to us that the road into Avenia was shortly ahead. I ordered him to stop where we wouldn't be noticed, and once there, we exited the carriage. We emptied enough of the crates to pry up the false floor. The space inside was smaller than I'd imagined it would be, but if it was any larger, it would've been noticeable from the outside.

"This won't fit the three of you," I told Tobias.

Tobias quietly gestured toward Fink, reminding me that at the last minute I'd insisted he must come along too. Even if the space could've been made larger, there had been no time to change the design.

"It will have to fit us," Amarinda said.

"I'll stay out, if necessary," Tobias offered. "Our priority is the princess's safety, and Fink can guide her through Avenia toward Bymar."

"No," Amarinda said. "A way must be found for us all to get through that border."

"I'll stay out," Fink said. We put up a protest, but above our voices, he added, "I'm Avenian, and I'm young. They won't see me as a threat." He turned to me. "Jaron, you know I'm right."

A lump formed in my throat. "You're the closest thing I have to family, Fink."

Something glimmered in his eyes. "Then that makes me a prince . . . almost. If the king risks everything for Carthya, then I should too."

Difficult as it was, I nodded my permission at him, and then said, "Avenia will search this carriage. Tell them the driver allowed you to ride in here on your way home. Make sure they notice the crate of wine, but tell them it's strong and they shouldn't take it."

"That'll only make them more determined to take it." Then Amarinda's face lit up when she understood. "More Ayagall?"

"They'll be sick for a week."

Tobias climbed inside the carriage first, and maneuvered his body to make room for the princess.

"I may have come to Carthya because of a promise and a treaty," she whispered, "but I will return again because my heart remains here."

"Then I will see you soon." I kissed Amarinda's cheek and

embraced her warmly. When we parted, I attempted to calm the worry in her eyes with a smile and assurance that all was well, though I admit, I wasn't entirely certain of that myself.

I helped her into the carriage, although it was necessary for her to cradle closely into Tobias for them to fit, with his arm outstretched for a more comfortable place to rest her head. There was no way Fink would have fit in there too.

Once they were in, I reminded Tobias of his sacred obligation to protect Amarinda, with his life if necessary. He promised to do his best, but never looked at me as he spoke. Perhaps he was uncomfortable in such a tight and awkward position. Or, I wondered, maybe his discomfort came from the other body so intimately fit against his. In an emergency, Tobias could release another door beneath them, but until then, the false floor was placed over the top of them and the crates were replaced.

Fink stopped before climbing in and turned back to me. "Jaron, I'm scared."

Considering the danger involved in this next phase of his journey, I understood how he felt. But I also had an idea how to help with that, something I'd considered doing for a while anyway. I withdrew my sword and stood tall. "Kneel," I commanded him.

He stared up at me, confused, until I motioned for him to fall to his knees. When he did, with my sword I touched on his right shoulder and then his left. "As king of Carthya, and the head of the house of Artolius, I dub you, Fink, into my house, and as a knight of the kingdom."

"Really?" His smile grew wider than I'd ever seen it. "I'll be a good knight."

As he rose to his feet, I sheathed my sword. "The actual ceremony is longer, but I doubt you could sit through the whole thing anyway. This will have to do for now. You are charged with protecting a princess. She needs you to be strong, and I know you will be. Get her home safe, and don't be afraid."

"I'm glad you made me a knight, but that's not what I meant before," he said. "When I said I was scared, Jaron, I'm scared for you."

I had not expected that. The fear in my heart was for Carthya, and for those around me who were in so much danger. But perhaps I was afraid for myself as well. I told him to be brave enough for us both. Then I shut the door and ordered the driver to move on. Once they drove away, I climbed on Mystic's back and rode to where I could view the carriage for as long as possible. Eventually it vanished and the dust settled. Their next stop would be at the border of Avenia, directly under the watchful eye of soldiers who could reap untold rewards for capturing the princess. Amarinda's fate now lay with a regent who couldn't wield a sword against his own shadow, and a young knight who could barely lift a sword with both hands.

## · FIVE ·

Half-Moon Pass was a narrow corridor through the steep mountains of Gelyn. So named for its crescent-shaped trail, the pass was the sole connection for travel between our two countries.

Gelyn had long maintained a small garrison of around three hundred men at the mouth of the pass. Roden's job was to draw small groups of men away from the garrison, capture them, and gradually take control of the entire border. Once that was accomplished, they were to lie in wait for other Gelynians to come.

I wasn't sure when things had gone wrong. The note from Roden indicated they had taken control of the garrison, and even held up under fighting against the first wave of soldiers to come through the pass. But that battle left him with only eighteen men, and the next group was on their way. Now, as I approached the battle from a distance, I hoped the additional men I'd sent that morning would make a difference.

As I drew closer, the clashing sounds of blades, the cries of the injured, and the odors of sweat and blood rushed at me in feral waves. Immediately, I withdrew my sword and charged forward.

The worst of the battle seemed to have already passed, and far too many of my own men lay dead on the ground. I had been the one to send them here, and could not dismiss their sacrifices as easily as looking away. We had to win this battle before the sun rose again, or their deaths would be for nothing.

I reached the garrison in the shadows of the setting sun, but there was still enough light for me to take in the struggle of my armies against the leather-clad men of Gelyn. We seemed to have the advantage, but the battle was far from over. The garrison had been designed to feed and bed soldiers, but now served as a series of small structures where the courageous could fight and the weak could hide. Surrounding the few buildings were tall, ragged cliffs with occasional ledges overlooking the land. It had been my intention to go as deeply into the center of the battle as possible, but I got no closer than to the empty horse corral before I was drawn into the fighting.

I quickly recognized one of the soldiers who had left with Roden a few weeks before. We had no time for a proper greeting, but with our combined strength, we were able to buy ourselves a few seconds to catch our breath.

"Where's Roden?" I dreaded to hear that he had fallen, as I saw no sign of him anywhere here with his men.

The soldier only cocked his head up to a ridge. "The captain might be on one of the ridges behind the garrison, but wherever he is now, he's done us no good."

"Why not?" I scanned the area, hoping to see him. "Isn't he fighting?"

"Yes, my king, he fights," the man answered. "But we have many fighters. What we lack is a leader."

I wanted to ask more, but we were pulled again into the battle. Despite the fact that Gelynians were not accustomed to fighting, I realized that perhaps I had underestimated their strength before. Instead of swords, they fought with pikes and halberds, and it required us to change our strategies. They could swing or thrust with the sharp end of their pikes before we could get close enough to do any damage to them. However, I soon realized that their weapons also challenged their ability to fight in any direction but forward. So I focused my attacks on the men whose backs were toward me and did my best to avoid the rest.

As I plunged deeper into the action, I realized that Carthya held the advantage against this wave of men. Clearly we had fought hard and well, though without the additional soldiers I'd sent, we surely would have been sunk. The tide had turned in our favor, but I wanted this battle ended before more lives were lost.

On a hill ahead of me, several of our archers had gathered in a semicircle, watching for trouble and helping where they could. They were invaluable, but it cost a full dozen of my soldiers to guard them, and we were losing too many from the halberds as the Gelynians charged directly at them.

I pressed my way toward the archers, then I pointed to the ledges on the cliffs behind us. "Get yourselves up there,"

I shouted above the noise surrounding us. "You'll be far more useful and will need no protection."

"We lack the king's talent for climbing," one archer said.

"Lately, the king lacks the same talent," I said. "But that's where you need to be."

The archer nodded, and then directed his men to follow him. Once they ran for the ledges, I jumped down to join the others, pausing only to wince at the pain that bolted up my leg. "Where's the captain?" I cried.

The swordsman beside me smirked. "Roden is your captain, not ours. We all know why he was given that position."

His reaction caused me to pause. "Oh? Why is that?"

"He's your friend, sire. Maybe you trust him, but you can't expect us to."

Actually, yes, I could expect it, and I did. But my retort was lost in the shrieks of several Gelynians charging for us at once. The man next to me tripped and fell, but I held them back until he joined me again. Hoping to draw the Gelynians away from our archers, who were still climbing, I ran deeper into the garrison.

The buildings that served Gelyn's border vigils were small, but sturdily built from rock and thick planks of wood. They ran in two parallel lines and had a wide space in the center where men could eat, train, and march. That area was congested now with my men and theirs, all of them fighting nearly on top of one another, and so I darted right, through a narrow path between two buildings. There I hoped to make an escape behind the garrison and come out in a better position. However, this path led me to a dead end. As I considered my circumstances, I realized I'd made a mistake coming this way. A bad one.

More men had followed me than I'd anticipated, and when I could run no farther, I faced an outhouse with a steep and rocky hill behind it. Without the option of climbing, there was no escape from this area. So I continued to fight, but the Gelynians were pressing me closer to the hill, far from any help.

"They called you 'sire' back there," one Gelynian shouted at me. "Is it possible we have the boy king here?"

"Yeah, I'm here," I said. "But thinking you have me is a delusion. Does the fish have a bear just because it's within reach of the claws?"

I thought that was a good remark, but it seemed to go over their heads, and became a waste of a perfectly good insult. I consoled myself by getting a deep jab into the gut of one of the larger men. At least they paid attention to that.

I used the chance to begin scrambling up some rocks where I'd be out of reach of their pikes. If they tried to follow I could kick at their weapons, or better yet, just drop other rocks down on them. It wasn't the most graceful fighting style, but in that moment, grace was the furthest thought from my mind.

Except my weaker right leg collapsed as I neared the top of the rocks and I landed back on the roof of the outhouse, nearly falling through it, which would've been unfortunate for any number of reasons. The men below me grabbed one leg and then another, pulling me back to them. I tried kicking, but it didn't do much good. Maybe they did have me, after all.

Then I recognized the cry of a familiar voice. A pair of boots appeared above me and an armful of rocks cascaded over my head and down onto the men below. I would've pointed out that I'd had that same idea already, but I supposed it didn't matter who dropped the rocks, only that it happened.

Arms reached down and braced mine. As I was helped up from the shed onto the top of the ledge, I grinned and said to Roden, "If a battle like this is how you welcome me when we're friends, I can only imagine what it would've been if we were still enemies."

## SIX

Temporarily out of the path of any Gelynians, Roden quickly embraced me, and then said, "What are you doing here? When I asked for more soldiers, I didn't intend for you to come."

"Yes, but I was bored." We paused to hear the Gelynian commanders calling for surrender. The battle must've been closer to its end than I'd realized. Roden started to move toward the hill to join in the victory, but I pressed him back with my arm. "Your men can finish this. We need a place to talk."

He sighed. "We can talk. But as you probably noticed already, they're not my men." Then he motioned me down the ridge to a quiet cove that didn't appear to have seen any fighting.

Once we were alone, I sat on one of the smoother rocks and invited him to sit as well. He shifted the weight on his feet, as if he felt more comfortable poised for battle. I understood that, but the fight was over and he and I needed to talk before the next one came.

Finally, he sheathed his sword, and then sat with his hands clasped together. He glanced at me briefly, then hung his head, and scraped at the ground with his boot.

We sat in silence until he finally said, "The night before we took this garrison, I overheard the men talking. They knew it would be hard, and risky, and most of them expected to fail. I almost stepped from the shadows just then, to assure them that I'd fight at their side until the end. But then they said if we failed, it would be my fault, that I had no business being their captain." When he looked up at me, his eyes were filled with sadness and doubt. "They're right, Jaron."

For some reason, a memory from childhood came to my mind of standing before my father as he sat on his throne, staring down at me in full disapproval. Earlier that day, I had taken all the coins from the offerings dish at the church. Stolen them, he said, like a common thief. Looking back now, I knew my actions had embarrassed my father, but all I understood then was his anger. I couldn't explain that I had given the coins to a young widow in town who'd been threatened with debtors' prison. Much as I wanted my father to understand my reasons, I worried I might get her in trouble too. In front of the entire court, he had told me I was nothing like a prince should be.

Uneasy with the memory, I stood and reminded myself that this talk was for Roden and not me. With a shrug, I said, "You know my flaws, Roden. I make plans that don't work, mistrust my closest friends, and do stupid things when the easier option should be obvious. I'm wrong all the time. But I am not wrong about you."

"I'm a terrible captain!" Roden said. "You can't convince me otherwise."

"Oh no, I agree with that," I said. "You are terrible."

He drew back. "Is that meant to encourage me?"

Once again, my memories transported me back over the years. "After my father sent me away, I sometimes overheard people talking about the missing prince, about me. At first, I had expected to hear sadness, how much they mourned my loss. They were sad, yes, but not in the way I thought. They didn't miss me, only my mistakes, my pranks, whatever I'd done that gave them a story worth laughing about. These were people who had bowed when I entered a room, but they never loved me and certainly never respected me."

"I see." Roden nodded. "You had no business being a prince."

"Nor a king. Before I went to the pirates, do you know why Gregor was able to so easily manipulate my regents?"

"Because they were ridiculous and stupid."

"Well . . . yes. But they weren't evil. All they knew about me was the boy my father had sent away from the castle. If I were still that boy, then they shouldn't have allowed me to rule. If they didn't trust me to lead, that was my fault."

Now Roden stood. "But they follow you now — they bow because they respect *you*, not just your title. It's different for me. I am not worthy of my position, and you know it."

"How dare you doubt me?" My anger was sudden, but justified. "Why do you think I went to the pirates? For the pleasure of their company? For entertainment? It certainly did no favors to my health. I came for you, Roden. I risked my life for *you*. So don't you ever again disrespect the risks I took by claiming you weren't worth it!"

"I'm only a displaced orphan," he mumbled.

"So am I!" Then my voice softened. "But I'm also a king, and you are my captain. Doubt yourself, if you must, but you will not question me!"

He stepped back, then lowered his head. "I can read a battle and I can swing a sword, and my strategies are good if anyone will listen. But they don't. I can't do this job if they won't give me respect."

"Nobody gives you respect in this life. You must take it, you must earn it, and then you must hold it sacred, because no matter how hard respect is to attain, it can be lost in an instant." I nodded my head toward the garrison. "Go get it, Roden. People won't follow a leader who doesn't know where he's going. Show them that you do."

Roden nodded, and then started walking beside me back down the hill toward the garrison. "I do know where we're going, and I will get us there. Jaron, with this army, I'm going to hold this border until all of Gelyn surrenders to you."

# · SEVEN ·

By the time we returned to camp, the dead were being separated from the wounded, and the healthy prisoners had been disarmed and placed in an enclosed area of the garrison that seemed to serve as a temporary prison whenever the need arose. They looked crowded and uncomfortable in there, but I figured they had survived the battle, and we would treat them better than they'd do for us. They had nothing to complain about.

"Call your men to attention," I said to Roden. "Talk to them as their captain."

"And say what?"

"Well, they did just win a major battle," I scowled. "You might mention that."

He called the men into lines, but someone replied that first they were building a fire for the bodies. Roden glanced over at me and I arched an eyebrow, waiting to see what he'd do. He called again for his men, but this time he was roundly ignored. I had no intention of helping him here. In fact, stepping in would be the worst thing I could do. It'd suggest to the men that he needed my help, that they only had to obey him when I was nearby. So I stood back and waited.

The fire was being built just outside the garrison. The bodies of the dead had not yet been placed — a strong, hot fire was needed first. On this rocky soil, it would be the most respectful end we could give them.

Beside me, Roden watched it too. Many of the men working at the fire were the ones who had been with him from the first attack. They were good warriors, some whom I had admired since my earliest years. A few of them had even taught me at times. But at the moment, they were in the wrong.

Finally, Roden nodded his head as if he had come to a decision. He grabbed a bucket and walked out of camp. Only a minute or two later, he returned, this time with the bucket so full that water sloshed from all sides as he carried it. He walked directly up to the fire, and just as the first sparks were beginning to take hold, he splashed it all over the wood, making sure plenty splashed onto the men too.

I choked back a laugh, slightly shocked and greatly amused. Really, that was better than I'd expected from him.

The men immediately responded by withdrawing their swords. Roden raised his as well and a sort of standoff began. I started forward — it felt natural that I should. But again, I reined myself in so that Roden could speak. Still, I kept a hand near my own sword and hoped he knew what he was doing.

Now that he had their attention, Roden shouted, "I am your captain, and I have given you an order!"

The men kicked at the dirt, clearly not convinced, but they lowered their weapons.

"You will all form a line," Roden said. "The king is with us and he will see you now."

I wasn't sure if they lined up because Roden was demanding it, or out of deference to me. But either way, the men immediately created two rows on either side of the garrison's narrow courtyard.

Roden began by addressing the men. "You fought well," he said. "Another battle is coming soon and so I hope you will get some rest tonight."

He looked over at me and I muttered, "That was the worst speech anyone has ever given. Ever. Work on that too."

He only rolled his eyes and then followed at my side as we walked down one row, assessing the health of each man and trying to get a picture of what strength still remained.

As I passed, one older man touched my arm. I stopped to give him my full attention and he immediately went to one knee. "King Jaron, do you remember me?" he asked. I shook my head, and he said, "When you were ten years old, your father commissioned me to make you a gift, a sword."

"You're the swordsmith! I do remember now." I'd used the sword in a duel against King Humfrey of Mendenwal, who now waged war against us. Conner had duplicated that same sword as part of his plan to install a false prince upon the throne. It was too small for my use now, but I still had it amongst my most valued possessions. Still looking at the swordsmith, I said, "You stood in the great hall when my father gave it to me. That sword has served me well."

"Yes, sire." With a cautious smile, he added, "I confess, I urged your father to give you a different gift, a horse or a journal for writing. But he only said that you'd use the horse to run away or the journal as kindling for a fire somewhere in the castle. He wanted the sword to encourage you to take your studies more seriously."

"And I did." Then I grinned back at him, as mischievous as ever. "Though you should know that I found other horses to help me run away and still started my share of fires."

His laugh didn't come as easily, and ended with an expression of sadness. "I remember the boy you were. So when you became king, I doubted you. But I was wrong, and I beg your forgiveness."

I angled my head toward Roden. "You will not be equally wrong regarding my captain, I hope."

"No, sire."

Roden and I continued walking until we reached the area where the remaining Gelynians had been corralled. The walls around them were smooth and tall, and iron bars were set between rock and mortar walls. There was barely enough space for them to sit and not enough to lie down unless they agreed to stack themselves up. Buckets of water had already been provided for their thirst and they would be given any food we could spare. Hopefully they would not need to be in there for long.

"Remain at peace and you will live until Gelyn's final surrender," I said to them. "But there are consequences if you cause any trouble before then."

I started to walk on, but a tall soldier with the markings of being their captain stepped forward and said, "We won't be imprisoned for long. We're only the advance group. Gelyn will pour out the whole of its strength with the army that is still coming."

"The whole of what strength?" I asked. "Gelyn fights like bedridden grandmothers, only with longer knitting needles."

"They're not three days behind us," he said. "And Mendenwal is coming too. Once we have defeated your men here, we will attack Drylliad and destroy everything there that moves."

I snorted. "Your needles pierce walls now?"

"No, but their cannon does. It's probably crossing the plains of Carthya as we speak."

That stopped me. I'd heard that Mendenwal had been experimenting with cannons, and I didn't like the idea of one being tested on my castle. They were more common in other lands, I'd heard, but something entirely new to this region. My hope had been for Carthya to develop its own cannon, but there hadn't been time. Now, the blast from a single weapon could bring down whole walls. Even with all our protections, Drylliad could be overrun in minutes.

Certain that my worries would be revealed if our conversation continued, I instructed Roden to learn what he could from the man, then said I needed a private place to think and rest.

Except the man called after me, "I confess that I am surprised to see you here, Jaron. Avenia's king thought your people would protect you better than this."

"My people do protect me," I said, still walking away. "And I protect them."

"Oh? What about the girl King Vargan captured? Did you protect her? I heard her described as a servant girl rumored to have caught your eye."

I turned on my heel and returned to him. "You know about that?"

He motioned to the prison behind him. "Promise me a private room with food and a bed. I'll give your men no trouble, but I cannot stay in here."

I nodded at Roden, who gave the man his promise. Then he said, "My king heard it directly from Avenia's top commander. That girl was central to Vargan's plans to bring a quick end to the war. After he took her, he would allow someone to escape to be sure you got the news of it. That would lead him to his real target."

In an attempt to seem indifferent, I shook my head. "Obviously, I didn't go to rescue her, so his plan to capture me failed."

But the soldier laughed in my face. "Arrogant boy! He never expected to capture you. Naturally, you wouldn't be allowed to go."

"Then what?"

"It would be too risky for you to send an entire army to rescue her — Avenia could kill the girl before your men got through. So Vargan figured you would send a very small group of your finest warriors — someone you'd trust with her life. That's who he wants. Your most trusted man."

Mott. I had sent Mott.

"Why?" I asked.

"Once he's captured, Avenia will force him to reveal all your strategies, everything Avenia needs to know to win this war. And if he won't talk, then Vargan will remind him of his responsibility for the life of the servant girl. They will stop at nothing until he breaks or she is dead." His smile became outright laughter. "So which would you have him choose, Jaron? The girl you pretend not to love, or this country you are sworn to protect?"

I stumbled away without responding. Any answer I might have given risked turning my heart to stone.

Roden caught up to me once we had moved farther from the men. "Don't walk away. We have to talk about what he said."

"Why? Can you change it?" My mind raced as I struggled with the Gelynian's question. I thought Vargan's plans were for me, so Mott would have the better chance of moving safely through the Avenian camp. But no, even if he was careful, Mott would enter that camp with no idea that the vigils there were watching for him.

Mott wouldn't tell them my strategies for the war, no matter what they might do to him. But it wasn't only his life at stake. What would he do when Imogen was threatened?

Roden asked, "How much does he know, Jaron?"

"Enough to bring Carthya to its knees." Mott had asked me to trust him, and so I had. And now both he and Imogen would pay for that.

"Let me take some of the men from here." Roden grabbed my arm to slow me from walking. "We'll rescue them both."

"And give them more targets for our secrets?" I slowed, but did not stop. "Within three days, Gelyn's army will arrive here. They *cannot* cross into Carthya. For that, you will need every man we have. Even then, it won't be enough unless Bymar gets here in time."

"Then what will you —" Roden's jaw went slack and he started shaking his head. "Jaron, you can't. You're our king."

"I may wear a crown, but in my heart I am still a thief. Nobody would know better how to get into that camp." Before he could protest further, I added, "Have my horse made ready by morning. I leave at dawn."

## · EIGHT ·

Roden was waiting beside my horse when I emerged from a tent early the following morning.

"Did you sleep?" he asked me.

I ignored that and instead gestured around the area. "Who attended to my horse? Where are your men?"

With a sigh, he said, "They were tired."

"Roden, you'll never —"

But he anticipated my reprimand and cut me off. "The order to rest came from me, not them. I promise that I will learn how to lead them, how to be your captain. But you must let me do it in my own way."

All I could do was nod back at him. If anything, I was far more flawed as a leader than he seemed to be, and it was hard enough to find my own way forward. So I embraced him for a farewell and a wish for his success, and then swung into Mystic's saddle.

"Let me come with you," Roden said. "My horse is ready to ride."

"Thank you." I meant that with far more sincerity than my tone could offer. "But it's not wise for us both to go. Just in case . . ."

"As long as you keep fighting, I will too," he said. "Whatever comes next, for either of us."

"Help is coming soon." My words came from hope rather than certainty, but I wanted him to believe it. "Tobias and Amarinda will get through to Bymar. She will convince them to send her armies here to join you."

Roden squinted against the morning sun as he stared up at me. "The princess has to cross through Avenia first. We both know how dangerous that is, and Tobias won't be any help if they're caught. If they don't make it —"

"Whether Bymar comes or not, you must hold this border," I said to him. "The combined strength of Avenia and Mendenwal might still destroy us, but at least we have some chance. If Gelyn gets through, there is no hope. None."

Roden brushed a hand down Mystic's neck, and then gathered the reins into his fist. "It's bad enough that the king I've sworn to protect is going to Avenia on his own. Can you at least promise me that you know what you're doing, that you're undistracted?"

I steeled my voice and answered, "This is what I want. My head is in this."

He frowned. "And what of your heart?" I turned away, but he added, "Jaron, are you in love with Imogen?"

That brought a sigh from me. "It's complicated."

But Roden only shook his head. "I have no one in my life. No family, no girl. For me, love isn't complicated at all."

I stared through empty air until I lost focus of the world. "I cannot love her."

"Of course you can. I know she already —"

"No, Roden, I cannot love her. That choice was never given to me." There was a silence before I added, "And if I cannot love her, then I will not ask her to feel anything for me."

"I've seen the way she looks at you. Whatever she says, whatever she has made you believe, she cannot choose to feel nothing for you."

But that's exactly what she had done. The last time we were together, she had denied loving me, and in fact had suggested almost the opposite. I shook those thoughts from my head and said, "Nor did she choose to die in a plot to uncover my secrets. I will free her, and return her to her life. There can be nothing more."

After a delay, he said, "I knew you could lie, Jaron. I just didn't think you'd lie to yourself." He frowned as he placed the reins into my hand. "After Gelyn surrenders, I will head back toward Drylliad. Now, go do what you must."

I wanted to brush off his accusation with the ease of dismissing a servant, but I couldn't. His words affected me more than he might have guessed. I dipped my head at Roden, and then urged Mystic to carry me away. At first I headed south, directly toward Libeth, but the words of the Gelynian commander echoed in my mind. Mendenwal had a cannon, which could rip my cities apart before we even had the chance to defend ourselves. It was probably at this time passing through the plains of Carthya, north of my castle. The land was vast through here, but for something of that size, they would have to take a main road.

I felt torn in my decision like never before. If I did not turn west, I risked additional harm to Mott and Imogen. But if I did not turn east, the cannon would reach Drylliad. Everyone we had sent there with the promise of safety would be killed.

In the end, I closed my eyes and whispered a request for Mott and Imogen to hold out for one day more, then rode east. I wasn't exactly sure how I could possibly steal a cannon, but I loved the idea of trying. Wherever there were hills, I kept to them and spent the ride scanning the horizon for signs of an army on the march. But for as far as I could see, there was nothing.

By early afternoon, Mystic began to slow. Despite my hurry, I knew he needed a rest. So I found a thick copse of trees in a basin of rolling hills with a small stream flowing through it. Mystic and I both lapped up all we could drink, and I refilled my waterskin for the upcoming ride, then shared with him some of the food rations from Roden's camp. I would've saved more for myself, but the truth was, they were stale and tasteless, and Mystic seemed to like them more than I did.

I was about to get back into the saddle to continue forward when the sounds of a large team of horses and the heavy creaking of metal caught my attention. I had been searching so hard for the cannon, the possibility of it finding me prompted a mischievous smile. I left Mystic in the trees and crept as close as I dared so that I might sneak a glimpse.

Several men on horses lined the road and continued forward until an order was shouted for them to halt. They wore the yellow and white colors of Mendenwal, unusual colors for an army. I hated the thought that we might be defeated by soldiers who looked as if they were wearing daisies. Once they stopped, a gap showed in their ranks and between them I saw a large black cannon being pulled on wheels by a long team of horses. I couldn't imagine the weight of it, other than to count the animals and guess at the strain they were bearing for this weapon. But at least I'd found it.

"The horses are exhausted," a man in the lines shouted. "They won't pull any farther today."

"This is good enough," another man shouted back. "I'd rather not bring the cannon into camp anyway. You'll find the rest of our men in another mile. Ride on and tell the captain we'll test the cannon here, firing into the hillside."

As the men carried out his orders to unhitch the team of horses and ride onward, I used the opportunity to sneak even closer. However, before I could get much nearer, two men walked up the hillside, evaluating the slope as a target for the test-firing of the cannon. I ducked behind a rock and realized quickly they were only on the other side of it. If either of them took more than a couple of steps to the left or right, they could look down and see me hiding there. As the men continued talking, I stifled my breaths, certain the only reason they couldn't detect me was because of the noise their men were making down on the road.

"At least we caught up to the others before they got much farther into Carthya," one man said.

"You idiot, we didn't catch up to anyone," his companion snarled. "They were ordered to wait for us here until Avenia arrived. Their king wants to know the cannon is solid before we drag it all the way to Drylliad."

"I wish someone else was testing it. A cousin of mine was nearly killed when the last cannon exploded. The gunners were worse than killed, you know. Blown to pieces so their own mother wouldn't know 'em."

"Hush! If you talk like that, nobody will volunteer to test this one."

"Not me anyway." There was a shuffling of feet, and then he added, "I'm not going to wait here when the others leave. They'll think it's a sign I'm volunteering."

"You'll be punished if you leave this post."

"But not blown up. I won't agree to test it, and if you'd seen my cousin, you wouldn't either."

"All right, let's go. It's not like anyone could drag it off, eh?"

Laughing, the men walked back down the hill. Only minutes later, I heard their horses being ridden away. I waited in the silence, wondering if it was a trap. But when I dared to look, there was only the cannon on the road and the empty hitch. Behind them was another wagon that seemed to be carrying supplies for the cannon. No sense in bringing that along if it was needed here for testing, rather than at the camp.

Once I determined I was alone, I snuck the rest of the way toward the cannon. It was larger than a battle horse and cast in iron. I ran my hand along the rough, cool metal, and then ducked behind it to investigate the supplies being transported with it.

The second wagon carried instruments for the cannon's use, including a ramrod, a sponge, and a dozen or more cannonballs. Tightly woven bags were stacked in the closest corner. A few empty sacks lay beneath three or four others that were packed full of black granules.

I knew what those granules were. When I had been with the pirates, they had captured a ship filled with mining supplies. When Roden and I left the pirates, we had taken with us a bag of this same substance so that we might learn more about its power and potential. Tobias told us it was gunpowder, capable of creating explosions that had never before been seen in these lands.

Roden and I decided to test it one night and invited Tobias along, but he flatly refused us and told us we were insane. Maybe he was right. Even the small amount we used downed several trees and created a fire that might've burned down half my kingdom if we hadn't been saved by a passing rainstorm.

In the days after, Tobias began creating designs for us to build our own cannon. He explained how the gunpowder would be stuffed down the barrel of the cannon with the ramrod, followed by the heavy iron ball. When the gunpowder was lit through a fuse, it would explode and the ball would fire out.

One shot could do all the damage of a battering ram and destroy fortresses that would take an entire army to topple. Even one cannon could change the course of a war.

The problem was that I had no hope of stealing it. Mystic was a strong horse, but on his own he couldn't budge this weapon an inch. Worse still, time was not on my side. I had no idea when Mendenwal would return for their cannon, but I guessed it couldn't be long.

If I couldn't steal it, I had to destroy it.

I closed my eyes, trying to recall everything Tobias had taught me from his studies. The conversation I'd just overheard came to mind, of the soldier whose cousin was nearly killed while testing an earlier cannon model. Why? What had gone wrong with the test?

Back when I suggested to Tobias that we simply mold a cannon and see if it worked, he had warned me that the danger lay in how the metal was cast. If it wasn't thick enough, or welded together well enough to withstand the explosion inside, it would fail. Perhaps the injured cousin had been too close to a cannon when it failed.

The problem was that the cannon in front of me looked very thick and very strong. It would take far more than a normal burst of gunpowder to destroy it.

Then I smiled. No, a *normal* burst wouldn't be powerful enough. But who said it had to be limited to that?

I opened the closest sack of gunpowder and scooped a generous portion into the barrel, then rammed it into the breech.

Once I was certain it was packed in tightly, I replaced the ramrod and scoop exactly as they had been before. I started to close up the sack, then realized I was passing up an enormous opportunity. I scooped as much gunpowder as I dared to steal into an extra bag, then refastened the bag and made my escape back to Mystic.

Unless they carefully checked their cannon, Mendenwal had no idea they were now testing a loaded weapon.

I rode away, retracing my ride back toward Avenia. Less than an hour later, as I reached the arch of another gentle hill, the ground quaked violently enough to startle Mystic to his hind legs, and a thick plume of black smoke rose into the air several miles behind me.

I turned to look back and grinned. Avenia and Mendenwal were still terrible threats to Carthya. But they no longer had a cannon.

## · NINE ·

It was early evening before I found the place where Imogen was being held. The hastily assembled camp lay just on the Avenian side of the border near Libeth, but a hill descending toward the camp allowed me a good view of the interior. The swamplands surrounding Libeth butted up to the camp's northern boundary. Due to its reputation for thick underbrush and poisonous snakes, no one would dare attempt any crossing of the swamp by foot, and it wasn't much easier by boat. The other perimeters were surrounded by tall mounds of earth or iron bars with razor ends. It was a larger camp than I'd anticipated, with several buildings and tents of all sizes.

"Your Majesty?"

I swiveled around, sword drawn, as two men approached me. Realizing they had caught me off guard, they raised their hands in a gesture of peace and then each quickly fell to one knee.

When I recognized them, I replaced my sword and asked them to rise. The man who had spoken was Henry Evendell, a talented archer with a good heart who often stood as a vigil at my castle. I didn't know the second man well, but Evendell introduced him as Herbert, a new but ambitious soldier, also from Drylliad. Both men had bows slung over their shoulders and quivers on their backs.

"Where's Mott?" I asked.

Out of respect, Evendell inclined his head before speaking again. "He entered the camp this morning, sire, hoping to get to a tent we thought looked different from the others. But we've seen no sign of him for hours, and we're concerned that he may have been captured."

"Show me the tent." Evendell pointed it out to me and I squinted, trying to see it better. Several vigils stood around it now. Either a royal was inside, or more likely, a valuable prisoner.

"Did he leave you with orders?" I asked them.

Evendell and Herbert eyed each other, and then Evendell answered, "Before coming here, we secured a small boat near the swamp, on the north end of camp. Once Mott came out with the lady Imogen, we were to use our arrows to clear a path for their escape into that boat."

"Has there been any sign of her?"

Both Evendell and Herbert shook their heads. Herbert mumbled something that I couldn't hear and I told him to speak up. Then he said, "There was one more order, sire, but you won't like it."

Whatever it was, by the squeamish expression on his face, I already didn't like it.

"Mott warned us you might come," he continued. "If you did, he asked us to remind you of your responsibilities for the safety of the kingdom. Not for him, or the lady Imogen."

Which was a fine idea, except that Mott's capture had just become the biggest threat to the safety of my kingdom. Also, I had never obeyed Mott before. I couldn't think of any reason to start now.

"We have to get both of them back," I said. "You have no idea where Imogen is being held?"

Evendell started to apologize and shake his head, but Herbert lifted his arm and pointed straight ahead. I followed his line to see a group of Avenian soldiers emerge from a tent deep inside the camp. In the center of that group was Imogen, her hands bound and mouth gagged. She seemed uninjured, which was a relief, and the gag didn't really surprise me. Although we were friends, she'd still scolded me often enough. I could only imagine the blistering words she'd have for an enemy.

My panic rose when I saw Mott being led from the tent Evendell had pointed out. His hands were also bound, and he was limping. For anyone else, the number of blades on him would've been too much. But not for Mott. He was strong and fast, and if there were any fewer weapons, he could've fought them all and won.

From a third position in the camp, I saw a man walk forward with a barbed whip in his hands. His purpose immediately became clear. Mott would be asked questions about Carthya's strategies in the war. If he refused to answer, that whip would be used on Imogen. They would force Mott to talk, or things would get worse. Much worse.

Reinforcing my fears, once Imogen and Mott were brought together into a small clearing, he was made to sit in a chair where more ropes went around his arms and feet. The soldiers escorting Imogen turned her to face a crude whipping post, then began retying her arms separately on each side of the wood.

Quickly, I turned to Evendell and Herbert. "Which of you is better with the bow?"

Evendell cocked his head and I told him to build a small fire and then gave him his instructions. Herbert was to come with me. He and I ran down the hill into a narrow valley of the camp, using the growing evening shadows to keep us hidden.

The closer we drew, the more we became aware of the bustle everywhere inside the camp. Vigils stood watch both at the gates and at elevated posts, and were stationed beside several tents within the camp. It would be impossible to get much closer without being spotted and likely shot.

Everything that happened next would have to be done quickly. Herbert nocked an arrow and moved into position. Hopefully, Evendell hadn't lost us in the waning light and would be watching too.

I was spotted soon after I began running for a quiet area of the wall. An Avenian at watch called out for me to stop, but a whoosh hissed through the air and Herbert's arrow found him. Others would be alerted now, but I didn't need much more time.

At the wall's base, I reached into the sack of gunpowder I'd stolen earlier that day. I withdrew a generous amount and laid it in a heap, then ran away as quickly as I could. Seconds later, Evendell sent a flaming arrow directly onto the heap. The gunpowder instantly exploded the entire wall. I was thrown off my feet and rolled behind a nearby rock to protect myself from falling debris. When the worst had passed, I peeked over at the collapsed wall and widely scattered wreckage. Perhaps I'd used too much gunpowder that time.

I went at a full sprint back toward the wall. Those who had survived began shouting for help, but Herbert remained watchful and fired off arrows at anyone who took notice of me. Once inside, I realized there was far more attention being paid to the destruction of the wall than the cause of it. If I kept my head down, I would be able to pass right through the crowd.

I climbed the ladder of an abandoned watchtower until I could see Mott and Imogen. The soldiers with them had gathered in close to guard their prisoners, or perhaps to protect one another. There were more than I could fight, and far too many people who could hurt my friends before I could stop them.

I climbed down again and took shelter behind a building to consider my next move. A quick glance inside the nearest window revealed it was full of weapons, in my opinion far more than Avenia needed. I dumped more of the gunpowder next to the building and then ran as if my life depended on it. Mostly because, well, it did. Just as had happened before, I wasn't nearly far enough away before a flaming arrow hit it and the building exploded. This time, I didn't shelter myself as well and got a nasty scrape on one arm, not to mention a chunk of rock nearly landed on me. If both Evendell and I survived this, we would have to discuss his timing when explosives were involved.

By then, general chaos had erupted in the camp. Soldiers were being ordered to the places I'd already destroyed, but several others were running as far from it as they could get. The confusion helped me, but what I really needed was to get at the soldiers around Mott and Imogen.

So my last use of gunpowder went to another nearby supply building, this one full of food and blankets. I left the entire bag beside it, and then gave a signal to Evendell. This time, he allowed me more distance before he lit the explosive. When it blew, I heard orders for all available soldiers to surround the camp and prepare for an invasion.

I rather liked that. My invasion had already happened, and the thing I wanted most was for them to clear out the center and move to the flanks of their camp.

A hand tapped my shoulder and I turned to see Herbert next to me. All I had asked of him was to stay in a safe position where he could pick off anyone who prevented my entrance into the camp. But he had gone beyond that and followed me inside. I nodded at him in thanks for his loyalty and motioned for him to come with me.

Mott and Imogen had not been entirely abandoned. One young soldier stood behind Mott's chair with a crude sword pressed against his prisoner's chest, waiting for whatever terror he expected to come at him. Two other larger soldiers guarded

Imogen. The man with the whip and the remaining soldiers had been ordered away.

I quietly instructed Herbert to position himself with a solid view of Imogen while I prepared to sneak up behind Mott. Our timing would have to be perfect, and Herbert would have to be fast because he had two targets.

The instant I crept from the shadows, Herbert fired his first arrow, hitting one of Imogen's vigils. By then I was directly behind the boy standing watch over Mott. With my left hand, I brought a knife to his neck, as my right hand steadied his arm holding the blade against Mott's chest. The boy stiffened, and without a word I pulled that arm back and lowered it. When I looked up again, Herbert had downed the second soldier beside Imogen. He would now watch this area until Mott and Imogen were free.

The boy behind Mott released his sword into my hand carefully and squeaked, "Please don't kill me."

My memory flew back to several months ago, when the orphan Latamer had begged me for the very same favor. I had never intended any harm toward Latamer, and not toward this boy either.

With my knife still at the boy's neck, I told him that if he tried any tricks, an arrow was already nocked with his name on it. He agreed to cooperate and I ordered him to untie Mott.

While he worked, Mott said, "I'm sorry, Jaron. The trap was for me."

"We were both tricked."

"I knew it was you when I heard those explosions."

I flashed him a grin. "Imagine the possibilities if I'd had more gunpowder."

Mott didn't act impressed, but I knew he was. They were fine explosions.

Then I ran over to Imogen, whose honey brown eyes blazed with disapproval. I knew she'd be angry with me — she often was. I rarely blamed her for that since, admittedly, I usually deserved it. But this time, it wasn't the sort of anger I could laugh off. We remained in a very dangerous situation.

I first removed the gag from her mouth, and when I did, I felt overwhelmed by a sudden desire to kiss her. The pull was stronger than anything I'd ever felt before, and was a feeling I didn't entirely understand. But I held back and instead asked, "Are you hurt?"

Ignoring that, she said, "You know what they'd do to Mott and me just for information. What do you think they'll do to you?"

"If we get out of here, none of us will have to find out."

"No, Jaron, please just go! This place is a trap. *I* am the trap!"

Her body wiggled while she argued, and though her legs were free, she was complicating my attempts to reach her tied hands. I said, "You can help me or not, but I won't leave without you!"

She huffed, and then went still so that I could reach her ropes. While I sliced at them, I said, "Once we're free, we'll run toward the swamp. Mott has a boat waiting there."

"We won't make it. Not all of us."

"We're just going to run. Don't look back. Just run."

"They were asking Mott about you, but at first he wouldn't tell." Imogen bit into her lip with worry. "Once they brought me here, and the whip, he told them he would cooperate. I begged him not to. I hate that they used me against you. I'd rather be dead than be the cause of your downfall."

I hesitated long enough to look squarely at her. "Never say that. I need you alive." I went back to work and added, "I'm nearly through the rope. Get ready to run."

She had one hand free by then and used it to comb her fingers through my hair, brushing the strands away from my face. Thick and brown, it had been cleaned up from the coarse chopping I had given it before I went to the pirates. Now I wished it were longer so there could be more for her fingers to get lost in. Even here, I felt drawn to her touch and had to force myself to concentrate on the rope.

"When you're finished, let me have your knife," she said. "I can fight too."

Once her other hand was free, she gave me a warm embrace. I thought about Roden's comment that I had been lying to myself about Imogen. Maybe she had told herself some lies as well.

Before I could speak, she whispered, "Whatever happens next, promise me that you will choose to live."

Behind us, Mott finally tore free from his binds. When Herbert went to help him stand, the young Avenian who had untied him immediately ducked into the shadows and escaped.

Mott grabbed the boy's sword from me and said, "We must hurry. He'll tell everyone we're here."

I put my knife in Imogen's hands, aware of my fingers brushing against hers, and then pulled her along with me. "Go!"

We weren't even out of the trees before a new group of soldiers rushed at us. Herbert continued firing arrows into the clearing, doing what he could to open a path for us. I guessed that Evendell was somewhere outside of the camp, watching for us as well. Mott yelled at me to leave, and as he fought, Imogen and I broke through the group and headed toward a hill.

Even more soldiers appeared, and I told Imogen to get to the top where Evendell could see her and protect her. Once she went down the other side, she'd be out of sight with a clear path toward the boat. I swung at whoever was closest to me, found my mark often enough, and dodged attempts to leave similar marks on me. When the crowd thinned to only a few, I broke through them to follow Imogen.

By then, she was nearly at the top of the hill. But instead of running down the other side, Imogen paused to look back at me. A soldier came out of nowhere and lunged for her, but her knife was faster and she left him clutching at his bleeding leg.

"King Jaron is down there!" a heavy man at the crest of the same hill yelled. "That's him! Shoot him!" He pointed directly at me, then an archer nearby raised his bow and nocked an arrow. Where was Evendell, or Herbert, to fire at him first? I needed a place to hide, but the hillside was bare. I was in trouble.

Imogen must've heard the order too. The archer's eye was on me, so he didn't see her coming when she crashed into him. His arrow that had been intended for me flew far off course. Imogen picked herself up, but the heavier man grabbed her arm. She bit down on his flesh, and when he released her, she ran again.

I yelled as I ran up the hillside, hoping to draw their attention back to me, but their anger was focused on Imogen now. The archer drew another arrow and lined it up with her as she ran away along the spine of the hill. She turned back, just long enough to look for me again.

Despite the noise and confusion throughout the camp, a whoosh through the air became louder than all else. The archer's arrow found its mark high in her chest. Still turned toward me, her face twisted with pain, and then she fell from the top of the hill. Her body rolled down the other side and out of my sight.

I continued running, certain that I could find her and save her again. Somehow.

But even as I ran, I heard a soldier call from the other side of the hill. "We've got the girl! She's dead."

And with those words, my entire world collapsed.

# · TEN ·

Whatever happened next was a blur. I didn't take another step after hearing of Imogen's death, and might've fallen to my knees. Either that, or a soldier in pursuit pushed me there.

I wasn't sure how many men surrounded me next. Was it fifty or a hundred? It couldn't possibly matter because I wasn't fighting back. I had lost any sense of how to fight back, or why I should try.

Imogen wasn't dead. She couldn't be, because I had just spoken to her. Only moments ago she had run her fingers through my hair, and was very much alive. All I had to do was find her and then surely I would discover the wound wasn't as bad as I had thought. We could still run from here, together.

Except that I had seen for myself where the arrow pierced her chest. Blood had poured from the wound — far too much of it and far too quickly. She could've been gone before her body touched the ground.

One of the soldiers hit me hard across the jaw, but kept me braced so that he could add to it and punch my left eye. I gave him no resistance as he continued to beat me, and in fact, I barely felt it. I couldn't see how he thought any pain to my flesh mattered at all in comparison to the rending of my heart.

They eventually got me on the ground, wrenched my sword from my grasp, and tore off my jerkin. Two men immediately began fighting over the leather but were ordered to preserve it whole for the commander. I was carefully searched for any tricks I might've carried with me, then my hands and legs were chained together. Without care for the pinch in my shoulders, they rolled me onto my back, presumably so that I could see the commander who had captured me. Perhaps they didn't realize that my left eye was already swelling shut, and that I had better things to look at with my right. I turned my head to avoid him and felt the sole of his boot on my cheek, pressing my face even farther to the side.

"So this is the boy king who has caused us so much trouble?" he sneered. "I'm not much impressed."

He removed the boot, then bent on one knee beside me. I kept my head turned away from him but felt his hot breath as he spoke. "I wish I could report that the girl died quickly and without pain," he said. "But I found her alive at the bottom of the hill — barely. She begged me to have mercy on you. I told her I had no such intentions. And in the last breath of her life, she asked me to give you a message, from her heart straight to yours."

This time I did look at him, though from his tone I knew he was bringing me anything but words of love. He grinned wickedly and showed me two of his fingers, wet with blood.

Her blood. He ripped at my undershirt until he got my bare chest and brushed his fingers across the skin, creating two red lines there. It stung like acid, and hurt almost as much as if he'd stabbed me.

"Get him inside and locked down," the commander ordered. "No rescuer will come within a mile of him!"

Someone pulled a dark sack over my head, and then they picked me up and carried me away by the chains. Several minutes later, I was deposited in a nearly black room filled with cold air that suggested I was in some underground location.

From there, I was transferred to irons fixed on the wall. It eased my situation somewhat because there was enough length on the chains that I could move my arms in front of me and slide to a sitting position. But nothing else improved. In the privacy of the room, one of the men who had carried me there kicked at my legs and gut, cursing me and telling me he'd had friends on the wall I exploded. He kept at it until another voice finally told him to stop.

After that, I withdrew into my own mind. I kept going back to those final moments. Imogen's expression while I untied her. There was fear and doubt, but it was more than that. Anger that I'd rescued her, but maybe relief as well. Roden had said that Imogen looked at me as if she loved me. Had there been love anywhere in her expression?

I didn't know. All I could think about was why she had stopped the archer. Why couldn't she have just kept running and saved herself?

Aware that I wasn't giving him any attention, the man who had kicked me before started at it again, harder this time. His foot connected with the very spot where Roden had broken my leg, and the pain of it forced a reaction from me.

"Ah, you have a weakness there," he said. "I'll remember that."

"All of you are dismissed." That voice belonged to the person who had kept a boot to my face. The men who responded called him Commander Kippenger.

I heard the room empty, then noted the sound of a knife being removed from its sheath. He placed the blade at the base of my neck and I hoped he'd make my death quick. My heart already felt as though it were full of holes, so he couldn't make it worse. I just wanted it over fast.

But that was not his intention. He ran the knife back down my torn undershirt and sliced it off me in pieces. I wished he had removed the blood too. I couldn't bear to feel it on my skin. Then he reached down and pulled the king's ring off my finger. Finally, he removed my boots, I assumed to keep me from running away. I had no thought to even try. When all was finished, he pulled the sack off my head. I should have blinked as my eyes adjusted to the light, but there was so little, no adjustment was needed.

I was in a hastily dug prison cell, almost entirely buried underground, and lined with rough wooden boards to hold back the earth. The only existing light came through cracks in the roof high above us, but those gaps also leaked dirt and water and likely invited rats inside as well. Due to the nearness of the swamplands, the ground beneath me was muddy at best. Yet the irons on my wrists and ankles were anchored deep in the wall. I couldn't pull free from them, even if I had the will to attempt it.

Kippenger was tall, with dark blond hair and a prominent nose. I supposed there'd be women who found him handsome if they didn't stare too long and see his flaws. Namely that he was obviously a cruel sort of devil who seemed to take my capture as his personal badge of honor.

"There," he said once he stood back to look at me. "Whatever you were before, you are nothing now. To the rest of the world, you will be dead. King Vargan is on his way here. He thought he was coming for the interrogation of your servant, but he'll be pleased to see we now have a much higher prize."

I didn't answer. I didn't care.

"Vargan will spread word of your death to the farthest reaches of these lands," he continued. "Robbed of their king, within days Carthya will be extinguished like a candle in a breeze."

My mind was already wandering again. I wondered whether Herbert and Evendell had survived. If Mott had gotten away, if he had seen what happened to Imogen. If he had seen me. And what they'd do to me here if I refused to surrender in this war. The blame for the destruction of my country lay solely at my feet.

And I had no will to make any of it better.

## · ELEVEN ·

The most difficult time to be hungry is when the pangs first start. When the body realizes it's missed a meal and signals that it wants food. But after a while it gives up asking; it gives up expecting anything. The pangs will return, of course, and the hunger never goes away. But once a person has reached this stage, he has bigger problems than the next meal.

Hunger was the least of my concerns.

In the first couple of days following my capture, I was left almost entirely alone. My prison was well guarded — I knew that from the conversations that filtered down through the boards over my head. But I remained in the darkness, was given nothing to eat, and had only the muddy water that dripped from the earth above to drink. The few visits I did get were only to be sure I was still there, and to add to my injuries in whatever way entertained the vigils. In all that time, I never fought back, never said a word, never gave a single indication I registered their presence. As far as I was concerned, if they were going to tell everyone I was dead, I might as well behave that way.

On the morning of the third day, their treatment changed. A couple of Vargan's soldiers came with a bowl of soup they insisted I eat. I gave them a thorough description of where they could shove it and waved it away. The taller of the men threw the bowl at me, as if I cared about that, and they left.

Later that evening, a plate was carried in with a chunk of stale bread and a cup of dirty water. I tossed the bread into the corner, hoping the rats would prefer chewing on it rather than getting any closer to me. I tried to hit someone when I threw the cup, but didn't manage to throw even as far as the vigil's feet.

Commander Kippenger was immediately summoned, and yelled a lot about how much trouble he'd be in if I didn't start eating. Somehow, that single fact made the hunger easier to bear.

The next morning, a woman was sent in with a towel that she used to wash me up. I begged her to wipe whatever was left of Imogen's blood off my chest and she did. Only then did I feel able to breathe again.

"I helped take care of the girl once they brought her here," the woman said. "They offered her every possible reward for information about you, but she always refused."

It hurt to hear about Imogen, yet I realized not hearing about her was worse. I had spent much of the past two days thinking back on things the priests of the churches had taught about an afterlife. If they were right, that all good people became saints in heaven, then surely that was where Imogen now rested. My family would be there as well. Whether it was true or not, I chose to believe that's where she was, happy and free from any worries or pain. It helped.

After the woman left, a chair was brought into the room. A herald outside announced the presence of King Vargan, though by the prickle of my skin, I'd already sensed him nearby. Moments later he entered my prison.

In his youth, Vargan had been a commanding presence, but time had worn away at him like seawater against a sand-castle. His gray hair was tied back and he had thick round spectacles that enlarged his dark-saddled eyes. A servant accompanying him discreetly mentioned the spectacles and Vargan quickly removed them, as if he hadn't wanted anyone to see. When he gave them to his servant, he was then handed a cloth, which he pressed to his nose. I found that odd, since it hadn't even occurred to me how it must smell in here. He stood in the doorway, stretched his back, and then studied me as he walked forward. Eventually he settled into his chair, though he still hadn't spoken a word, and I had yet to acknowledge him.

"I'm told you won't eat," he said finally.

"Avenian food tastes like salted dung," I muttered.

"I expected some humility. I could let you die in here."

"I wish you would."

He shifted his weight and looked me over. "Captivity has been hard on you. You look terrible."

"So do you. At least I have an excuse."

He chuckled softly. "The boy king single-handedly invades my country, causes the death of the girl he loves, and now is mine to treat in any manner I see fit. As you were told, we immediately sent word of your death far and wide, along with an offer to your prime regent for peaceful surrender."

"I'm glad you're offering," I said. "He'll happily accept your surrender."

He chuckled again. "When we met on the night of your family's funeral, I said that I liked you, and I do. You're a spirited young man, greatly in need of discipline, but with many qualities I admire. I wish we could've been friends."

I said nothing. My wishes for him were far less kind.

"Your position in this war isn't good, Jaron. The best choice for any of your men is to put down their swords. There will be a heavy price for their loyalty, and I hope you won't require that of them any longer. Do you think I'm not serious? The two archers who came with you are dead. Did you know that? They stayed to help you when they ought to have run."

I had figured they must be gone, but it was still terrible news. I took note that he didn't mention Mott. Perhaps there was a chance he had somehow escaped.

Vargan continued, "If it was only my army, you would still be outmatched, both in strength and in numbers, but there is also Gelyn and Mendenwal against you. I heard about your fight with the captain of your guard. Now he's left and taken the finest of your soldiers from what I'm told. Your remaining armies are scattered, without the strength to defend any single area. And I have you, still in mourning for that girl."

He referred to Imogen as "that girl," which was an insult to her. Yet I preferred that to hearing him use her name. He had no right to speak it, not after what he'd done.

Vargan leaned forward and clasped his hands together. "We've waited as long as we can to bury her. I wonder if you want to see her body, to see where the arrow struck. You may wish for the chance to mourn properly."

Still I remained silent. The thought had occurred several times to ask to see her, but ultimately I knew seeing her that way, having that one last memory, would destroy me even faster.

Vargan shrugged indifferently. "We know nothing for her gravestone other than her first name. She died in battle, and deserves more than that."

Amarinda would want Imogen adopted into her own house. I was sure of that. "She was Imogen of Bultain," I mumbled. "That was her name."

He nodded. "And is there any epitaph you want added?"

The words had already formed in my mind, and yet I waited until I was looking directly at him before I said, "Here lies Imogen of Bultain. Whose death prompted a revenge that marked the final days of King Vargan."

Vargan's face hardened and he stood. "Consider yourself lucky I don't bury you beside her. Because of your insolence, she will have no gravestone. There will be no memory of her ever having been here."

If only memories could be abandoned so easily.

"I took her!" Vargan yelled. "And before this is over, I'll take everything from you."

"There's nothing left," I mumbled.

"Are you sure of that? You'll give me whatever I want, or you'll learn what it means to lose everything. Mott, that servant you care so much about. I will let you watch every minute of his slow execution. Rulon Harlowe — he's like a father to you, isn't he? It won't take much to end his life. And the princess. She'll be lucky to escape with as little pain as that kitchen noble you loved."

By then, he had my attention. Coming from anyone else, those might have only been threats designed to frighten me. But Vargan would relish the chance to carry them out. If I didn't cooperate with him, using one person after another, he would destroy me.

He called for his vigils, then pointed at me and said, "Let the devils humble him. The next time I see this boy, I want him eager to bow at my feet. He will not defy me!"

The vigils bowed to their king and some of them escorted him up the stairs. The others came closer to me, pounding fists into their hands, preparing to carry out Vargan's orders.

# · TWELVE ·

My world had blurred between dreams and reality. Imogen still lived in one world, and nothing but pain existed in the other. Because of that, I spent the greater part of each day clinging to every possible memory of her. That alone kept me alive.

One memory returned to me over and over, a moment I both cherished and hated. When I had untied Imogen from the post, her fingers had combed through my hair. Despite any indifference she had ever shown me, every word she had uttered to make me believe there was nothing but friendship between us, her touch had changed all of that. And if I could have cut off the memory there and thought nothing further, I would have done it. But it was always followed, *always*, by the image of her twisted expression when the arrow pierced her chest, and the crumpled collapse of her body before it vanished over the hill. That memory had been burned into my mind, and was worse than anything Commander Kippenger or his henchmen could do to me.

Imogen's last words begged me to choose to live. Why couldn't she have done the same?

Vargan had left his soldiers with the invitation to torture me at will, and I had expected it would take on the worst form they could design. At first they were cruel to me, every bone in my body knew that. But I was becoming weak from lack of food and no more responsive than a rag doll. They began interrogating me for information, and repaid my silence with total humiliation.

Kippenger even devised a game meant to entertain the simple minds of his men. He placed a single garlin on a flat, embedded rock at the top of my prison walls and ordered me to retrieve it.

I glanced up at the coin, then turned away. The distance wasn't far — maybe double my height — but it seemed like more. Reaching the garlin while in these chains would be difficult, if not impossible, and I certainly couldn't see the point of trying.

But Kippenger wanted to play. "Reach the coin, boy," he said, "and I'll let you buy your freedom with it."

Still I didn't move. Not until his vigil, a brute the others called Terrowic, pulled out his sword and ordered me to climb up for the coin. It hurt to rise to my feet, but I figured that sword would be worse.

The earth surrounding me was soft in some places, but there were also roots and other embedded rocks that could provide holds to help me reach the coin. I still doubted whether I could reach it — if the chains didn't pull me down, my weaker leg would surely fail me.

After another of Terrowic's threats, I dug my fingers into the dirt to grab a root, and made my feet climb. The instant I did, Terrowic struck the back of my legs with the broad side of his sword.

I lost my grip and fell backward to the ground. Terrowic stood over me and laughed, then Kippenger ordered me to climb again. After a few more threats I got back to my feet, but climbed no farther before Terrowic hit my legs again. This happened a third time as well, but by the fourth, I only rolled to face the walls and ignored them. Kippenger didn't take too kindly to my refusal, but I was his prisoner, not his entertainment. I would not play these games.

Kippenger leaned over me as I lay on the ground. "They call you the Ascendant King. So climb. Rise up and get that coin."

"Remove the chains."

He laughed, mocking me. "Ah, but that's just the point, isn't it? You will never be free of those chains. You cannot reach that coin. You can't even stand unless I allow it. If a single garlin is beyond your reach, then how can you ever reach freedom? You will never rise again."

I turned to look at the coin once more and then closed my eyes. Maybe he was right.

By the next day, Kippenger had forgotten about the coin. But he returned with a new strategy. The same woman who had washed me a couple of days earlier came in with a bowl of soup. Kippenger followed her in and ordered me to eat it. I didn't even look at him until he ordered two other soldiers into the room. One held a stiff rod. I readied myself for more punishment, but instead he ordered the woman to turn and lean against the wall. She gasped in fear and looked at me.

Immediately, the bowl was in my hands. "Let her leave. I'll eat." To prove my sincerity I took a sip. Perhaps it was only because I had become so hungry, but the soup tasted like a gift from the saints. I intended to finish it all, and if he offered more, I'd accept it.

Much as I wished things could be different for me, Imogen had been right before: I could not give up here. I had to make the choice to live.

After I began eating, Kippenger ordered the woman and soldiers to leave. Knowing what would likely come once I finished the soup, I took my time. But after I set the bowl down, he said, "You won't eat to save yourself, but you will to save a stranger. How interesting." He watched me a moment longer, then continued, "Back in Carthya, you have a large number of soldiers stationed on a bluff, far from any fighting, and overlooking a lake that no longer exists. Why is that?"

"You've asked me this already."

"And you refused to answer. So I'm asking again. Why is your army there?"

"It should be obvious," I said without looking at him. "They're waiting for the lake to come back. Perhaps you could join them and go swimming."

He kicked me in the side, adding to a bruise already there, and then crouched to face me. "Why not work with me? Why not save yourself this pain?"

"You're not causing me any," I replied. That wasn't entirely true — I was still gasping, after all — but I felt better for saying it.

"If I can't hurt you, then you force me to bring in somebody I can hurt." He rose to his full height, and then whistled to his vigils outside. Like obedient dogs to his call, they pattered down the stairs. Only this time, they had someone else with them.

"Tobias." He raised his head when I breathed his name and I saw the remnants of a bloody nose on his face. As good as it was to see him, my heart was already pounding. If Tobias was here, then where were Fink and Amarinda?

His eyes widened when he saw me and he shook his head in disbelief. "Jaron? You're alive? But they said —"

"I am alive. Or something close to it."

Kippenger's voice became louder. "I'll ask you again, Jaron. Why is your army on that bluff?"

I set my jaw forward, but said nothing. Kippenger used my silence as a reason to backhand Tobias with a force I knew would leave its mark. Tobias yelped in pain, then collapsed to the ground, unconscious.

The vigils grabbed his arms to lift him again, but Kippenger said, "What's the point now? We'll wait until he wakes up, so Jaron can hear his cries."

They manacled Tobias to another set of chains across from me and left him with his face half buried in the cold mud. Kippenger pointed at him, warning that if I didn't cooperate, he would do the same to Tobias as he had to Imogen.

When Kippenger and his men left, I softly called out Tobias's name again. He only stirred at first, but I called to him once more, louder the second time.

Without opening his eyes, he whispered, "Is it safe?"

I coughed out a quiet laugh. "Of course not. You know where we are, don't you?"

Now Tobias opened his eyes and maneuvered his way to a seated position. "How'd you know I was awake?"

"People who've fainted don't peek when they think no one's watching." He half smiled back at me, and then, with more seriousness, I added, "You thought I was dead?"

He nodded somberly. "They're parading your clothes around for everyone to see, ripped and covered in blood. They hope it'll discourage your people from fighting."

With a humph, I said, "Well, as you can plainly see, I'm not nearly as dead as Avenia claims."

"You don't look far from it."

I liked his joke, but in truth, I didn't feel far from it either.

"Were Mott and Imogen able to escape, then?"

Answering was harder than I had thought it would be, and I had to force the words out. "There's been no word on Mott since I came. I haven't dared ask about him. Imogen didn't . . . isn't . . ."

Tobias nodded and opened his mouth to say something, then closed it. Whatever he was going to say, condolences, or pity, or further questions, I didn't want any of it. So before he could change his mind, I closed my eyes to rest them and then asked, "Where are Amarinda and Fink? Please tell me they made it to Bymar."

The silence was long enough that it forced me to look at Tobias again. He was shaking his head. "We got past the border guards without too much problem. They took most of the food, but let our driver pass through. We were almost to Isel when a group of thieves attacked the carriage. There wasn't time to get back into the holding below, so when an opportunity came, we ran and hid near the road while our driver held them off. A group of Avenian soldiers was passing and heard the commotion. They captured a few of the thieves and our driver. The thieves told them about our having escaped, and the soldiers soon realized our carriage might have held the princess. They ordered our driver to talk, but he only expressed his allegiance to Carthya and refused to answer any further questions."

I shook my head. Loyalty was invaluable, but amongst those soldiers, it meant that I already knew how that man's story had ended.

Tobias continued, "That's when the soldiers told the driver about your death. They even showed him a piece of your clothing. Amarinda and I were watching from a distance. We recognized it as the same clothes you had worn when we were last together."

"Fink saw them too?"

"We all saw it, Jaron, and it was all any of us could do in that moment to keep from crying out. Fink even rose to attack them but I held him back." Tobias licked his lips. "It was the worst news of my life, and no better for the others. It took several minutes after the soldiers left before Amarinda felt well enough to walk."

"Toward Bymar?"

Again, Tobias shook his head. "I tried to persuade Amarinda to go, but she knew it wouldn't be long before word spread of your death. She felt that Carthyans would look to the throne for leadership and that someone had to be sitting on it. So she insisted on walking back to Drylliad."

The idea of that was insane. If the soldiers who stopped those thieves knew the princess was in Avenia, they'd turn the country inside out to search for her. And Isel was their closest escape. Retracing their steps all the way back to Carthya was far too dangerous, and I told Tobias so.

"I agree," he protested. "But she's the princess and I'm her servant. If she wanted to return to Carthya, I had no choice but to follow. Fink went on to Bymar, to beg them to come to Carthya's aid."

"What?" I exploded with anger and had to remind myself to stay quiet. "You sent him off alone?"

"He insisted he could do it. And he is Avenian, so his chances of getting past any soldiers are decent. We had no choice, Jaron."

Maybe not, but I still didn't like it. "How'd you get captured?" I asked him.

"She and I were asleep one night and I heard a noise in the darkness. I crept out to investigate and the soldiers found me. By the time they dragged me back to where I'd slept, she was gone, along with any trace of her trail."

I felt terrified for what had happened to the princess since then, and by the expression on Tobias's face, he felt the same way. The thought of what would happen if she was also captured was unbearable, made even worse since I had become so helpless here.

No more. It was time to break free from this place.

# · THIRTEEN ·

Despite my best intentions to find an escape from the Avenian camp, the realities of our situation complicated those plans. Now that they had Tobias for leverage, their work on me intensified. Even if the opportunity for escape arose, my strength to accomplish it was dwindling. Tobias offered to help where he could, but his treatment was little better than mine, and without my cooperation, things would only get worse for him.

In the same area from where I had released Mott and Imogen, Tobias and I were questioned about the plans for the war, this time by the lumpish troll, Terrowic, and another of Kippenger's men. It was hard enough just to be there, with a clear view of the hill where Imogen had stood only days before. I repeatedly scanned the ridge, hoping against reason to see her, and then my focus would be taken again, back for another of their endless lines of questions.

"How many soldiers have you kept in Drylliad?" Terrowic asked.

"Don't answer that!" Tobias begged, which earned him another punch to his gut. He doubled over, choking on his breath, and I felt the same pain within me.

"Give us a number." The smaller one who spoke had a large mole on his chin that I constantly stared at with disgust, mostly because I knew my staring bothered him. "We'll drag it out of you if we must."

"No, you can't do that," I mumbled. It wasn't their intentions I doubted, only the reality that there was nothing in me anymore. All of that had drained out, leaving behind only the dregs of any spirit I might have had once.

"We can do more than you think," Terrowic said. "My king has been secretly corresponding with someone I'm told you know well. A nobleman named Bevin Conner."

"*Ex*-noble," I muttered. And it was no secret. I'd already made the connection between Conner and Vargan.

"Conner told us about the kitchen noble in Libeth, about your armies, and your fight with the captain of your guard. So even if you don't want to talk, we'll still learn what we want."

Then I wouldn't talk. I tried turning away, but he ordered someone to get a whip.

Whether it was for me or for Tobias, I couldn't allow it to happen. So I called him back. "My commanders will expect you to get this information from me," I said. "They'll change all our plans. Don't you see how useless this is?"

"We'll determine what's useless." Terrowic had half the brains of anyone else in this camp, but made up for it by doubling the strength of his hits. He was round and fleshy, so at first I had underestimated him. But no longer. The worst of everything I'd received here had come from him.

"I'm certain that you understand uselessness better than anyone," I said. "But I've had enough of this. Let me talk to the commander."

Terrowic frowned. "You can't trick a person who sees the red rose."

Whatever that meant. Maybe he only had a third of a brain instead. He raised his hand against Tobias again, but I yelled, "Enough! Go get him now!" He paused and I added, "Get the commander, or I'll tell him you think his daughters look like toads."

"I never said —"

"You did, last night. You should speak more carefully when passing my dungeon."

Terrowic lowered his hand, then told his companion to watch over us until he and the commander returned. While Terrowic stomped away, the mole man merely stood off to one side where he could watch the women pass by with their heavy loads of washing. It didn't seem like the most interesting view to me, but maybe that was only because I had bigger issues on my mind.

With mole man distracted, I took a deep breath, hoping it would bring me some relief. When that failed to provide anything but more worry, I turned to Tobias. "I need to smile. Tell me something not awful."

"Now?"

"There might never be a better time."

"Okay." He grinned as a story came to his mind. "The first two days after we began walking back to Carthya, after hearing of your death, both Amarinda and I were miserable."

I arched an eyebrow. "This is the worst good story I've ever heard."

"Hush. It's coming." Tobias's eyes glazed as he was transported to that day. "Amarinda barely spoke a word for all that time, and I had no idea what I might say to her. It rained that night, and she and I were forced to take shelter beneath some thick underbrush. It was cold and so dark we could barely see our own fingers, and the night seemed to last forever."

"I'm beginning to wonder if you understand what 'not awful' means," I muttered.

"Hush!" Tobias smiled again. "But the next morning was beautiful. It was warm and sunny, with everything brightened by the rain. Even in Avenia, it looked to be a perfect day for walking. We hunted around for anything we might find to eat. The princess saw a large bush of wild berries and, in her hunger, hurried toward it. She was so eager, in fact, that she failed to notice the ground beneath her. She tripped on an exposed root and fell directly into a thick mud patch. The more she struggled to get out, the dirtier she became. I waded in to help her but fell also. By the time we were both out, there wasn't an inch of our bodies not covered in mud."

I chuckled. In all my time with Amarinda, I had never seen her make the slightest ungraceful movement of her hand, much less her entire body. Since I had once commented that she had dirt on her face, the possibilities for jokes now were endless. Now that I knew she wasn't perfect, perhaps there was a future for her and me after all.

"Did you ever get the berries?" I asked.

"Eventually." He smiled again. "At first, we were too filthy for eating. So we walked farther off the trail until we found a pool where the night's storm had created a vibrant waterfall. Hours seemed to pass as we stood beneath the water to get clean again, and it took some time for our clothes to dry. Then we ate."

I lost my smile and clicked my tongue, but he quickly shook his head. "Forgive the way that sounded. It wasn't what you're thinking."

He started to say more, but by then Terrowic had returned with Commander Kippenger, who didn't look at all pleased to be summoned here.

"We need a place to talk," I said. "Privately."

"Why not here?"

I glanced around and rolled my eyes toward Tobias and Kippenger's men. "Because it's not private, obviously." He started to turn away, but I added, "I'll give you what you want. But only if it's just you and me."

"No!" Tobias said. "Jaron, what are you doing?"

"Saving your life." I turned back to Kippenger. "Well?"

He nodded at Terrowic and mole man. "One of you, take Jaron's friend back to the dungeon. The other will wait here while this boy king and I talk."

Tobias yelled my name as they unchained him, but I wouldn't even look at him. He didn't have to understand my decisions, or like them; they were my decisions to make.

It was much later that evening when Terrowic brought me back to the dungeon. My time with Kippenger hadn't gone as well as I had hoped, and by then, I was exhausted and ached so badly that I couldn't even sit up while he rechained me. Tobias begged for some soup for me, but Terrowic refused him. It didn't matter. I didn't have the strength to eat it anyway.

"While he's held captive, you're responsible for his life," Tobias protested. "He's entitled to some basic decency."

"He's entitled to nothing," Terrowic replied. "If your king wanted basic decency, he should have included that in his bargain."

"What bargain did he make?" Tobias turned to me. "Jaron, what bargain?"

"I told them everything." It took all my willpower to force myself to a seated position. "Well, almost everything. I gave them enough to negotiate your release. When I see you safely away in the morning, I'll tell them the rest."

"No! Jaron, you didn't!"

"What else am I supposed to do?" I yelled back. "Watch as they punish you for my silence? They'll eventually get me to talk anyway, but you'll be dead by then. At least this way, you'll live."

"And what about you?" he asked.

"They won't let me go," I whispered. "You know that. Not at any price."

The reality of that was overwhelming, and I slumped against the cold rock wall. He looked me over with an expression of sympathy that I hated more than if he'd felt disappointment in me, or even anger. I turned away from him, but that didn't protect me from the wretched feeling of being pitied.

"Tell me you're not broken," he said. "I know it must feel that way, but you can rise from this."

"How would you know?" I snapped. "Do you bear the weight of an entire kingdom on your shoulders? Has an enemy country focused all its resources on destroying you?"

"No."

"And did they take someone you love?"

"No, she's —" Then Tobias caught himself and immediately switched. "Jaron, did you love Imogen?"

If he hoped for a confession, he wouldn't get it. I rolled toward the wall and closed my eyes. "I loved everyone who's been taken from me. So don't tell me when I'm allowed to break."

# · FOURTEEN ·

Tobias was supposed to have been released early the next morning, but when I dragged myself out of a deep sleep, he was at the end of a whispered conversation with Commander Kippenger. After the commander left, I asked Tobias what they had been discussing.

"I'm a regent of your court," Tobias said. "That gives me some value as a prisoner."

This was not the time for vanity. "You have more value to Carthya alive," I said. "You should be on your way there already."

"I agreed to stay, in exchange for some real food and a blanket for you. As part of my terms, they're also giving you today to rest."

I wished I were strong enough to refuse the offer and force him to leave, but I wasn't. I desperately needed the food by then and I was almost constantly numb with cold. So I nodded back at him. Even if I disagreed with his decision, I was grateful for it.

The food was brought soon after, but it was done as a mockery to me. A thick cut of meat and large chunk of bread were offered on a heavy silver bowl fit for a king. For as little as

I'd eaten over the past few days, I knew the meat would be too much for my stomach. I tried nibbling on the bread, but it felt just as uneasy inside me.

I kicked the bowl over to Tobias. "You should have this."

"No," he said, kicking it back to me. "Jaron, that's for you."

"I can't eat it, and they know that." I sent the bowl to him again. "It takes a lot of effort to push this over to you, so just take it, please."

He reached for the bowl, but only stared at it. "I made a deal with them. This isn't what I wanted."

"I have the blanket, and that's enough. Now eat. At least one of us needs our strength." The food smelled so good that it renewed all the hunger pangs within me. So I wrapped myself in the blanket and lay down to sleep.

I remained that way until late in the day when Kippenger came into the dungeon and announced that King Vargan had returned to speak with me. "You promised to answer the rest of our questions," he said. "The king wishes to ask them himself."

I didn't even open my eyes to reply. "That agreement was only if Tobias left safely."

"He is still here because of the agreement he made on your behalf! Now get to your feet. King Vargan is extending a hand of friendship to you. He invites you to share tea with him."

The tea appealed to me, but I had no interest in the kind of friendship he was offering.

Terrowic returned, and this time he was carrying a black livery coat crossed in red, similar to his own uniform. I eyed it, but remained silent. I slowly rose to my feet, mostly to avoid the kicks he was so generous in giving me.

With a nasty glare on his face, Terrowic began unlocking the irons that had bound me to the wall. Then he tossed the coat my way. "Put that on."

"Wear Avenian colors on my back? You must be joking. Get me something else."

He pointed to Tobias, who sat silently in his corner of the dungeon. "If you won't, I can break his arm."

"Or you could say please. Have you no thought other than cruelty?" I reached for the coat, and then held it out to him. "I'm a king and you're a servant. You should dress me."

Terrowic nearly hit me again, but Kippenger grabbed his arm first. "You're nothing but stinkrot to us. Put that on."

With a sigh, I slipped the coat over my shoulders. I didn't bother with belting it closed, but Kippenger cinched it tight for me, then ordered my wrists to be chained again. I held them together without fighting. Once I was bound, Terrowic ordered me to follow him.

"I can't walk," I said. "You should know that. You beat me the worst."

If they hadn't liked me when I was unresponsive, I certainly wasn't gaining any friends now. Kippenger huffed and ordered his soldier to carry me to Vargan.

"I'll do no such thing. He can walk just fine."

"I watched how you treated him yesterday. Even if he can walk, with those bruises it'll take an hour to get him there. Pick him up."

With the gentle manners one might expect from a rabid bulldog, Terrowic threw me over his shoulder. That's when I finally saw my opportunity. We weren't even out of the prison before I had the keys from around his waist slipped down the sleeve of my coat.

The king was housed in a hastily assembled but elegantly decorated brick building with three steps leading to the entrance. The soldier dropped me on the ground in front of them and told me I'd walk from here or get dragged in by my feet. I got up, but immediately collapsed forward onto the middle step. That was my moment to let the keys fall inside the coat, held up by the tight belt. Before he had the chance to kick me properly, I stood again and limped to the top. That part was not an act. Walking was genuinely painful.

Vargan was seated beside a simple wood table that looked completely out of place for someone dressed in so much royal finery. The spectacles were gone this time, but he had two red marks on either side of his nose, indicating he had recently been wearing them. And he wore his gray hair straight down today, which made him look even older than usual. A good decade past death, at least.

The entire back of the room was masked by a heavy embroidered curtain that draped onto the floor. I briefly wondered what was behind it, and then decided I didn't much care. Vargan was surrounded by at least twenty highly decorated soldiers, each of them a human armory. I wanted to believe so many men were needed as protection from my tricks, but I had no tricks left. Both my strength and will to fight were failing. A kitten could've guarded Vargan from me.

When I entered, he motioned to a chair across the table, inviting me to join him. I stood in place until the soldiers at my heels pushed me forward. I shuffled to the table and, without looking at him, dropped heavily onto the chair.

Vargan studied me with an expression of disgust and finally offered me a plate of bread and sliced cheese that had been set between us. He waited for me to look at him, and I gave him the finest acknowledgment I could, which mostly consisted of me gathering spit in my mouth in case he happened to lean in closer.

Instead, Vargan sat back in his chair. "Tonight, Avenia will begin a march into Carthya. Thanks to the information you provided my commander yesterday, I know exactly where to attack, and how. I have a hundred men for each of yours. Everyone who stands against me will die."

My eyes darted up to him, then back to the table. Nothing more.

That angered him, and he got louder. "Don't you care what's happening out there? To your country, your people?"

Of course I cared. If he looked at me and saw only the scars of my flesh and callous tone of my words, then he knew nothing of who I really was. Who I'd always been.

"You made a bargain with my commander, and you owe me some information. However, we both know that once you give it to me, there won't be any reason to keep you alive." Vargan did lean forward then, but it was too late. I had swallowed the spit. "So I'm making you an offer instead. Work with me to end this war. Together, we'll save thousands of lives, including your own."

He paused so I could give him some response. I declined to so much as blink.

So he continued, "Carthya will become a tributary to Avenia. I will become emperor of these lands. You will still be a king, although subject to my rule. We can negotiate terms for the tributes, in exchange for peace between us." Another pause, then he said, "I know you don't want to hear any of this, but I warned you on the night of your family's funeral. You could've had peace from me then — I wasn't asking for much. But you ignored my warnings, you played games with the loyalty of my pirates. You had to make it worse."

Despite everything, I smiled a little. Making things worse was one of my few talents.

"I have shown my ability to take whatever I want from you, and I'll take Carthya as well, if I have to. But I'd much rather we came to an agreement. With your signature on a treaty, there can never be any question of the arrangement between our countries."

This time when I failed to answer, Vargan leaned forward enough to reach me. I turned my face away, but he pinched my cheeks with his meaty fingers and forced me to look at him. "I'm offering you peace, and a chance to live. This is the only way you'll leave this camp alive."

He was close enough now that when I spit, it hit him directly in the eye. I had aimed for his cheek, but this was better.

"If I care nothing for my own life," I said bitterly, "just imagine how I feel about yours."

He cursed and backhanded me hard enough to nearly knock me off my chair, but I didn't care. I had insulted him worse.

"I told you to humble him," Vargan said to his men. "Does he look humble?"

In all fairness to his soldiers, until the moment I spit on their king, I probably had looked pretty humble. But this also meant I had more punishment coming my way. The spitting was still worth it.

Vargan started to say something else, but Kippenger had been waiting outside the building and burst inside. He gave a hurried bow to Vargan, then said, "Pardon me, Your Excellency, but a diplomat has come from Carthya inquiring about King Jaron's death. He begs to see you at once."

My head whipped around. What diplomat?

Terrowic was immediately beside my chair and put a knife to my throat.

"Take him behind the curtain and keep him quiet there," Vargan ordered. "I want this boy king to understand exactly what's at stake if he doesn't cooperate."

At knifepoint, two other soldiers dragged me to the head of the room and behind the curtain where there was nothing but stacked crates of supplies for the war. Terrowic whispered again what he'd do if I breathed a word, and it didn't sound very pleasant. But there'd be no trouble from me. More than anyone in this room, I wanted to know who had come.

As it turned out, I'd have recognized the voice from any distance, and I wished it could've been almost anyone else.

"King Vargan, I bring you sad greetings from the kingdom of Carthya, where our people are in mourning. As is my duty at this time, I have come to inquire about the body of our monarch, King Jaron." That was Harlowe's voice.

I wanted to cry out, to tell him I was this close and a lot more alive than I was being given credit for. But I knew what would happen to both of us if I so much as cleared my throat.

For reasons I couldn't fathom, Harlowe had willingly walked into Avenian hands. And now, if I didn't cooperate, Vargan would take him from me too.

# · FIFTEEN ·

Vargan seized on this new opportunity the way a snake might snatch a mouse. He would force me to act, but I didn't know how to fix this. It would have been hard enough to get both Tobias and myself out of here. Now Harlowe too? How many others from my kingdom would collect in that dungeon? I didn't want their company, not here, and no matter how hard they tried to help me, it didn't make anything easier.

The key to my chains was still hidden inside my coat, but I'd have no chance at freedom before one of the many vigils here killed me, and then Harlowe next. So I stood silently and in full cooperation. For now.

"You wish to have Jaron's body?" Vargan said to Harlowe. "For what purpose?"

"His title is *King* Jaron," Harlowe replied calmly. "And naturally, we wish to bury him, according to Carthyan traditions."

Vargan let a long silence pass, probably in some attempt to intimidate my prime regent. Well, he could stare at Harlowe for as long as he wanted, but I knew Harlowe wouldn't blink.

Eventually, Vargan gave up and said, "It's a pity Jaron's dead. Otherwise, I'd have offered you the chance to trade places with him, to give your life for his."

"And I'd have accepted," Harlowe said.

"Yes, but would Jaron allow you to do that?" Vargan's laugh was dark and coarse. He was speaking to Harlowe, but his message was for my ears. "Would he let you die to save himself?"

"I would insist on it," Harlowe said. "If Jaron were here, I would beg him to find a way to remain alive, even at my expense."

"And *if* he were here," Vargan said, "I would offer him a way to save you both. Bring him out!"

The vigils at my sides shoved me back through the curtain and into the main room. I hadn't been prepared to move so suddenly, and so although I was in bad shape, stumbling into the room probably made my condition look worse. Harlowe sat up straighter when he saw me, but the expression on his face was one of deep sadness, not surprise. I tried to understand that. Obviously, he must have known all along that I was alive, but how? Harlowe immediately left his chair and bowed at my feet, a move that infuriated Vargan.

"You will bow to me before this is finished!" Vargan growled. "Both of you will."

Harlowe rose again and in his anger seemed to have grown in size, towering over Vargan. He gestured at me with his hand. "Look at him, the suffering he's clearly endured here! If you allowed such treatment of a royal, then you are not worthy to demand anything of him!"

"He illegally entered Avenia and attacked this camp," Vargan countered. "Are those the actions of a king or a mercenary? Jaron is my prisoner, and believe me, he has received far more kindness than he deserved."

Harlowe stepped forward to further the argument, but I mumbled his name to get his attention. Shaking my head, I said, "Go home, *now*, while you can, and let me handle things here. Tell the people I'm well."

"But you're not," Harlowe said. "I will not leave your side."

Vargan chuckled. "Noble words from both of you, but about choices neither of you have." He tilted his head in an order for his vigils to advance on Harlowe. They pulled his arms behind him and almost instantly had him in chains similar to mine.

"King Jaron, just before your regent arrived, I was about to give orders concerning you. Can you guess what for?"

"You want to set me free, to save yourself any embarrassment after I escape."

His eyes narrowed. "I was about to order your execution. But I suggest we start with your prime regent instead. Your younger regent will follow."

"No!"

"Then do as I say! Sign the papers making Carthya a tribute to Avenia."

I glanced at Harlowe, but read nothing from his expression. He had to know I couldn't sign them.

At Vargan's gesture, the man holding Harlowe withdrew a knife and placed it at his neck. Harlowe cocked his head away, but his eyes were on me. They were calm, or at least, more at peace than I felt.

Then Vargan said, "You will watch him die, Jaron, here and now. And you will know that all of this could have been prevented if you would only bow to me!"

Still, I did not respond. Finally, Vargan said, "Kill him."

"I need time!" I shouted. "King Vargan, you ask everything of me. The least you could do is give me an hour of privacy with my two regents to discuss your proposal. I need their advice." Vargan looked unconvinced, but I added, "I promise to make the best possible use of that time."

Vargan waved us away, back to the same prison where I'd been held before. Vigils led me away first, with Harlowe not far behind. Terrowic, the man from whom I'd stolen the keys, suddenly began patting around for them.

"I've lost my keys," he said to the other vigil with me.

"Again? The king will have your head if he finds out."

"My vigils never lose their keys," I muttered. "In Carthya, we're not that stupid."

He dug his fingers deeper into my arm and picked up his pace. I nearly lost my footing with the increased speed, but managed to keep up. I didn't want to stumble again and worry Harlowe. He already seemed concerned enough.

There had only been two sets of chains attached to the wall. Tobias was still bound to one, and when I walked in with Harlowe, he sat up in surprise but said nothing. They returned me to the other chains. With no other alternative, Harlowe was taken to a corner and ordered to sit and not move. Quite pleased with themselves for having taken an additional member of my court, the vigils folded their arms and stood back against the wall.

"We won't speak a word until you're gone," I said. "Your king promised us an hour of privacy to discuss his proposal. Do you want to explain the delay, or shall I?"

The vigils looked at each other, then exited. When I was sure they had gone, I immediately asked Harlowe, "How did you know I was alive?"

"Mott has stayed hidden close to the camp all this time, but he couldn't get anywhere near you. We didn't know about Tobias, but I'm glad he's been here to help you."

"I'd have done more for him, if I could have," Tobias said.

Harlowe smiled at him. "And for that, you have an entire kingdom's gratitude." Then he turned back to me. "We couldn't rescue you, so we decided to force you to rescue yourself."

"If I could escape, I'd have done it already. You sacrificed yourself for nothing!"

"I've made no sacrifice, Your Majesty. We will all escape here safely. I know you well enough to see when your mind is working. Now, tell me your plan."

My last plan had ended with Imogen's death. I didn't trust that I could do any better for Harlowe and Tobias this time. However, doing nothing had a very definite outcome for us all. Something had to happen.

Although it required a bit of maneuvering, I was able to withdraw the key from my coat and free myself. Then I freed

Tobias, who crept over to Harlowe and set to work at his chains.

"Can either of you fight?" I asked. "I'm afraid I won't be much help to you here."

"You know how I am at fighting," Tobias said. "But I'll do what I can."

"Then I'll be strong enough for all of us," Harlowe said.

When the guards returned an hour later, we were back in our places, chained to the wall. Or rather, the chains were around our wrists, but not locked.

As soon as they entered, I asked Terrowic, "Did you find your keys?"

He scrunched up one side of his face and moved farther into the cell. "Why?"

"Because if a prisoner found them, you'd be in a lot of trouble."

Then he understood. He lunged for me, but I rolled away and he hit the wall. From where he had been hiding behind the door, Tobias leapt forward and swung the chains he had worn at the vigil's head. With a large cracking sound, Terrowic tumbled to the ground, unconscious.

"Did you see that?" Tobias asked. "I did that!"

Harlowe quickly helped Tobias remove the man's livery, and Tobias slipped it on over his clothes.

We started for the door, but footsteps pounded down toward us from other vigils who had heard the commotion. We were trapped.

# · SIXTEEN ·

Vigils began filling my dungeon room. I started into the center of them, but Harlowe pressed me back. Then, from up higher on the stairs, we heard bodies thump to the ground. Caught by surprise, the men who had entered the cell were easy prey for Harlowe, holding Terrowic's sword. Moments later, Mott darted through the door with a baselard in one hand and longsword in the other. He had on the same helmet as the other Avenian soldiers, and was dressed in the same black and red coat as I wore, though his wasn't belted.

He saw Tobias first and raised his brows in surprise. But then he saw me and frowned. "What have they done to you?" Before I could answer, he remembered his business and said, "We won't have long. Let's go."

Tobias and I leaned down and grabbed the helmets and daggers from two men who had fallen. We had no time to disguise Harlowe, but I hoped with our uniforms and weapons it would appear that we were vigils escorting him as a prisoner.

Once outside the dungeon, Mott helped me onto a horse he had tethered nearby, then climbed up in front of me and told me to keep my head down. He had a second horse for Harlowe, who leapt into the saddle with more agility than I'd ever have guessed he was capable of. Tobias rode behind him, and even put his dagger out to make it appear as if Harlowe was his captive. Amazingly, almost without the notice of other soldiers in the area, we rode away.

Mott wasn't taking us toward the main entrance of the camp, but rather, toward the swamp. We passed several tents, but fewer soldiers than I'd have expected. Then somewhere behind us the camp suddenly burst into activity and I knew our absence had been discovered. Mott only rode faster, trying to stay ahead of the alarm to search for me without drawing any attention our way.

We stopped in a quiet area near the swamp where the ground was already mucky and where cattails and duckweed grew thick and dense. Mott jumped off the horse, then pulled me into his arms. I insisted that I could walk but he continued carrying me deeper into the water and dropped me into a small boat hidden there. Harlowe and Tobias climbed in behind us and the coxswain immediately ordered the two rowers into action. I noticed one of them used his oar to bat away at something before we moved. If we were lucky, it was only a snake.

They folded a thick blanket over my shoulders and Harlowe directed me to a seat at the center of the boat while we silently backed away from the shore. Kneeling before me in the boat, he slid wool socks and leather boots onto my feet and asked if I had any injuries requiring immediate attention. When I shook my head, Harlowe handed me a flask and told me to drink slowly. The hot tea was like a balm to the little energy still flowing within me. The liquid took on the bitter smell of the sulphur rising in vapors from the swamp, but I didn't care. I drank it gratefully while Harlowe sat quietly beside me. Tobias was somewhere behind us, watching for anyone who had followed.

Night came faster within the swamp, or at least it seemed that way. The plants atop the water were so thick in places that they often forced us to back up in search of clearer routes. The foul odors were nauseating, held in by the tall trees that crowded the shorelines. When we were far enough north of Vargan's camp, the coxswain ordered lamps to be placed in the front of the boat, but they only made the shadows more menacing and the black water look deeper. I turned away from it and buried myself deeper into the blanket.

"Are you cold, Your Majesty?" Harlowe felt behind him in the boat. "We have more blankets."

"I'm fine. Nothing more is needed." When he met my eyes, I added, "Thank you, for what you did back there."

"Thank Mott. This was his idea."

I turned around to look at Mott, who was already watching me. I nodded at him, a weak attempt to communicate the gratitude I felt. His smile back at me was grim.

"Two men helped me get inside the camp," I murmured. "Both were archers —"

"They didn't get out," Mott said. "I'm sorry, Jaron."

So Vargan had told me the truth about their fate. Hearing the news again didn't lessen the sorrow I felt for their loss, or my regret that I didn't achieve more for the price of their lives.

It was impossible now to see anything beyond the light of the lanterns, but I suspected there was little here worth seeing. I tried to ignore the creaks and moans that gave life to this swamp and drank more of the tea. I'd gone so long without any substantial amount of food, my stomach was having trouble with the liquid. But it was giving me much needed warmth inside, so I continued to draw from the flask.

"I wish you could see this place in the sunlight," Harlowe said. "Perhaps you'd tell me whether it's as ugly as I've always thought it is."

A corner of my mouth turned up. I hadn't seen much of the swamp, but I'd smelled more of it than I cared to. I could already give him my opinion.

"My family has always lived here," Harlowe continued, "but as soon as I was grown, I wanted to leave, to make my home as far from this ugly place as possible. I did leave for a while, and years ago on my travels met a lovely girl named Havanila. She felt that Libeth needed us, and insisted there was beauty in the swamp. That's the way she was — someone who only saw beauty around her."

"Havanila. I've never heard that name before."

"It's where my granddaughter's name comes from." Harlowe returned to his thoughts again, and then said, "I lost my dear Havanila a year ago, far too soon."

I took another sip of the tea. It was clear from the tone of his voice how much he had loved her. How much he still loved her. I wondered which was worse: to love someone who passes too early. Or to never love at all.

"How did she die?" Beyond my curiosity, the question was meant to distract my own thoughts.

The creases in Harlowe's face deepened as he considered his answer. Finally he said, "I believe it was sadness. You see, there have been three losses in my family. You know of the death of my oldest son, Mathis, a few months ago. Perhaps I've never told you, but you remind me a little of him. There are some slight physical similarities, but the likeness is really in your character. Like you, he was stubborn and willful, and hard to discipline. Despite his challenges, I loved him dearly."

I thought of my own father, the endless battles over his attempts to control me, mold me, and make me see the world through his eyes. And me, resisting all of that, every time. I wanted to believe that despite the troubles I had caused my father, he had loved me just as dearly as Harlowe loved his son.

Harlowe continued, "You may not know, but Mathis had a younger brother. When he was still an infant, he was stolen away by his nurse, an Avenian woman who demanded a large ransom for his return. I would've paid it, but never heard from the woman again. It was a terrible winter that year — likely neither of them survived it on the run. My wife never fully recovered from that loss; I'm sure that sorrow eventually led to her death. But I take comfort that if she cannot be with me, at least she is with my sons now in the afterlife."

"You believe in the afterlife, then?" I asked.

His eyes remained steady on me. "I know it exists. My family waits for me there."

*As my family waits for me.*

"I suppose I'm telling you this because although I would never aspire to the role of a king, sometimes I think of you as my own son. I had to go after you in that camp, because I could not bear to lose you too."

No response came to my mind, so I only wrapped the blanket tighter again. After a long rest, I asked for news of any developments in the war.

"There's been no word yet from Kerwyn," Harlowe said. "Let us hope that means he is continuing to work with King Humfrey of Mendenwal, and nothing worse."

"Their army broke through our borders three days ago," I said. "They tore through our defenses near Benton and moved northward."

Harlowe reacted with surprise. "Yes, they brought thousands of soldiers, numbers Carthya could never compete against. But how did you know?"

"Nobody thought I would ever leave that camp," I said. "They weren't always as cautious as they ought to have been in their conversations near me. I know far more than Vargan would like to believe. What I don't know is Mendenwal's plans now that they're here."

"I might be able to help with that," Harlowe offered. "One of our spies intercepted a message from Mendenwal to Avenia. The bulk of Mendenwal's armies are taking up camp at Falstan Lake, where they'll wait for further instructions from Avenia."

"Then you must send more of our men to Falstan Lake too. We have a good camp in the highlands above the lake."

"We don't have nearly enough men to win a battle there, sire."

"That battle won't be about numbers. And no one should act until I can get there."

Tobias, who had been listening, cut in. "Are you sure, Jaron? You may have information now about Avenia. But they know us better too. In your bargain with Commander Kippenger, you told him all your strategies."

I turned enough to grin at him. "Did I? Why else have I practiced lying in my life, but for that moment?"

Tobias chuckled. "You gave him false plans?"

"Is that an accusation, Tobias? Do you doubt that I am burying the wealth of Carthya in secret caves in the hills of Benton?"

"There are no hills around Benton," Tobias said. "Nor caves."

I arched an eyebrow. "Maybe that's what makes them so secret. Do you doubt that I am melting our warriors' swords and using the metal for armor? Or that I am seeking peace with Mendenwal by offering to give my future child to their king?

Do you? Because Kippenger didn't doubt any of it. I learned from them, but they got nothing from us."

While the others laughed, Harlowe picked up our old conversation. "We can get you to Falstan Lake, if you wish. But I urge you to first take time to rest."

"I'll rest on my way there. Make sure it's widely known throughout Carthya that I am alive, and that I'll be at Falstan Lake."

"If I send out word, our enemies will hear it too," Harlowe warned.

"I'm counting on that. But I won't be there right away. There's something I must do first." I turned and asked Mott, "Do we have weapons with us?"

Mott reached in front of him in the boat and withdrew my sword and its sheath. "I was able to get this when they put it in storage a couple of nights ago." I held out my hand for it, but he only lowered it near him again. Normally, I'd have insisted on taking it, but that seemed like too much effort, and it would've been hard to hold anyway. Then Mott gestured to a wrapped bundle near him in the boat. "More weapons are in there too, though we shouldn't need them. We'll cross back into Carthya soon. Then get as far as we can from this place."

I shook my head. "Turn the boat around. We need a safe place to land inside Avenia."

Mott grimaced and his fists clenched. Something about me kept Mott at the edge of his temper, or beyond. At least this time I understood why, and tried to hedge the argument by saying, "I have reasons."

He wanted to yell at me — I knew that, and he would've been justified in doing so — but he only took a deep breath and said, "Remember where we are, Jaron. We are nearly to Carthya, where we can dock safely. Your orders will take us deeper inside Avenia."

"We'll dock in Avenia, preferably on their western shore." Mott groaned, and Harlowe started to object, but I said, "It's a safer plan anyway. It won't be hard for Vargan to get men on the Carthyan side of the swamp. They could be waiting for me there. Nobody expects me to stay in Avenia."

"There's a reason nobody expects it," Mott said. "It's too foolish, even for you."

I turned back to Harlowe, to give him the details he would need for this next phase of the war. "Of course, Your Majesty," he said once I had finished. "But at least tell me why you're staying in Avenia."

I shared a look with Tobias and Mott before I said, "We're going to the pirates. It's time they answered the call of their king."

# · SEVENTEEN ·

Our landing at an Avenian dock was so easy, I almost wanted to remind Mott that I had made the better choice. Of course, we had a dangerous road ahead and so it was too early for any celebration. Mott, Tobias, and I were still dressed as Avenian soldiers, which would help us move through the countryside without trouble. At least, I hoped there wouldn't be trouble. Much as I tried to hide it, Mott clearly understood that I was in no condition for a fight.

The three of us left the boat; then I ordered the rowers and coxswain to return my prime regent safely to Drylliad. I reminded Harlowe of my strategies, but was firm that his first priority was to send out a search for Princess Amarinda. If Fink made it to Bymar, then I hoped he would either stay there where it was safe, or return to Carthya in the company of Bymar's army and under their protection.

To avoid any argument, I explained only what was necessary of my plans. Mott's mouth was pinched in a thin line of disapproval and Harlowe didn't look much happier. Tobias clearly thought I had gone insane during my time in captivity, and as that wasn't entirely impossible, I didn't contradict him. In the end, they agreed to all that I asked, and Harlowe made Mott and Tobias promise to keep me safe. Mott replied that he could protect me from everyone but myself, which I thought was a fair compromise.

After Harlowe left, Mott, Tobias, and I obtained some food and three sturdy horses from a farmer on the outskirts of the swamp. Vargan's camp was farther south than our position, and I hoped our path would keep us far from there. I couldn't stomach the thought of returning, willingly or not.

Gradually the sun rose at our backs. We were heading west at a slower pace than I wanted, but Mott insisted I preserve my strength and recover from the past several days. Patience had never been a virtue that interested me, and certainly one I had never courted. But for now, it was a necessary one. When night fell, I arranged for an inn where we could spend the night with a good sleep. With our black and red uniforms, and my Avenian accent, nobody gave us a second look.

I felt much better the following morning, and even managed a meal of real food, or the closest thing to it in Avenia. Once we were on the road again, Tobias asked, "Shouldn't we turn farther south to reach Tarblade?"

"We have another stop first," I said.

Mott groaned. "You remember we're deep in enemy territory, correct?"

"The people here aren't my enemy," I said. "Only their king. I need to send a message."

"Carried in the hands of an Avenian? Jaron, you might not consider these people your enemy, but they won't look so kindly upon you. If you had a message to send, it should've gone with Harlowe yesterday."

"A fine idea, if I'd have thought of it yesterday," I snapped.

We rode for another half hour before we came to the edge of the thieves' camp, the place where I had first been taken on my way to the pirates. It had always been a bustle of activity, and I'd expected the same liveliness now.

But it was different this time.

I left my sword in place as we rode into camp, but had my hand ready, just in case. The few men still there came to their feet to greet us, but they looked more like scavengers than thieves. A few were armed, but nobody went for their weapons. I recognized a few men but most of them were new faces. I had no friends here.

"You've picked us over enough!" a drunken man shouted through blurred words. "None of us here can fight — the last group of soldiers knew that and left us alone."

With some nervousness, Mott and Tobias looked at each other, and I remembered how we were dressed.

"What happened to the others who were here?" I asked. "Did they volunteer to fight?"

"Volunteered at the point of a blade," a man said. "They took everyone who might be of use."

Another man sauntered forward, staring at me. "How old are you, boy? You're no soldier. Or no leader amongst them, if you are."

"No leader amongst Avenian soldiers, no." When I removed my helmet, there was enough of a reaction that it was clear some of them knew me. "My name is Jaron. I am the king of Carthya, king of the Avenian pirates, and a friend of Erick's, who was in charge here. If you don't wish to fight for Vargan, then join me now. Ride with me and let's leave this place."

"Or we could capture you and earn a lifetime of gold from Vargan," the man nearest to us said.

I snorted. "Don't be ridiculous. If you had the ability to capture me, you'd have already been recruited."

They gave up and half turned away from me. "We're Avenian," another thief said, sitting back down beside his fire. "We'll stay here."

"As you wish. But that's a thin stew in your pot, and I can help thicken it. If you're hungry, I'll pay your fastest rider to deliver a message back to Carthya for me."

"No," Tobias hissed. "You can't trust these men." But I only ignored him.

The man closest to me lifted his hands to his hips. "I'm the fastest rider here. What's your message?"

"It goes to my commander in Drylliad." I eyed him steadily. "Can you deliver it?"

He held my gaze. "On my word of honor as a thief."

Which, at best, was a contradiction in terms. Continuing, I said, "Good enough, I suppose. Tell him that during my time in captivity, I was forced to reveal our key strategies in this war, so everything must change. I need every spare man moved to Drylliad to protect the castle, and I want every trap ready in that city. I also want the wealth of Carthya moved to a place called Farthenwood. It'll be safer there." I leaned in to him. "Now promise me that this message will reach my castle."

"That's a pretty dangerous message." He nodded at a single garlin clasped in my fist. "I hope you're planning on paying more than that."

I stuffed the coin back into my pocket. That one wasn't for him. "No doubt Vargan would consider this message far more valuable than what I can afford to pay you here. But my companion will give you a few garlins now, and you may ask for many more once you've reached Drylliad."

I gestured to Mott, who reached into his saddlebag and withdrew a handful of coins for the man. He pocketed the money and then told the other thieves to get his horse ready.

There was nothing more to keep us here now. I wished the men well and told them we had to be on our way. After we rode off, Mott said, "While in captivity, you lied to Avenia about our plans."

"Yes."

"And now you wish to change all our actual plans to fit those lies?"

"It seemed like a good idea."

He stared at me for a moment, and then shrugged. "I hope you know what you're doing."

"If I don't, then you'll always be there to point out my mistakes."

I smiled from the corner of my mouth and Mott chuckled lightly. The joke eased the tension that had been between us since my rescue, and even Tobias relaxed somewhat. After another few hours, we stopped to give the horses a rest and for us to share some of the food we had brought with us from the inn. In the warmth of the day, we took shade beneath the canopy of a tall yew tree that overlooked the coast of the Eranbole Sea in the distance. It was uncommonly beautiful and I longed to one day board a ship and set sail across it.

Before taking bites for themselves, both Mott and Tobias leaned against the trunk and allowed me to eat as greedily as I needed to. It helped to return my strength, though it wasn't nearly enough for the conversation I had been avoiding since my escape.

When it couldn't be delayed any longer, I asked Mott, "Did I do the right thing, coming after you in that camp?"

"No." He sighed heavily and looked sideways at me. "But it wasn't the wrong thing either. The night you rescued me, from the minute they brought Imogen there, I knew I would tell them everything they wanted. I'd have failed you, Jaron."

"I'd have done no better. I didn't even last long when they put Tobias against me and he isn't nearly as pretty."

Tobias snorted a laugh and said he wouldn't even try to disagree with that.

We rested awhile, and then Mott said, "About Imogen —"

My eyes had been closed, thinking again of that last moment with her. "I thought I could save her. And you as well."

"You did save me. She might have gotten away too, but she wouldn't leave you behind any more than you'd have left her."

"She took the arrow intended for me. She gave her life for mine."

"And you risked yours for us. Why didn't you send someone else in? We have other warriors capable of that rescue."

"I knew Avenia was looking for information, and if anyone was captured they'd dredge my plans from them, as they would've done with you. But if I became their captive, I knew I could give them the exact information I wanted. Which I did."

Tobias shook his head. "If you were going to lie, why not just tell them at first, before they had to beat it out of you?"

"They'd never have believed me if I made it that simple." My voice softened as I felt again their strikes and blows. "They had to beat it out of me so that they would accept my lies. It was going to happen anyway. At least we got something from it." The price for misdirecting them had been very high, so much that it had nearly killed me. But we had an advantage now in the war. Avenia would waste a great deal of energy chasing shadows that did not exist.

Little more was spoken until we were back on the road again. Then my thoughts inevitably turned back to Imogen. I said, "The arrow hit below her shoulder, but might've missed her heart. If she survived the fall, then they would've tried to heal her, so they could use her against me."

"Then why didn't that happen?" Tobias spoke gently, knowing his words would add to the crushing ache within me. "If she survived, of course they would've used her and not me. So why didn't they?"

I already knew the answer, though I couldn't find it in me to speak the words. She had said it herself when we were together. Even if she had survived, she would try to die. She would choose that, rather than allow herself to become a weapon against me.

But this understanding only stirred my frustrations. "Why did she stop that archer? All she had to do was run."

Mott pressed his lips together, then with the same calmness as Tobias had used, said, "She stopped him because that's who she was. Don't be angry for what was best about her."

Maybe he was right, but I still wasn't sure that Imogen had been. I dropped my head and said, "Give me hope, Mott. Is there any chance of her being alive?"

He rode for a minute, probably replaying that moment just as I was. His eyes were closed and his face was tense. At last, he said, "I saw her fall from the hill, and I ran toward her, but she was quickly surrounded. They removed the arrow and then called for the wagon to get her."

"A medical wagon?"

He shook his head slowly, as if that simple movement took effort. "For the burial of the dead. That's where they put her. I'm sorry, Jaron."

We went silent. Until that moment, I had almost convinced myself that he would have seen something that could give me hope, one small possibility for her survival. But that wagon would've been called for only one purpose.

Finally, I said, "Her mother lives in Tithio, I think."

"Once we're back in Carthya, I'll arrange for a message to be sent to her," Mott offered.

"No, I'll do that. I owe her mother that much." The garlin from my pocket was in my hand again. I started to run it over my knuckles, then changed my mind and replaced it. "Every part of me hurts, Mott."

"You've been through a lot. But with enough time, all wounds will heal."

"I'm not talking about cuts and bruises."

"Neither am I."

"Oh."

"Jaron, she saved you because you have to save us. She did the right thing for Carthya. But only if you turn her death into purpose, and win this war."

I knew that was what I had to do, and yet it didn't make the task ahead of me any less impossible. I only understood now that despite the odds, I still had to succeed.

Little more was said until I pointed to a wide field on our right and directed Mott to have his sword ready. Tobias removed his too, for what good it might do us. Almost under my breath, I said, "Be alert. This is Tarblade."

# · EIGHTEEN ·

Tarblade Bay was the well-disguised home of the Avenian pirates. It was easy enough to spot from the sea, though any unfortunate sailor who came close enough to discover it was sure to be captured and killed. By land, most travelers could move right past the camp and not realize it was there. I had been here just a couple of months ago, and even then had to concentrate to be sure we were in the right place.

Anyone who found it necessary to ride into the pirates' camp would do so with their sword held out, blade down, to show the pirates he intended no harm. I certainly intended no harm, but I wasn't holding my sword out either. I would ride in as their king.

The pirates on the edge of camp recognized me immediately and things quickly flew into action. I heard shouts for Erick to come forward, and people calling my name, though it wasn't in the friendly way I would've preferred.

Erick had been the leader of the thieves and was the one who had brought me to the pirates. Eventually, I became the pirates' king, but left Erick in charge of them here. It was very good news to see he was still their leader. Based upon the expressions staring up at me, I suspected the only reason I remained king of the pirates was that I hadn't been here for them to challenge me to the death.

"Are you sure you know what you're doing?" Mott asked as we rode deeper into Tarblade.

"I'm sure I don't," I replied. "Keep your sword ready."

My reception wasn't any warmer once Erick emerged from his hut. He looked much as he did when I first saw him a few months ago, tall and lean with short, fading red hair, and penetrating blue eyes. Some things were new. He had a few recent cuts on his face, and a ragged scar replaced a line of the closely shaved beard along his jawline. He heaved a deep breath when he saw me, then muttered something to a couple of the pirates near him, who left in the direction of the kitchen.

"Who's this?" Erick asked me, gesturing at Mott and Tobias. "We don't like visitors at Tarblade. You know that."

"They're not visiting. These are my friends and will be welcomed as such." I was well aware of the danger in my words. It wasn't yet clear whether *I* would be welcomed here as a friend.

Mott and Erick acknowledged each other with curt nods. Tobias attempted it, but he was so nervous his spine had forgotten how to bend. I slid off my horse and said to Erick, "You look like you chose the wrong side in a fight."

"You look worse." Erick and I headed toward the kitchen as well, with Mott and Tobias leading our horses behind us. "Why are you here?"

"You must know why. Avenia has begun the war. I have the oaths of these pirates that if war came, they would fight for me. I'm here to call for the fulfillment of that promise."

Erick stopped, his face twisted in doubt. "Do you think the pirates wanted to give you that oath?"

"Whatever their feelings, they did give it, and they will keep it."

"It's taken everything I have to remain as their leader. Jaron, I came to power after only days here, and only because you gave me this position. They might follow me, but they'll cheer once someone finally takes my place. If they have such little respect for me, then you must know how they feel about you."

Did he think I had deluded myself about that? I felt my temper warming. "If you knew everything Carthya might lose in this war — everything I've already lost — then you would understand how little I care about whether either of us has friends here. Gather the pirates, Erick. I will talk to them myself."

"I'll gather them. But tell your dark-skinned friend to keep his sword ready. He might need it." Then Erick nodded at Tobias, who was fumbling with the grip on his weapon. "And tell that boy to lower his sword so he doesn't hurt anyone with it. In the meantime, get yourselves something to eat. I've seen corpses that look healthier than you do."

He gestured to a table nearby where Serena, a kitchen girl who had helped me in my lowest moment with the pirates before, was already setting down bowls of stew for us. She smiled warmly at me and invited me to sit.

I sat, eager for the food, with Tobias next by my side. Mott remained on his feet and only sat when I told him he looked like he wanted a fight. He poked at his stew a little, then saw I had finished mine in only a few bites and passed his bowl over to me. "For once don't argue with me," he said. "Just eat."

I was too hungry to argue. And I was nearly finished with his stew when the pirates began arriving. Mott was on his feet first, but I wasn't far behind. They gathered in a group slightly lower on the slope than where we stood. I recognized many of them. These were the men who had inflicted wounds upon me once they discovered my true identity. They had also cheered in favor of their former king, Devlin, when I fought him. Off to one side I saw the pirate who had kicked my broken leg while I was fighting Roden — the worst physical pain I had ever endured. I'd always remember him.

Erick joined me at my side and said to the gathered men, "Not all of you were here when King Jaron of Carthya came to the pirates. But you've heard the story, no doubt, and know of his strength, his courage —"

"What courage?" someone yelled from the crowd. "He passed himself off as a thief named Sage. We'd have killed him if he'd told us the truth."

"What better reason to lie?" Erick responded. "Forget whatever you think about this boy, whatever feelings you have about how he became king here. Because whether you like it or not, Jaron is your king. And each of you took an oath that you would follow him. He's come back now, and he needs our help.

I ask you all to listen to him." He turned to me and more quietly said, "If it turns ugly, I won't be able to stop them."

I nodded at him, and then stepped forward. "War has come to my country. I need your help."

"You ask us to fight against our home country?" another man yelled.

His anger was pure hypocrisy. With equal intensity, I answered, "You steal from your fellow countrymen, terrify their families, and kill anyone who crosses you. Now you want to claim that you are loyal to Avenia? I know as well as you that Tarblade is your one and only home, not Avenia. You are pirates, and I am your king. If I say that you will fight for Carthya, then you will."

"You don't have to be the king." The man who spoke was nearly as wide as he was tall, and appeared carved from solid stone. A matted black beard fell from his chin and every line of his face was creased in dirt. In my current state, he could crush me like a twig. Actually, even at my best, he could probably still do that.

Erick pressed between us. "You'll have to go through me first."

"And me," Mott said, raising his sword. Tobias said nothing, but stood beside them with a hand on his sword.

I pushed past them all. "If you want to challenge me as king, then that's your right. I will answer the challenge. But not yet. I have a duty to Carthya, and I must see this war through to the end."

Grumbling could be heard throughout the crowd. I withdrew my sword and felt surprised by the weight of it. Perhaps over the last several days, I had become weaker than I'd realized. Still, I held it high and hoped my arms could keep it steady enough to persuade them that I could fight, if I had to.

"Do you forget who I am?" I asked. "What I did here in this very spot? I am not asking for your help. I'm not here to debate whether you should follow me. I came to give you my orders, calling on your sworn oaths to follow me. It's the same oath I took to become a pirate, which means I am bound to answer when the pirates are in need. You will collect any men who are out to sea, and you will gather whatever supplies you need for travel. Erick will have my plans and I will see you on the battlefield."

"We know what Carthya is up against," a man in the far corner said. "It's too dangerous."

I smirked back at him. "If you wanted a safe life, you should've become a midwife, or maybe a tailor. Unless pricking your finger on a spindle also rattles your nerves. I cannot guarantee that everyone will survive. But for those who do, I promise you a battle worthy of a true pirate's blade."

Silence fell over the group. Gradually a few of them shifted on their feet, and quiet mumblings escaped in whispers and loud breaths. I decided to leave while we were ahead.

"Sleep well tonight. You'll be traveling soon." Then I strode away without looking back. I hoped I had said enough to persuade them. The longer they debated, the less inclined they'd be to do as I'd asked.

Erick walked with me long enough to hear the details of my plans for the pirates, but a loud argument was already erupting behind us. "We haven't seen you in months, and now you come to ask them to die? It's too much, Jaron."

"I asked them to fight, with the hope that they'll live to see victory declared. Nothing more."

"I'll do what I can, but you had better make your plans as if we're not there."

"I already have a plan, and it relies on them. Get the pirates there, Erick." My smile turned somber again. "They must keep their promises."

"Well, even if they don't, I will keep mine." Erick reached for my hand and added, "Whatever they choose, you will see me there as you asked."

I shook his hand, and then turned to leave the camp, flanked by Mott and Tobias. Erick stayed behind to take part in the pirates' rising argument. I couldn't pick apart their words, but my orders were clearly not being received as well as I would've liked.

We found our horses and left Tarblade by the shortest route possible. Once it was safely behind us, Tobias said to me, "Please tell me we're leaving Avenia now."

"We are. We're going to Falstan Lake, or what's left of it." I yawned and checked the darkening skies for some idea of the time. "We'll have to find a place to sleep tonight. But we should be there sometime tomorrow."

A beat passed, then Mott said, "Jaron, do you really think the pirates will come?"

"I don't know," I mumbled. "I really don't know."

# · NINETEEN ·

The next morning, Mott and Tobias allowed me to sleep as long as I wanted, and when I finally awoke, I was surprised by how high the sun had risen.

"I suppose I'm still recovering," I said as I broke into a long yawn. "I expected to be past all that by now."

"After only two days?" Tobias arched an eyebrow. "Does it bother you much on those moments when you remember you're only human?"

"Very much, actually." I chuckled and looked over to Mott. "How much food does this inn have? I think we might wish to order it all."

He dipped his head at my request, said he would ask for as much as they would give us, and then left.

An hour later, we were well stocked with good food, and on our way again. It would be some time before the wounds I had suffered in the Avenian camp were healed, and perhaps some would never heal, but life was returning to me, and I was eager to rejoin my armies.

After another half day's ride, we crossed into Carthya. It was a tremendous relief to be on my own soil again, assuming Avenia hadn't yet stolen it from me, of course. Once we were there, we took the opportunity to get some rest. Tobias and I left our horses in Mott's care, then wandered up a hill to see if we could spot the bluff overlooking Falstan Lake. My eyes went first to the horizon in search of my camp, but we were still too far away.

However, Tobias's mind seemed to be moving in a different direction. "Where do you suppose she is?" he asked.

"Amarinda could have made it back to Drylliad by now," I said. "And if not, Harlowe will have sent out orders to search for her everywhere."

"So will Vargan." He shook his head, clearly angry with himself. "I promised to protect her, and I didn't. If anything happens —"

"Trust her to protect herself. She is intelligent and resourceful, and stronger than she's ever been given credit for."

"I know all that!" Tobias nearly spat the words at me. "I know who she is, and probably better than you!"

I turned to him and might've been harsher if the worry wasn't etched so deeply into the lines of his face. In a gentle tone, I only said, "We will find her, Tobias."

We fell silent then, and my attention went down the hill to a trail that looked as if it had been worn by hundreds of footsteps. I doubted they were Carthyan — no commander of mine would've led our soldiers on a march this close to Avenia's border. It was too risky.

But someone — likely soldiers of Avenia or Mendenwal — had recently come through here.

We ducked low, just in case they were near, and then watched and waited. Within a few minutes, Mott joined us and we debated whether to follow their trail or to proceed to Falstan in an entirely different direction.

"Wait a minute." Tobias held up his hand to silence us. "Just wait. Do you hear that?"

If I listened carefully, then I did hear something. It sounded like a moan, rising up the hillside from somewhere near the trail below.

Tobias rose up tall, clearly with the intention of going down to investigate, but Mott pulled him back.

"He sounds injured," Tobias hissed. "We have to help if he is."

"He's an enemy," Mott said. "You'll help him get well enough to return to the battlefield and kill more of our men."

"But that man isn't our enemy." Tobias turned to me. "Isn't that what you said before, that only their king is your enemy?"

I had said that. But had I truly meant it? It was certainly possible that the moaning was a trap to lure us in, which was the last thing I wanted to face. If we met on the battlefield, that man and I would have to engage in a fight where only one of us walked away. But if he was injured and helpless, off the field of war, did I then have an obligation to try to save his life?

Obligation or not, I couldn't just leave him to die. During my time with the pirates, I had promised myself that I would not go down the dark paths they had followed. I would not become as they were.

So I nodded my permission at Tobias, then Mott and I pulled out our swords to accompany him down the hillside. This didn't feel like a trick, but we had to be cautious nonetheless.

Tobias saw the man first, and to my surprise, he started laughing. We caught up to him and couldn't help but join in. This man — this supposed enemy — wasn't much older than I, and had all the ferocity of a frightened lamb. He had become caught in a hunter's rope that had grabbed his leg and whisked him upside down and into the air. Everything that wasn't attached to him had fallen out of his reach, including a poorly made sword that barely looked sharp enough to skewer a plum. He wore a livery similar to our own, and must have been upside down for so long that his face had now become as red as his hair. Truly, he was a ridiculous sight.

When he saw us coming, he hailed us as friends and said, "I beg you to help. Please, get me down."

I walked around the area, beating at nearby bushes to be sure no one else was hiding there. He rotated his weight until he turned to Mott, the oldest of our group and the one he would naturally suspect was in charge.

"I've been here over a day, sir, and the pain is becoming intolerable. As a fellow Avenian, I beg you to help me."

With my Avenian accent, I asked, "What is your name?"

"Mavis Tock. My father is a candlemaker, in the south."

"Ah, then you must have learned your fighting skills from him. How did you get into this position? Are you being punished?"

"No."

"Are you being hunted?" I squinted at him. "Or are you the bait?"

"We were marching but I was terribly thirsty. So when I heard a stream, I snuck away to get a drink. When I ran to catch up to the others, faster than I knew it, I became caught in this trap. By then, everyone was too far to hear me calling for help. I'm not even sure anyone knows I'm missing."

Tobias removed his knife and went to cut him down, but I pressed him back with my hand. "Where was your group going?"

"North. Apparently, the armies of Gelyn were stopped at the border by a small group of Carthyans. I heard that Gelyn would've won, but Bymar arrived at the last moment and sealed Gelyn's doom."

So Bymar had come? That was excellent news on two fronts. It meant that Roden had achieved a victory at the border, and also that Fink had gotten through safely. But since Mavis still assumed we were from Avenia, I only shook my head and said, "Carthyans are horrid people, aren't they? What right do they have to defend themselves in this war?"

Mavis nodded, then frowned as if confused. He finally gave up and simply asked, "I'm really hurting. Can you help me down?"

With my permission, Mott strode forward and used his sword to cut the rope on the boy's leg. He tumbled to the ground, but we immediately noticed the blood around his ankle where the rope had sliced into his flesh.

Tobias darted toward him and began examining it. "How'd this happen?"

Mavis took a look at it and his eyes rolled in his head, forcing him to lie back again. "I tried for hours to wiggle my way free. It hurt, but I had no idea it was so bad."

Tobias pulled a handkerchief from his pocket, one I recognized as belonging to Amarinda, and I wondered why he should have it. He ran toward the sound of water and reappeared moments later with it dripping wet. He wrung it out, then knelt before Mavis to wash his leg.

"We should go," Mott whispered as he leaned over to me. "We've freed him, and there's nothing more required of us."

"What if your roles were reversed? Wouldn't you hope for more from him?"

"Of course." Frustrated, Mott kicked his boot against the ground. "It's just that I don't like the feeling of being on this trail, so exposed."

I didn't like it either, but Tobias looked up at me and shook his head. Now that he had washed the blood from Mavis's ankle, it became apparent how bad the injury was. The rope had cut deeply into the flesh and probably would become incredibly painful once full feeling returned to his leg. Even now, Mavis was beginning to show signs of strain and held on to his thigh, as if that would help.

Tobias stood and then pulled me aside. "If we do nothing, it'll become infected. He'll lose the leg, and since he won't be able to walk on it, he'll possibly lose his life too."

"There's nothing we can do about that," I said. "Cutting him down is one thing, but we're not physicians. We have no provisions to help him."

"I've been studying medicine." Tobias smiled meekly, almost as if he was embarrassed to admit it. "I figured with you as our king, knowing how to heal injuries would be a good idea. Please, Jaron, let me help him."

I nodded and Tobias immediately set to work, asking Mott to return to our horses for a clean rag and a waterskin. Turning to me, he described a plant with thick, pointed leaves that would need to be cut free and gathered. He said it had a gel inside that Mavis needed.

"Where do I find it?"

"Near water, and in full sun."

I nodded at him and hurried toward the stream. After Mott and Tobias had kept such a careful watch over me these past few days, it was disconcerting to be alone and my senses were heightened. We were so close to Avenia. Surely others in his group would eventually notice Mavis's absence and come back to look for him.

I scanned the ground, looking for any plant that fit Tobias's description, and questioning my decision to spend so much precious time here. It was the right thing to do. I knew that, and yet Mott's suggestion that I was strengthening an enemy also lingered in my mind. Mavis might not be any sort of warrior, but that didn't mean he was incapable of doing us damage.

Finally, I had wandered far enough downstream that I saw Tobias's plant. I pulled out my knife to collect some of the leaves, but from this angle, something caught my eye, a sparkle of ruby, cut in the shape of a diamond. That was odd.

When I turned to look at it, I immediately recognized the object the ruby was attached to. It was a shoe, but not just any ordinary shoe. With nothing better to do while riding in Tobias's escape carriage so many days ago, I had stared at that same ruby for some time, and I knew it now. This shoe belonged to Amarinda. The princess had at some point been in this exact place.

# · TWENTY ·

I grabbed the shoe and leapt to my feet, hoping for any sign of her, or at least some clue as to where she might be now. Nothing indicated how long the shoe had been here or what direction she had traveled. Was it possible she had passed through as a captive of Mavis's army?

I cut the leaves, then ran back to Tobias. Mott was already there with him and stood vigil, listening and watching for anyone's approach while Tobias continued washing Mavis's ankle. I pushed past him and thrust the shoe in Mavis's face. "Do you know where this came from?"

Mavis's eyes widened, though it wasn't clear whether he recognized the shoe, or because he was surprised to see a woman's shoe of that quality in a place like this.

"I asked you a question!" I yelled. "Now answer me!"

"You're not Avenian," he replied coolly. "That was easy enough to figure out. You lost your accent just now and these two others with you have the accent of Carthya. You are the youngest of them all. Why do you give the orders?" His eyes brushed over me, resting briefly on my forearm with the mark of the pirates, the bruises that were still visible on my face, and the sword in my hand. "I know who you are . . . Jaron."

So Mavis was not as stupid as I had thought. Either that, or I was less clever than I wanted to believe. Neither improved my opinion of myself, or boosted my hopes to pass through this area unnoticed.

In his protective way, Mott walked toward us, but I didn't think Mavis was in a position to harm me. I knelt beside him with the shoe still in one hand and the plant he so desperately needed in my other.

"Help me," I said. "Then I will help you."

His eyes remained focused on the plant. "I see. Either I tell you what I know about that shoe, or you will let me die. Is that right? Carthyans are no better than Avenians."

"You dare say that, after we rescued you, knowing who you are? You are on my soil. You attacked us!"

Mavis turned away. "I follow my orders without question, as a good soldier would. You ask the same from your soldiers."

"No, I ask them to be good people. That way, if they follow my orders, I will know I am doing the right thing." Tobias extended his hand, and I thrust the plant leaves at him. "Do what you must for this boy and let's be on our way."

But Tobias only gripped the leaves tighter. "If he knows about Amarinda —"

"He wants to play games with us. We'd do better to just pick up her trail while it's still fresh. So wrap his leg and we'll go."

Tobias stripped open the leaves to reveal a sticky yellow gel. He ran his fingers through it and then applied the gel to Mavis's leg. Mavis arched his back as it stung the wound, but the worst of the pain seemed to pass once Tobias wrapped it with a rag from Mott's saddlebag.

Tobias handed the boy the remaining leaves. "You need to check that wound often and keep this gel on it until you're entirely healed. It might not stop the infection entirely, but if you do as I say, it should keep you out of danger."

With that, Tobias stood and we hurried to our horses. Mott even lifted his saddlebag and found a spare roll, which he tossed to the boy to eat. "You are in our debt now," Mott said. "Remember that."

"I'm the lowest soldier of Avenia," Mavis said. "I cannot repay anything to a king."

"You'll find a way," I said.

"Let's leave." Tobias started away with his horse. "We must hurry."

Mott and I followed, but before we had gone far, Mavis called after us, saying, "We saw the girl who wore that shoe and chased after her, but she got away. I don't know where she is now, but she's not with my army."

I met his eyes and nodded in gratitude. Then without a word, I turned and hurried after Mott and Tobias, already on their way to find the princess.

# · TWENTY-ONE ·

ott had told me once that he was skilled in tracking, but I hadn't appreciated his claim until I saw him at work. Once we lost the princess's footsteps in the soft soil around the stream, he got off his horse and began showing me how he worked.

There were some things I already understood — to look for crushed grasses or bent twigs that indicated a person had passed that way. But Mott used a stick to measure the distance in her stride and then used that information to estimate where her footsteps should fall to find the trail again. It was slow work, requiring our horses to be led on foot, but after we had gone some distance, the indents suggested she was walking, not running, and the prints were less than a day old. If we kept at it, we should find her.

We continued this way for several hours, until the sun began to sink in the sky, and along with it our hopes of finding her before nightfall. That decision was sealed when we came upon another stream with no visible footsteps on the other side.

"She could've walked in the water, upstream or down, and exited anywhere." Mott's frustrations were clear. "It's too dark for us to follow now. We should make camp and start again tomorrow."

"We must keep going or she'll get even farther away," Tobias said. "Let's try upstream. That would take her closer to Drylliad."

"And closer to the soldiers who chased her," I reminded him. "She's already much farther south than I'd have expected. She may go south yet again."

Faced with one choice no more certain than the other, Tobias reluctantly agreed to make camp. Mott prepared us a fire while Tobias and I put together a simple stew. After eating, we sat around the fire with little to say. Tobias went to sleep first, insisting we begin again at first light. Mott followed shortly after, and I lay down near the dwindling fire, but sleep would not come. I should have arrived at Falstan Lake that day, and although I had no regrets for helping Mavis, and certainly the search for the princess was a priority, I still felt disconnected from the war I was supposed to be leading. I worried that my country was collapsing from the center, even as I rode uselessly in circles around the action.

Finally, I drifted off, but it was a restless sleep filled with haunted dreams that kept me on edge. In them, Amarinda was on the same ridge in the camp where Imogen had fallen, begging me to come after her. Telling me that she was intelligent and strong and would fight for me. Then I heard the whoosh of an arrow—

I woke up with a start, sweat on my brow. But I soon realized it wasn't the dream that had awoken me. Something near us had made a noise.

The horses were tied close by, but not immediate to our camp. Whatever the noise had been, it was minor, but something clearly had disturbed them.

As silently as possible, I reached for my sword and got to my feet. I poked at Mott and Tobias and, when they awoke, motioned for them to follow me. We had only taken a few steps when we caught the sound of our horses on the run. We gave pursuit, Mott racing far ahead of Tobias and myself. One of the horses must've pulled free. Mott caught it and, jumping into its saddle, set off to get ahead of the thief and force him back this way.

Tobias and I kept running in the direction of the noise. I yelled at Tobias to run to the right, in case our horse thief circled back that way. The thief continued forward, but another of our horses escaped and veered toward Tobias. He was able to grab the reins and calm the horse enough to climb on its back, then he set off as well, leaving me alone.

It wasn't long before I lost sight of him, and Mott was already too far away. I wasn't sure which way I should go until several minutes later when I heard Tobias yell, "Help! I see him!"

They were coming toward me, and I ran to intercept. The thief would come upon me first and be greeted by the sharp end of my sword.

Only it didn't happen that way. When Tobias cried for help, our thief responded.

"Tobias?"

That was the princess's voice.

Still running forward, I saw her approach in the moonlight. Amarinda had stolen our horses, and now that she recognized a friendly voice, she immediately turned back to race toward Tobias. When they were close, she slid from her horse, as did he. I was near enough then to call out to her, but something silenced me. Somehow, this reunion belonged to them, and not me. So I only watched as the princess called Tobias's name and ran to embrace him. Several days ago, when I had seen them pressed together in the small space of the escape carriage, they had looked uncomfortable and awkward. Clearly, that had passed now.

"How did you get here?" she asked. "When you were captured, I thought" — her voice choked — "I thought they'd do to you what they did to Jaron."

Tobias saw me behind them and released her as if she burned him. With an eye on me, he said, "My lady, what they told us about Jaron was a lie."

Then he turned her to face me, and she stared a moment as if unable to believe her own eyes. The light from above was fairly dim, but her long brown hair tumbled in tangles down her back, her fine dress was torn and stained, and she was limping from having only one shoe to wear. She was dirty and ragged and clearly exhausted. Through all that, she was as beautiful as ever.

"Jaron?" She stumbled forward in disbelief. "Is this possible? They said you were dead."

"I nearly was."

"But how —" Amarinda was close enough then to touch me, and her face melted in sympathy. She reached out a hand to brush a lock of hair from my face. The hair had covered a dark bruise on my temple, a personal gift from the vigil Terrowic to me. "Jaron, what did they do to you?"

Rather than answer, I took her hand and kissed it, then asked, "Tell me of yourself. What do you need?"

She smiled. "All is well, my lord, but I am hungry."

"We have food at our camp."

"I know. I smelled it cooking earlier tonight, and in fact, that's how I found your camp. But when I got there, I saw the Avenian uniforms, and the horses packed with Avenian saddles. I had no idea it was you. My plan was to release the horses, and when you all went after them, to sneak into camp for some food."

"It was a risky plan."

"Yes, but I was very hungry. And taking this risk turned out better than I could've hoped."

By then, Tobias had brought his horse over to us. Despite the embrace he had just shared with her, he was awkward once again as he assisted her into the saddle. I climbed up next to ride with her back to camp. Her arms were around my waist, but I felt her turn back to look at Tobias as we rode off. It sealed in my mind a suspicion that had been growing for some time.

Tobias and the princess were in love.

# · TWENTY-TWO ·

Mott joined us soon after we arrived at camp, and was clearly as relieved as the rest of us to find the princess safe and unharmed. But I also caught him staring at me with his brows pressed low. Clearly, he understood that something was bothering me, but he knew better than to ask.

We built up the fire for her warmth, offered her tea, then Mott began warming her some food while Tobias and I reorganized the camp for her comfort and privacy. For his own safety, I would've preferred it if Tobias worked much farther away from me, but he seemed too focused on her return to be aware of my anger. While we worked, she told us the remainder of her story from the time Tobias had been captured.

"I knew I had to get inside Carthya's borders," she said as she ate. "But they were searching for me so heavily in the north, I was forced to go south. Finally, I was able to cross into Carthya and hoped to find some of our own people who would help me get to Drylliad."

"Everyone's gone to Drylliad already," I said. "It's not safe for the families out here on their own. And especially not safe for you. Why didn't you go on to Bymar, as we planned?"

My tone was harsher than it ought to have been and she would have been justified in replying with equal harshness. But instead, she softened her words. "They told us you were dead."

"I might've been! That's all the more reason to protect yourself!"

"No, it meant I had to return to the castle so that our people could be assured the throne still stands! If they know what they are fighting for, people will continue to fight, but if word spread of your death, they would start to wonder. I had to return so that I could provide them a purpose."

I stopped my work to steady my emotions. Whatever else I felt, words like that marked her as a true royal. There was no question of either her courage or nobility.

Tobias said, "The night before we left the castle, you asked her to rule if something happened to you, and to consider a husband from Carthya. She only did what you wanted, Jaron."

"Really?" I didn't need his help with this. He'd already helped me plenty. I felt my anger rise again. "Is this what either of you think I want?"

Amarinda drew in a breath to say something, catching my attention, but she remained silent. We continued staring at each other until Mott stood and said, "I'll check on the horses." He cocked his head at Tobias. "You should help me."

"Why?" Tobias clearly wasn't interested in going anywhere. "They've been fed and watered, and their knots are good."

"Because I told you to come and help!"

From the tone of Mott's voice, Tobias must've realized their leaving had nothing to do with the horses. But I didn't miss his glance back at Amarinda, full of sympathy that she was left alone with me, and regret that he would not be allowed to remain here with her.

I carried another log to the fire, then sat on a fallen tree trunk to watch it burn. This night seemed to have gone on forever, and all I wished for was that it might end. Before long, Amarinda came to sit near me, and we watched the fire together. Something needed to be said, but I had no idea where to begin.

Open as the sky was around us, I suddenly felt closed in, and my heart raced, though I couldn't be sure why. Was I angry? Not really, though I had every right to be. Hurt? Yes, though if she had believed me to be dead, her affections for Tobias weren't intended to cause me any sadness. Perhaps I felt displaced, as if I belonged nowhere, and to nobody. In all the glory of being a king, I was still an unwanted orphan of the streets.

Finally, she said, "While you were with the pirates, Tobias spent a long time trying to help me understand you."

I scoffed. "Yes, I can imagine that took many hours."

"It was more like many days." She smiled back at me, but not in a mocking way. I doubted she was capable of that sort of unkindness. "He told me that, back at Farthenwood, you once said you had no desire to be king. Was that true, or only part of your disguise as Sage?"

A quiet sigh escaped my lips. "Nothing I said at Farthenwood was more honest."

"We're very different people, Jaron, but in that one way, we're so much alike. You never wanted the crown, nor did I. In fact, in all my life, I have never been asked what I wanted."

How familiar that sounded. My own complaints weren't so different.

She continued, "From the moment of my birth, I was a betrothed princess, destined for your brother. When I was old enough, I left my home in Bymar and came to live in Drylliad, to get to know Darius better. Eventually, I gave my emotions to him and anticipated a life of happiness at his side. Then one morning he was dead. Gone. And almost as quickly I was expected to put aside everything I ever felt for Darius, to pretend that I wasn't completely hollow inside. On the same night that Darius's murder was confirmed, I was suddenly faced with betrothal to another husband, to you. I know that's how things had to be, but I don't think anyone understood how hard it was to face you, looking so much like Darius and yet serving as a constant reminder that he was gone."

"Please forgive me." I felt selfish to my core, to have dwelled so much on my own wishes and frustrations that, for all this time, I had failed to consider the pain she must have felt.

"There's nothing to forgive," she said. "The betrothal wasn't your desire any more than it was mine. Yet despite all that, we built a friendship. And then as the war began, you became the first to ever ask what I wanted for my life. To marry you, if I wanted, or to choose my own way. I thank you for that. In many ways, that is the most love anyone has ever shown me." She drew in a slow breath, and then said, "You promised never to lie to me, correct?"

"Yes."

"Then I must ask you a question and beg for your complete honesty." When I nodded, she said, "Before we left the castle, Kerwyn suggested that you and I should marry. Why did you accept his suggestion?"

I hadn't anticipated that question and, in fact, had barely thought about it since then. I struggled with finding the right words to answer her and finally said, "Because Kerwyn was right. If something happens to me during this war, it preserves your role as queen."

She pressed her lips together and then said, "For you, is that reason enough to begin a marriage?"

In a perfect world, there would only be one reason for marriage, when two people loved each other more than their own lives. But there were other realities of life, often requiring partnerships to be formed for more practical reasons. Marriages to gain a provider or a cook or a companion were common, and for many people, that was enough. Amarinda and I were supposed to marry because of a treaty worked out between our families. Maybe people did marry for reasons other than love, but when I thought about it, a treaty was the most ridiculous reason of them all.

"No," I said. "I would hope to marry for love, and no other reason."

She scooted closer to me and I felt the warmth of her presence. When she spoke, her voice was low and gentle. "Jaron, do you love me?"

She might as well have asked me to solve the mysteries of the universe. I'd never asked myself that question because I'd never needed the answer. As part of the terms of returning to the throne, it had always been settled that I must marry the princess. Why question what must happen?

But that was it — I had always felt that I *must* marry her. Never had I *wanted* that.

"Of course I love you." My words were like a confession, and it felt good to say them. "But as I would a sister, or a dearest friend. I am not *in love* with you." And with those words, any anger I had felt toward her and Tobias vanished. I could not blame her for withholding emotions that I did not feel either. And if I truly felt any affection for her, then her wishes would be my priority. I had to accept that her happiness came from someone other than me.

The tension in her released as well. "Tobias does not have your wit with words or strength with a sword. But he is good and kind, and I am myself when I'm with him."

I couldn't deny any of that. My opinion of Tobias had been dismal when we first met, but once he and I came to an understanding, he had served me as loyally as anyone could. Better still, he had become the truest of friends.

I said, "With his intelligence and his position as a regent, he should give you a comfortable life, though not a royal one."

She shrugged. "The life of a princess was a grand gift from the king of my country. But it was one I never asked for."

"You always fit the role perfectly."

"I will fit my new role well too. Because Tobias is a regent, if we marry, the treaty between our countries will remain secure."

Which was good to know, *if* I had a country left after this war ended. I took Amarinda's hand and kissed it, less saddened by her rejection than I would have expected. Perhaps it wasn't possible for her to break my heart because she had never held it. Or perhaps my heart was already in too many pieces from another greater loss.

I faked a smile that covered those heavy thoughts. "Tobias may be out there wondering if I'm going to order his execution. I think it might be fun to make him believe it."

"I doubt whether he'd enjoy that joke as much as you do." Amarinda's expression was serious, but I was sure I caught a small twinkle in her eye.

Eventually, Mott and Tobias returned. Mott stopped at the edge of camp, seeking permission to rejoin us. I guessed he had spoken to Tobias while they were gone. For, rather than entering, Tobias knelt where he was, with his head down. If he suspected I was angry enough to order his beheading, that wasn't the smartest position for him to take.

I walked over to Tobias, who said, "The darkest day of my life was when they told us you were dead. Please believe that, Jaron."

"I do. And I have only gratitude for all you did to help the princess once you heard that news. My blessings to you both."

Tobias lifted his head and smiled at Amarinda, who beamed back at him. She turned to me. "Thank you, my lord. Then may I extend my wishes for you and Imogen? Wherever she is now, she loves you, Jaron. She is meant for you."

At the mention of Imogen's name, I stiffened and tried to remember to breathe. Every time I thought about Imogen, I felt as though I were nothing but hollowed-out flesh. And I had no idea how to react now — it hadn't occurred to me that Amarinda didn't know.

Standing nearby, Mott leaned over and whispered into Amarinda's ear. Upon hearing the news, her mouth fell open and she let out a gasp of horror. Her eyes widened and tears spilled onto her cheeks like rivers of sorrow. "I thought if you escaped the camp, then she had too," she choked out. "No one told me." Still shaking her head, she staggered forward and closed me into an embrace, then held me tight.

I wasn't sure if I was comforting her, or the other way around. But as she cried on my shoulder, it allowed me to mourn as well, in a way I had desperately needed. When she finally released me, the sadness lingered, yet I felt cleansed from the worst of it. I took her hand, kissed it, and then placed it in Tobias's hand.

"She is always a royal," I told him. "Love her as nothing less."

He bowed humbly, then said, "We are forever in your debt. What can we do?"

"Back in Avenia's camp you asked if I was broken." I took a deep breath, in full recollection of how near I had come to my own end. "I was. But I am healing and I am ready to fight this war. Help me win, Tobias. Vargan must be stopped."

# · TWENTY-THREE ·

Long after Tobias and Amarinda had gone to sleep, I sat awake near the fire, exhausted but unable to sleep. While my fingers brushed over the single coin in my pocket, I watched the flames dance along the wood, and the smoke swirl into the air in whatever direction the wind sent it. What must it feel like, I wondered, to be something that drifts in one way or another, with no will of its own. From my earliest years, I had always been the very opposite of that, endlessly compelled to fight against whatever force seemed to push at me, even when it was for my own good. Such a fool I could be. I vowed to try to change that part of myself. But only on the condition that the rest of the world stopped trying to make me change it.

After some time of letting me be alone, Mott came to sit beside the fire as well. He nodded at Tobias and Amarinda, and in a hushed tone said, "That was a noble thing you did earlier tonight. I would've expected more anger from you."

"Why? They did nothing wrong, and deserve their happiness."

"You didn't feel that way earlier tonight."

"No, but I do now." I turned to face him so he could see my sincerity. "They should be happy. They have a long life ahead."

"So should you, Jaron."

I snorted softly. The odds of that weren't exactly in my favor.

But Mott only said, "If she were here, Imogen would tell you the same thing."

When I closed my eyes, her face came to my mind, as it always did, in the moment her fingers caressed my hair. More than once while in Vargan's prison, I had dreamed about her, that we were together somewhere in the afterlife and I was begging her forgiveness for my mistakes. And though the details of the dreams had receded from my mind like waves from a beach, I remained certain that she had made her peace with me.

When I opened my eyes again, I looked back at Mott and said, "I think she loved me."

"Of course she did."

"Why couldn't I see that before?"

"You always knew it. But you had the princess, your duty to the betrothal."

"That I did." I sighed and gazed into the fire again. "Villains and plots and enemies are simple things to me. But friendships are complicated, and love is harder still. It has wounded me deeper than a sword ever could."

"If you hurt deeply, then it means you love deeply too. Love is a powerful thing, Jaron. In the end, love will help you win this war."

I chuckled. "That'd be a fine new strategy, I think. When the enemy wields a sword against me, I'll simply express my love for them. They'll be so shocked, they'll collapse on the spot and the victory will be mine."

"I daresay you will be the first to claim victory that way." His soft laughter dimmed when he saw I had grown serious. He added, "Tomorrow we will rejoin the war. So it's time to decide who you are. Will you be carried off by this wind coming at us, or stand and face it?"

If only the complications of life could be simplified that way. I said, "This is no windstorm."

"It's *your* storm, and the future of us all depends on you now. So who are you? Sage, an orphan boy who cares only for himself? Or the undisciplined, rebellious prince your father sent away? Life has tested your resilience and strength and willpower, and you have succeeded in ways nobody ever thought possible. But the storm has never been worse, and it will either destroy you, or define you. When everything is taken from you, can you still stand before us as Jaron, the Ascendant King of Carthya?"

I closed my eyes again, but this time it wasn't to picture Imogen in my mind. I was remembering the moment of emerging from my carriage after returning from the pirates, with a bruised body and a broken leg. It had seemed as though the entire kingdom had come to welcome me home. They had bowed and hailed me as the Ascendant King. Meant to rise from the darkest night and bring dawn to my country. The forces against us in this war were overwhelming. But if I did not find a way out, our doom was guaranteed. There would never come a day when I didn't love Imogen, didn't ache to have her back again. But I would have to rise one more time.

"Let's get some sleep," I said to him. "Starting tomorrow, we're going to finish this war. We are going to save Carthya."

# · TWENTY-FOUR ·

The next morning, Mott was alone in camp when he suddenly found himself surrounded by a pack of Avenian soldiers who stormed in from all sides, took his sword, and forced him to his knees. The five men were armed and rowdy, and one of them said something about having come back to search for a missing soldier. Probably Mavis.

All the intruders were ugly — hardly unusual for Avenians, but it was the foulest of them all who spoke to Mott. He had a patch over one eye and thin, colorless hair that looked like winter grass sprouted from his uneven skull.

"Where's your king?" the man asked.

"Not far," Mott said. "And he won't be happy you're here. I suggest you leave now."

The man laughed, revealing blackened teeth. It was rather surprising that he still had any left. "One of our newer recruits got into some trouble near here. He told us about you."

"He told us about you too," I said from above them. Earlier that morning, I had edged up the limb of a tree to a solid perch where I could wait for their arrival. Being as unaware as they were unintelligent, they had failed to notice me when they came. "Though your recruit didn't get the description of your odor quite right. He said it was similar to a skunk's, but I think that's unkind to the skunk."

In my hand was a bow Mott had brought along with him. The arrow was already nocked and ready to pull back. I wasn't the best shot, but they were close enough that an accurate aim wouldn't be a problem. The man in the center put a knife to Mott's throat, and only then noticed his companions had already stepped away from him.

"You should drop that now, before you hurt yourselves." It was the most warning I intended to give.

One of the other men said, "Why? Even up there, we can still get you."

"In theory, yes. But you won't." I tilted my head to the trees behind them. Both Tobias and Amarinda were up there. Together they held a long rope that ran down the tree's trunk, with a hunter's knot on the end. When they pulled it, the rope went tight around the ankles of the Avenians, knocking them all to the ground and binding them together. It wasn't much different from what had happened to Mavis, and I hoped they appreciated the irony in that. When he saw that he had no support with him, the man behind Mott dropped his knife and held up his hands in surrender.

Mott stood and collected their weapons while I swung down from my branch and landed on the ground in front of them.

"You travel so loudly, we knew you were coming an hour ago. I was getting bored, waiting for you." Then I turned to the man who had spoken. "We lured you here like fish to a baited worm. Now, did you come for me?"

Fish Breath didn't seem interested in talking until Mott returned the favor and gave him a poke with his own knife.

He squealed and held his arms higher. "I already told you, we came for one of our own."

"And where is your army headed? To Falstan Lake?"

"I have nothing to say to a boy king," Fish Breath sneered.

"As you wish."

I nodded at Mott to drag him away, but he squirmed within Mott's grasp and shouted back, "You will not kill me!"

"Are you sure of that? Because I was just thinking that I might."

"Let me live, and I will give you information."

I made a show of thinking it over. "Well, if it's interesting, then I'll keep you alive. But if you waste my time, or tell me any lies, then you have no promise."

His eyes darted from left to right before he spoke, and when he did it was quieter than before, possibly so that wherever he was, King Vargan wouldn't hear the betrayal of secrets.

"Vargan is heading directly for the capital. Mendenwal is already there, on orders to destroy Drylliad and everyone within its walls. The victors will join those already encamped at Falstan Lake to end the war there."

Amarinda drew in a breath and reached for Tobias's hand. I looked from them over to Mott, debating whether this information was true.

"Has fighting begun in Drylliad?" I asked.

"If it hasn't, it will soon. I'm told the captain of your guard has formed a line near the city, and reinforced it with the armies of Bymar. They won't last long, though. Once we figure out how to breach their lines, it's an easy march into Drylliad."

My eyes narrowed as I studied him. "I think you're lying."

"I'm not! I heard this straight from a man named Kippenger, one of Vargan's top commanders."

Kippenger. I remembered that name like vinegar on my tongue.

I picked up a rock. "Which is your sword hand?"

Fish Breath trembled beneath my implied threat, but raised his left hand. "Please don't do that. You said you wouldn't kill me."

"And you said you wouldn't lie to me. You held your knife with your right hand before." I raised the rock higher now.

"That's all I know!" His panicked voice jumped nearly an octave. "Listen, you will find Mendenwal there, and my own king's armies with them in battle. He intends to destroy Drylliad."

I frowned at him and rubbed my chin, mostly because it seemed to make him nervous. "All right," I finally said. "I'll let you live, but you'd better hope there are others in your army willing to come look for you." Then I nodded at Mott. "Tie them up."

While Mott tied the men to the trees around our camp, Tobias and Amarinda came down to help him, and I collected our horses. We had to leave at once. When I last saw him, Roden hadn't yet figured out his role as captain. If he was no better, those lines outside Drylliad wouldn't last long.

After we left, Mott asked me, "Do you intend to go to Drylliad?"

"Of course. Drylliad must stand."

"That battle will be dangerous," Amarinda said. "Are you sure you're ready?"

With a grin, I told her, "I'll have more than ten minutes' notice that this battle is coming. In that way, this might be the most prepared I've ever been."

We rode as quickly as possible toward Drylliad, but once we came upon the Roving River, I turned to Tobias. "Can you and Amarinda get yourselves up to the camp at Falstan Lake?"

"Yes. But if you're headed toward Drylliad, I ought to go with you. We'll have injured men there, and I can care for them."

"What about Amarinda?" I asked.

"I can help Tobias," she answered. "Let me be of use in this war."

Her eyes met mine, and I said, "The terms of our betrothal may have changed, but not the terms of the throne. If something happens to me before this is over, I need you to take the reins as queen. You are already needed, and you must stay safe."

"I'll keep her safe, Jaron," Tobias promised. "Those terms haven't changed either."

I nodded back, then said to Amarinda, "You and Tobias will go to the Falstan camp and set up a tent for medical aid. Within a few days, we'll need it there just as much as where I'm going. Order the commander to send as many men to Drylliad as he can spare."

Amarinda nodded back at me, and then she and Tobias rode in one direction while Mott and I turned farther north.

We rode hard toward Drylliad, with heavy thoughts of the disaster that would unfold if the enemy breached those city walls. Harlowe was tasked with preparing an army to defend the city if necessary, but his options were limited. Many of the families who'd come seeking shelter inside the city were inexperienced in fighting anything other than the occasional wolf or wild dog attacking their herds, and most were women charged with protecting their children and elders, whose men had already joined the war.

Perhaps Harlowe would carry out his plan to pull men from the prisons. I wondered if they would fight for Carthya or abandon us at their first opportunity. But Harlowe had promised me he would not include Conner as part of those plans. No matter how desperate our situation became, I wouldn't trust Conner with my own life, or with the lives of my people.

It was late in the day when we approached the last hill before coming to Drylliad. Mott called my name and stopped, requiring me to stop as well.

He said, "I've been watching you since we left the Avenian camp. You're not as strong as you were before. I've seen the way you carry your sword, with two hands now rather than one."

All I could do was to stare straight forward. "I'm stronger each day. Besides, my will is as strong as always, and that matters more."

"But the battle is just on the other side of that hill."

"Yes, and if I must, I'll fight it with my sword in two hands."

He wasn't convinced. "Where's your armor and your shield?"

"Where's yours?" I countered. I let go of my irritation and only sighed. "No good king sends his people into battle unless he is there beside them."

"And no good servant lets him go alone."

I looked back at him, ever grateful. "You're no servant, Mott. Not to me, or to anyone. And there is no one I would rather ride into battle with than you."

"Then we'll go together," Mott said. "On to victory, my king."

"To victory."

We started forward again, and weren't too much farther along before the first sounds of war reached our ears. Mott and I looked at each other, withdrew our swords, and then rode into the fray.

## TWENTY-FIVE

Roden's defense was set up less than a mile outside the walls of Drylliad, and was visible from the minute we crossed the ridge. Although the soldiers of Bymar and Carthya were fighting against other soldiers out on the wide fields ahead of me, the Roving River far to our right became a sort of perimeter that Roden had determined could not be crossed by the enemy. Along the entire river, wide wooden canopies had been built to shield his men from incoming arrows, and the earth was dug up into tall mounds that would barricade against any attacks from straight ahead. The river was narrow here, but it was deep, and except for a few temporary bridges, nobody could cross it without going for a swim. That would make it difficult for the enemy to breach the lines, but not impossible.

I intended to make it impossible.

My purpose was to get inside the castle walls, or better yet, to get a messenger in there. But we had to hurry. So instead of diving into the heat of the battle, Mott and I rode farther to the south, encountering a few men on the outskirts. From what we could see, they were mostly from Mendenwal, but since we were still dressed as Avenians, their guard was low and they did not expect our swords when they came.

As we came closer to the lines, however, those same uniforms became our disadvantage. We rode toward a small glen that carried the Roving River beneath the castle walls out to the countryside. We were nearly into the glen when, from out of nowhere, a wall of women came running toward us, screaming and yelling to create confusion and distraction. It worked. Several of the women carried wooden poles, connected to each other by lengths of fabric about the size of a blanket. Before I could react or change course, the women ran on either side of my horse and Mott's as well. They passed us almost before we saw them coming, and used those stretched blankets to rip us both from our saddles.

With a hard thud, I landed on my back on the ground, while my horse rode away free. Mott had held on better than I did, but the women didn't give in until they had pulled him down near me.

Farther on, some younger girls caught our horses and swung into their saddles. Then yet another swarm produced swords, which they pressed against our chests, while others removed our weapons. We had been overcome by the mothers and daughters of Carthya, and nicely so. Perhaps they should be my commanders, I thought.

The woman threatening me was tall and simply dressed, and held her sword with confidence. "Invaders of our country, we sentence you to death, under the name of King Jaron of Carthya. Have you any last words?"

"Yes, I do, actually." I stripped off the helmet I wore so that she might see me better. "Before using that sword, you should know that my name *is* King Jaron of Carthya."

She reacted with a gasp and widening eyes, signs she recognized me, and praise the saints that she did. Begging for forgiveness, she removed the weapon from my chest and fell to her knees, as did all the others there.

Mott came over and helped me back to my feet, then I asked the women to rise. The one who had addressed me before said her name was Dawn.

"A name that carries feelings of peace and warmth," I said. "Your parents could not have known all you were capable of when they gave you that name."

She smiled back at me. "Few soldiers here know what we're capable of, Your Majesty. But Roden, the captain of your guard, trusted us to guard this this river. Should any of our people come this way needing to get inside the walls, we bring them in through the passage beneath your castle. But no one else will enter. Forgive us for not recognizing you."

"Actually, I'm grateful to have been part of your demonstration," I said, still rubbing my backside. "Down to my bones, I am impressed with you."

"Thank you, sire." Dawn hesitated and glanced at the other women. "My king, there were rumors about your fate in Avenia. Lord Harlowe assured us he had seen you alive. It gave us hope, but it's still a great relief to see you with my own eyes."

"It's a great relief to be seen." Then, speaking to all the women and their daughters, I said, "Will any of you volunteer to go up this river and into the castle?" This was the same way I had gone several months earlier to claim the throne, and I visualized it perfectly. "Once you're inside, you must tell the people the king requests every ounce of heating oil, animal fat, and pitch in the city. Upon my signal, they will pour it into this river."

"Why destroy all our oils?" a woman behind Dawn asked. "How will we cook, or light our lanterns?"

"We'll eat cold food in the dark if it saves our lives," Dawn said to her. "We obey the king."

"I'll send a signal when I'm ready," I said. "A single flaming arrow into the air, straight up." I looked over to the girls, as strong in heart as their mothers, though most were no older than Fink. "Who will do this for me?"

A smaller girl near the outside of the group raised her hand. From the comparison of their faces, I instantly knew this was Dawn's daughter. Confirming that, Dawn walked over and gently brushed a hand across the girl's shoulders, then crouched down to face her.

"There should not be any danger between us and the walls," Dawn said. "Still, you must run fast and don't look back. Once you get inside, tell them you have a message straight from the king."

The girl curtsied to me, then set off so quickly I doubted even the wind could catch her. I thanked the women, then we started back toward our horses, but I heard Dawn calling to us. In each of her hands were leather brigandines marked with the blue and gold colors of Carthya. Mine was a little large and Mott's a little small, but far better than our thinner Avenian coats.

"We sewed these ourselves," Dawn said as she fastened mine. "They may not be fit for a king, but they are good enough for the proud warriors of Carthya."

"That's all I ask," I said, happy to finally be rid of the Avenian colors. "How can we get behind the lines from here?"

Dawn explained our best possible route, and Mott and I rode that way, though it took us back amidst the fighting. Mott stayed ahead of me through most of it, protecting me with the might of several men. I did my part, but he had been right before. I often needed both hands on my sword, and felt tired sooner than I should have. I vowed that it would not be necessary in the next battle.

I couldn't guess at the numbers Mendenwal had here, but as far as I could tell, Avenia was nowhere to be found. Thankfully, Carthya was assisted by a large number of men from Bymar. Amarinda had told me once that their armies were cavalry, but I hadn't appreciated their skills until seeing them in battle.

A Bymarian soldier ahead of me fought both to his left and right as needed, and used his horse to fight forward. They acted as one, with the horse seeming to know instinctively what its master required. My skills weren't half so polished, and I promised myself that after the war I would seek out the Bymarians for training.

Mott shouted to the Bymarian soldier that he was here with me and that we needed his help to get behind the lines.

He turned to us. "Your captain has already called for a retreat behind those lines. The bridges across the trenches will be removed soon, and Mendenwal won't be far behind."

"Show us the way," I asked.

"I can, but it won't do much good. We'll be overrun before this night is over."

"No," I assured him. "We won't."

He pushed forward, and with Mott's help and mine, we cut a path toward the lines. Though I saw great courage in my men, the war itself was nothing but ugliness and horror. I resolved again to end it as soon as possible.

We were permitted through the lines where the men were being organized for their next round in battle. Our numbers were falling, and it wasn't hard to see that if they were sent out again, most of them would not return. Yet they were calm and focused, and ready for whatever might come. Once Mott and I got under the canopies, I was immediately recognized by several of the men. I asked where Roden was and they said the captain was in a tower at the center of the lines, waiting for the last possible moment to raise the bridges so that as many of our men as possible could get here to safety.

"What if Mendenwal gets across?" I asked one man.

"The captain says we are to hold this line just as we held the border of Gelyn."

"He's right." I stepped closer to him and asked, "How is the captain received by your armies now?"

The man thought about it a moment, then said, "I would give him my life, Your Majesty."

I would have asked more questions, but by then, Mott had found us some archers and we hurried along behind the crowded lines. I relayed my plan along the way, and with wide smiles they told me it wasn't likely to work, but they looked forward to trying anyway.

Word spread quickly that I had come, and a man approached me and said Captain Roden wondered if I had orders for him.

I asked, "How long do you think before Mendenwal is at our lines?"

"They've fallen back to regroup, sire. We'll hold them off with our trebuchets and archers, but that won't work for long. We expect them within the hour."

"Then tell the captain to keep our men inside these lines."

"But if we wait —"

"Yes, let's do that. Let's wait."

He was confused, but still bowed to me and then hurried away. Mott only smiled. He knew what I had in mind.

Throughout the following hour, we watched, waiting for Mendenwal to come. And so they did. In the fading light, we heard them long before we saw the tips of their helmets or wave of their colors. Mendenwal marched in lines and in perfect unison. They were coming for us. And they were coming quickly.

It was impossible to know how many men they had left, except that the noise of their march was growing.

Their advance was held together by the beat of drummers at the rear. Each roll of the drums pushed the battle nearer. Their drums grew louder, bolder. The message in the rhythm was clear. They would be here soon, and were bringing our defeat. The men near me stood on restless legs and some even looked around, as if wondering where we'd retreat to once Mendenwal came. I even overheard one comment that we'd be best to run to the castle now, and fight from there.

But by then, the rhythm of the approaching march had also reminded me of an old Carthyan anthem. Likely, many of my soldiers' mothers had sung it to them while they were young, as my mother had to me. I climbed a ladder to gain some height above the group, and then started singing.

> Let the winds blow, lad
> Let fall the deep snow.
> Let the stars fall, lad
> We'll answer the call.

Others joined me in the next verse, and suddenly the drumbeats that had seemed so threatening now strengthened us.

> Let the dark come, lad
> Ask not where it's from.

*After the fight, lad*
*We'll see morning's light.*

They continued singing, even when I turned away to watch the armies' approach. When I thought the time was right, I asked an archer to send a flaming arrow straight into the air. Whatever Mendenwal brought to us next, this fight was not over yet.

## · TWENTY-SIX ·

When I was younger, my brother and I used to carve small boats from wood and sail them on this same river. It took about fifteen minutes for them to leave the castle walls and make it to this stretch of water. I hoped the oils from Drylliad would carry at a similar pace.

It took Mendenwal almost twenty minutes to get past the worst from our archers and catapults. There was no way to know if the oils had made it this far — from this distance, the water wouldn't look any different. But the timing was good.

The soldiers of Mendenwal entered the river together, entire rows of men moving across it in time with the beat of their drums.

Once the trenches were full, I ordered the archers to light their arrows and then shoot. They weren't aiming for the men — there were far too many for us to get them all. They were to aim for the water.

The first few arrows entered the water and were immediately extinguished. But those in the next round found the patch of oil, which instantly lit the river as bright as the midday sun.

Fire traveled in ripples up and down the water, burning wherever it was fueled, and licking the men in its path. The soldiers scrambled to get away, but the flames would not be stopped so easily. The others who had not yet entered ran to avoid the flames now spreading to land. Within seconds, Mendenwal was awash in chaos, and their leaders were having trouble regaining control. The drumbeats, I noticed, were gone.

Once the fire burned itself out, I heard Roden shouting from his tower. I moved until I could see him, standing on the ladder so that he was as visible as possible.

"You came to these lines as farmers and tailors and merchants," he said. "But you stand here now as soldiers, in defense of your king, your country, and your families. Nothing is more sacred than their lives, and those who fall in their service will be carried to the afterlife on the wings of angels. Do not hesitate. Do not falter. Do not doubt that we will succeed. I will celebrate with you at the end of this night!"

With a loud whoop, he then sent all remaining men away from the lines again to finish the battle. I remained stunned for a moment. The Roden I had known was slow with words, full of self-doubt, and wouldn't have been able to inspire even the most eager warrior. Had such a speech really come from his mouth?

Yes, of course it had. Glimmers of this person had appeared at times when we were together at Farthenwood, even when he didn't know it. I knew this was in him, but just hadn't anticipated he would find his way this well or this quickly. Perhaps it was arrogant to congratulate myself on having chosen such an excellent captain, but I couldn't help it. He was exactly the leader I had expected him to be.

When I raised my sword and started to leave with the men, Mott asked me to stay back, for my own safety. I rolled my eyes to let him know I had no intention of that, and so without delay, he leapt over the mounds of earth at my side and we dove into the battle. The fighting was still hard, but it was obvious that many of Mendenwal's soldiers had run once the fire broke out. Their king wasn't here and their leaders were far too spread out now to be effective. Likely, many of them had no better idea why they were in this war than I did.

Within another hour, more Carthyans arrived from the same direction as Mott and I had come. Certainly, these were the extra soldiers from the Falstan camp, and they were fresh and eager to prove themselves. With their help, and Bymar's continuing support, a retreat was soon called by Mendenwal, and shouts of victory were raised through my armies. Mendenwal emptied from the field faster than I could have imagined possible, with Bymar and Carthya still in pursuit.

Roden found me shortly after. He was on horseback and looked exhausted, but as far as I could tell, he was uninjured. He had another horse with him, a smaller one, which he offered to me. I pointed out he should give me the larger horse that he was riding, but Roden insisted he was quite comfortable already and if I didn't want the small horse, he would find someone who did. As we laughed, Mott said he would stay behind and help with the wounded, then meet me again behind the lines.

I climbed onto the horse and Roden said, "You don't need to stay here tonight. Harlowe told me what you went through in Avenia. You'll rest better if I take you back to the castle."

"And miss all the fun?" I asked. "No, I've been away from my armies long enough. They will see me here." We rode farther, and then I asked, "Are they your armies too?"

He weighed that in silence, and just when I thought he had decided never to answer me, he said, "It is always your army, Jaron. But they are my men now."

"What changed?"

He shrugged. "I did. I realized that I couldn't expect them to think better of me than I thought of myself. So if I believed I was too young or stupid or inexperienced to be a captain, then that's all I would ever be."

"So what do you believe now?"

Refusing that question, he only chuckled instead. "I believe you need a solid meal. I'd think with the way Mott watches over you, that he'd be more concerned for your health, and stuff a meat pie in your mouth every time you open it."

I laughed along with him. "He'd probably like to try that, just to keep me from talking myself into trouble all the time."

"That's not a bad idea, you know. We have no meat pies behind our lines, but there will be good food to celebrate this victory."

"How are the people in Drylliad? Do they have enough food?"

Roden shrugged. "That's a constant concern. Far more people came to the city than anyone expected and shortages came with them. Lord Harlowe needed more supplies, but the men couldn't keep the walls open and defend them too."

"Then how —"

"You met the women at the river, didn't you?" When I said I had, he continued, "The women in Drylliad told us that if we could push the battle this far from the city walls, then they would keep the supply lines open. The men may have fought for this city, but it will be the women who save it."

They reminded me of Amarinda, who had risked her life to return to the throne in my absence. And Imogen, who had given her life to save mine. It would take entire lifetimes for the men of Carthya to deserve their women.

At supper that night, the soldiers toasted one another and celebrated Roden's name and mine for the strategies that gave us the win. I raised my own cup to them, but seeds of worry had sprouted in my mind and eventually I had to walk away. I couldn't quite explain what was wrong, but that only bothered me more.

When Roden followed me to ask about it, I said, "Does it feel like today's fight was too easy?"

"Easy?" Roden gestured toward the battlefield. "Do you know how many men fell out there? How close we came to losing?"

"Yes, and I don't take that lightly. But something about it just doesn't feel right."

Clearly angry now, Roden crossed directly in front of me. "If it feels easy to you, then it's because you've been apart from the war for too many days. Every man still here fought hard for his life and did his job while his brothers fell around him. Stay with us for longer than a day and you'll change your mind about how easy you think this was!"

I started to argue back but he stomped away. Mott came up to me, and when I tried to explain, he only took my empty bowl, insisting he would get me more to eat.

It was much later before I had it figured out, why the battle had felt easy. Mott was asleep by then, as were most of the men. Roden still hadn't returned, but there was another fire not far from ours where I suspected he had gone. Whether he was still angry or not, I would make him listen to me.

Mott and I had come here because of what Fish Breath had said, that the king of Avenia meant to break through these lines. I had noticed a few Avenians in the battle, but not many, and certainly not an army. Beyond that, King Vargan wasn't here, nor any sign of his banner.

Perhaps Fish Breath had lied to me, or perhaps the plans had changed since he heard them. Either way, it didn't matter. We'd fought Mendenwal here, but that's all it was — a fight. Vargan was letting me wear down my numbers while he remained in the background. Avenia was still out there somewhere, spreading destruction in my country like a silent plague. I had to find them. Because until I defeated Vargan, I could never end this war.

# · TWENTY-SEVEN ·

I heard Roden's voice long before I saw him. He wasn't speaking loudly, but everything else had become so quiet and still. I caught the sound of my name and silently moved toward him. He'd been angry for what he considered my insult to his skills in battle, and I could only imagine what he must have to say about me now.

I saw him in silhouette with his back toward the fire, and planted myself behind the trunk of a tree nearby where I wouldn't be seen. I vaguely recognized the man he was speaking to. It was the soldier from Bymar who had led us behind the lines, a commander in a fine uniform whom the others addressed as Lord Orison.

"Pardon my observation," Orison said. "But you are as young as your king. Why did Jaron choose you as his captain?"

"I'm still asking myself that question," Roden answered. "If you figure it out, please let me know."

I had already answered him weeks ago, when he and I had fought before the pirates. *Anyone fierce enough to threaten Carthya is strong enough to defend it,* I'd told him. And I had meant it. When it came to a battle, Roden did not blink.

"I only wonder because we all know how focused King Vargan is on recapturing your king. He has made those intentions very clear, and yet we both know what would happen to Jaron if Vargan gets hold of him again."

Roden nodded in agreement, but for my part, I didn't like the way the conversation was going.

Orison continued, "If this war became yours to command, could you do it?"

Roden shrugged. "Jaron won't let himself be captured again, and he knows how to survive on a battlefield."

"Yes, but if something did happen, *could* you command the war?"

There was a long silence while Roden thought it over. I pressed in closer, eager to hear what he had to say. Finally, Roden drew in a breath and said, "When Jaron first sent me to Gelyn, I was a boy with a sword, only pretending to be the captain of an army. But after several hard-fought battles, I am not that boy anymore."

No, he wasn't the same. But it still wasn't the answer Orison wanted.

After another pause, Roden continued, "I went to Gelyn with forty of Jaron's finest men. At first I thought I was there to teach them how to follow me, but that wasn't the plan at all. Instead, they were there to teach me how to lead them, to make me into the captain Jaron wanted. I will never have the courage or the wit of my king. But yes, if necessary, I could win this war for Carthya."

They took a few quiet sips of their drinks, then the Bymarian commander said, "I know little about Jaron, other than the stories Carthyans tell about him."

I rolled my eyes at that. The last thing I needed was for him to laugh at who I had once been. The war was hard enough; I didn't need to fight my own history as well.

But when Roden asked what stories, Orison replied, "I heard that the people of Carthya would follow your king to the devils' lair and back again. Is it true?"

"Yes, and I would be first amongst them," Roden answered. "I would follow Jaron wherever he goes, and trust with all my heart that he will win this war."

"How can you be sure?"

Roden's focus turned to the fire and he lowered his voice. "Some months ago, Jaron made his way to the pirates of Avenia. Their branding is on his right forearm. He tries to keep it covered, but sometimes a person catches a glimpse of it."

"I saw it earlier when he fought near me." Orison licked his lips, and then said, "I noticed you have the same mark too, by the way. There are rumors that Jaron is the pirates' king."

"He won't talk about it," Roden said, "but it's true. Do you know how he gained that title?"

Orison shrugged. "According to the story I heard, he fought the pirate king and won, though the battle ended with his broken leg."

"He lets people believe that, but that's not the real story." Now Roden faced his companion. "For a few short hours, I was that pirate king. And the battle didn't *end* with Jaron's broken leg. That's how it *began*. Jaron escaped from a secure room, climbed the face of a cliff, and defeated me in battle, all with a broken leg. Jaron may give up his life one day, but it will never be taken from him."

Orison let out a low whistle. "Why doesn't he tell the story? The people should know."

"Jaron thinks it'll turn his armies against me."

"Ah. He might be right, unfortunately." Orison was silent for a moment, and then asked, "How did you go from his enemy in battle to his captain?"

"Jaron never saw us as enemies. He risked his life to make me see that too." Roden shifted his position, as if suddenly uncomfortable with the turn of the conversation. "I owe him everything."

"As these men owe you. You are young still, but I look forward to watching you grow as their captain. I believe the day will come when you are one of the greatest leaders in all the lands."

"Only as long as I'm allowed to serve one of the greatest kings." Roden pondered that a moment, and then stood. "He was trying to tell me something earlier tonight. I'd better go find him."

He left the fire and came around the path where I had been hiding. Only now I was leaning against the tree, with my arms folded and a grin on my face that I knew would irritate him.

Roden licked his lips as he stared at me. "Tell me you didn't hear all that."

"*One* of the greatest kings?" My smile widened. "That's it? Why not *the* greatest?"

"This will only make your arrogance worse, I'm sure."

"Really? Do you think that's possible?"

He chuckled. "You can always make things worse, Jaron."

"I've thought the very same thing myself."

We were silent a moment before he said, "I shouldn't have become angry earlier. Why did you think the battle felt easy?"

I motioned for him to follow me to where it was quieter, and there explained to him what Fish Breath had said, and about the absence of Avenia's king. The more we talked about it, the more I was certain that something was very wrong. Vargan wanted Drylliad, of course, but he left Mendenwal to that task. He wouldn't care who lived or died in the battle because this city wasn't his real objective.

"The commander I just spoke to believes that Vargan wants to recapture you," Roden said.

"Well, he won't. I've had enough of Vargan to satisfy me for a lifetime."

There was silence again, and then Roden said, "How much of my conversation just now did you overhear?"

"From the time he asked if you could win this war. Why?"

"He told me something before that, something you won't like."

"What is it?"

Roden drew in a breath, and took long enough at it that I knew the news must be bad. "Fink made his way to Bymar. He's the one who got their soldiers here to fight."

"Yes, I know that. He went there on Amarinda's orders."

"Every day since we came back from the pirates, Fink pestered me to train him in sword fighting. I finally gave him a wooden sword and told him to come back when he grew a muscle or two."

"What about Fink?" I couldn't hide the concern in my voice, or dull the feelings of panic growing inside me.

"According to the commander, Fink was upset about your death but insisted to everyone it couldn't be true. So he traveled back through Avenia so he could go and find you himself. They believe he was captured at the border. Nobody has heard from him since." Roden sighed. "I should've taught him how to use that sword."

"They'll make Fink talk," I said. "And he'll lead them to Falstan Lake. It's the only place where Fink knows I have plans. Vargan wants me and he expects to find me there."

As I started to run away from him, Roden said, "If Vargan wants to find you at Falstan Lake, you really can't be going there."

"Oh yes," I responded. "That's exactly where he'll find me."

## · TWENTY-EIGHT ·

Before leaving for Falstan Lake, Mott, Roden, and I made a plan. Mott and I would leave immediately and arrive at the Falstan camp by dawn. Meanwhile, Roden would take his soldiers east in search of other troubles. Without doubt, he would find them.

Mott had argued that I should sleep for the night and we could start out fresh in the morning, but I told him it would be impossible for me to sleep, so nothing was gained that way. Besides, as my country continued filling with enemy soldiers, I believed we were safer traveling under the cover of darkness.

The ride to the Falstan camp was quiet and took less time than I had anticipated. The commander who welcomed us looked very much like Mott, except for a long braid of hair that went halfway down his back. He said that Mendenwal continued to maintain a camp nearby, but assured me there had been no sign of Avenia anywhere in the area. At least for now, all was quiet.

"I'm not wrong about this," I told Mott as the commander led us toward the tents. "Avenia will come."

"Avenia sent Mendenwal to do the hard work in yesterday's battle," Mott said. "Perhaps he's done that again here."

The commander stepped forward. "My king, you look exhausted. A tent has already been prepared for you, and we don't expect any trouble tonight."

"Please go to sleep," Mott said. "Tomorrow will be better if you can face it with a clear head. Besides," he added once I started to object, "I can't sleep if you won't, and I'm exhausted too."

I wasn't sure whether I would be able to sleep, but by then I was willing to try. The aches and stings from the battle had caught up to me and even ducking inside the tent felt like an impossible chore. I collapsed on the cot fully clothed and was asleep before Mott had left.

I slept solidly until first light, when I arose and got to work. I first exchanged the battle-stained coat from Dawn for a simple gray-laced shirt and a belt for my weapons. Then after eating a hearty meal, I went alone to survey the area, eventually finding myself at the overlook of Falstan Valley. Far below me, the Roving River emptied into this valley, creating a beautiful wide lake. Or, it used to, anyway.

The Roving River began somewhere in the mountains of Gelyn and wound southward through Carthya, supplying water to most of our people. This same river ran behind Farthenwood, and was where I had lain after taking a wild ride on one of Conner's untrained horses, and also where I had confessed my true identity to Mott. Dawn and the women of Drylliad now guarded this river near the castle walls.

As it left Drylliad, the Roving River gradually cut deeper into the earth, leaving high canyon walls on either side. I stood on one of those walls now, not far from my camp.

Falstan Lake, and the valley surrounding it, had been named for an early explorer of these lands. He had commented in his journal on the beautiful sight of coming upon the cool blue waters of the lake. Our people had enjoyed it ever since then. I, too, had many good memories of swinging into the waters from a rope hung from some of the tall trees on the shore.

But for well over a month, the lake bed had been dry. All that came through the caked valley floor now was a thin vein of river water, only a pale shadow of what it should have been.

Falstan Lake still existed, or at least, the water from the lake still existed. Except that instead of a wide, deep lake, it was bottled up in the canyon at my back, trapped behind a steep wall of rocks, logs, and mud. As the water rose higher, so did the dam of debris. Now it was nearly even with the earthen cliffs beneath my feet. From my angle, it looked as though an entire hillside somewhere upriver had collapsed and the debris had become lodged here.

As the commander had indicated the night before, Avenia was nowhere in sight, but Mendenwal was entrenched in their own camp not far from the lake's former bed. The soldiers of that camp had enough water for cooking and drinking, and to manage their animals. But little more. There certainly wasn't enough water for the men to bathe in, and I hoped the smell of so many sweaty and dirty soldiers was choking them. Not that

I was in a position to judge. After so many battles and the miles of dusty road in between, I needed my own bath. By now I was sure my odor offended even the devils, which was no small feat.

Mendenwal must have known our camp was here and yet they had not attacked. Why? Perhaps they were waiting for Vargan and his men. It surprised me that they waited at all. Mendenwal had thousands of men here, far more than we'd encountered near Drylliad. Surely they would look at our fewer numbers and see their advantage.

From what I could determine, Mendenwal had crowded their soldiers into a semi-sheltered knot of land that would be nearly impossible for my men to breach. They were near the dry lake bed, but surrounded by sheer slopes. It would be a long ride for us to approach from the south and attack from on top of the slopes. And I was certain the entrances to their camp were very well guarded should we attempt to enter it directly. The only way to defeat them was to draw them out. I had some ideas about that.

After a careful survey of the area, I returned to camp and held council with Mott, Tobias and Amarinda, and my military leaders. We described all we had seen in our battles, and they told me similar stories of their troubles. Little of what we discussed was encouraging.

Mott shared with the group a message that had come in from Drylliad earlier that morning, which was that the nearness of our battle yesterday had thrown the capital into disarray.

As we had suspected would be necessary, Harlowe had opened the prisons to anyone who swore an oath to act in defense of the country. But with the chaos in the city, the one prisoner who had not been offered the chance to fight had still escaped.

"Conner," I breathed. "Where's Conner?"

Of course, no one here could answer me, but his absence bothered me in every possible way. More so since I already knew Conner had been in communication with Vargan. I had no time to waste on wondering where he had gone, but clearly I had been wrong all this time to keep him alive. I hated the thought that he was free in the world, likely never to be captured again, and undoubtedly at work on more destruction.

Mott only shrugged in response to my question. Nor did anyone have news about Fink, which bothered me equally as much.

Next, we discussed Mendenwal's vast armies camped nearby and my commander's belief that they were readying for attack. Although I would've liked to wait for Avenia, it was vital that we make the first strike, before Mendenwal advanced. So with a map of the area spread across a table in my tent, I gave my lieutenants their orders. But the grim expressions on the faces around me very plainly showed their reluctance to carry them out, and in clear and respectful terms, a few of them even shared their specific concerns. Nothing of what they said to me was wrong, unfortunately. We *were* risking a lot, and also depending far too much on luck to see us through to victory. The confidence I had felt from the beginning faltered beneath their arguments.

"Will doubt be our enemy now?" I asked them. "Because doubt will defeat us far quicker than any army could. No plan is perfect, but that's no reason to give up. Unless someone has a better option, then we will go forward as planned." And hope against reason that I was not leading my men to their deaths.

One of my lieutenants leaned forward. "My king, we will follow you to the end. But we've seen their numbers. By my guess, we're outnumbered as much as five to one."

I sat back in my chair and smiled. "Only five to one? We might consider sending home half our army, then, so as not to intimidate them."

Uneasy laughter spread within the group and my grin widened. I couldn't let it show, but in truth, I was just as anxious about the upcoming battle as they were. Probably more.

By then we were coming to the end of a very long meeting, and I was tired. I was much stronger since escaping the Avenian camp, but yesterday had been a hard battle and tomorrow would demand even more from me. With so little sleep the night before, the weight of all I bore on my shoulders felt exhausting. I had only barely motioned for everyone to leave when Mott swept them out as if they carried the plague.

"You're a king's ideal nursemaid," I told him. "Defending me with a sword in one hand, and using the other to tuck me into bed for an afternoon nap."

Mott smiled. "Defending you takes both hands. So you may tuck yourself into bed, or do whatever is necessary to get some sleep."

"How can I?" My face fell, and I felt the urge to stand and pace the floor. "Even if everything goes well tomorrow, we both know that Avenia is still out there somewhere."

"Then what can I do?"

"Find me five men for tonight," I said. "Men who can climb."

Mott's brows pressed together. "Jaron, you haven't been able to climb since the injury to your leg."

"I never said I'd be climbing. Now, find me five. And warn everyone else to use this day to rest. We'll move before first light."

He gave me a bow, then backed out of the tent. "I'll find your men, but only if you rest too."

I lay down for a while, but did not sleep, then got up and ate a little while I studied maps of the area. My camp was higher in elevation, making it difficult for Mendenwal to launch a surprise attack against us, but it wasn't impossible either. There was a narrow and steep trail that led directly from their camp up to the ridges above them. It probably wouldn't support an entire army, but it was a fast route to my camp.

I considered joining the others outside to discuss the matter, except that Mott would've scolded me for not sleeping, and I didn't need that.

Tomorrow would prove to be a very important day. I sincerely hoped I wouldn't regret it.

---

As requested, five soldiers arrived at my tent that night shortly before dark. I had managed to get some sleep by then and felt ready for what lay ahead. As quietly as possible, I explained what I needed from each of them and the great danger involved, then invited any of them who wished to withdraw to do so. Not one man accepted the offer, which gave me increased pride in the courage of my military. However, before we left, I eliminated two of the men. One was because I knew he had a young family at home, and the other was quietly massaging his wrist. Whatever the cause of his discomfort, he was not the best fit for my plans.

I showed them a small wood-and-iron trunk that had come from Drylliad weeks earlier, then ordered the two strongest men to carry it to the ridge overlooking the former lake bed. As we walked, I explained in more detail the risks and challenges ahead. If the Mendenwal army had the sense of fungus rot, they were watching for our attack. So although the hill to the side of the dam was steep and slippery, they would have to descend it silently and in darkness, using little more than their wits and past experience with near vertical ground. Beyond that, they would have to lower the heavy trunk with them on ropes, and then wait until my signal to use it.

"Tell me you can do this," I said. "Everything hinges on you tomorrow."

The three men vowed with their lives to succeed. I had their loyalty; now I could only hope for their safety. We had no second chance if they failed.

Once they left, I returned to the camp where Mott stood with the heads of my armies, awaiting orders.

"How many men do we have here?" I asked.

One of my men responded, "Nearly a thousand, sire."

"Then I want our one hundred weakest men. Poorly armed, but on horseback."

"To sacrifice?" another captain asked doubtfully.

"Not at all," I countered. "To be the heroes of Carthya. They will win tomorrow's battle for us. When the moon is highest, have them meet outside my tent."

"What about the rest of us?" Mott asked.

"Everyone else should prepare to ride. We fight tomorrow."

I started to leave, but Mott caught up to me. "Jaron, your plan sounds reckless and dangerous. And if I know you at all, then it's probably impossible too."

"That sounds about right."

He chuckled. "Are you ready for what's coming?"

I smiled as I glanced sideways at him. "I am ready. Yesterday's battle was only a distraction from Vargan's larger plan. Tomorrow, the drift of this war is going to change."

# · TWENTY-NINE ·

I managed to sleep a little more that night, though I was already awake when a vigil came to tell me the one hundred men were gathered. Over a thick layer of chain mail, I wore a deep blue brigandine embroidered with the gold crest of Carthya and with metal plates riveted to the fabric to protect my arms and torso. Mott thoroughly disapproved of the outfit. He wanted me in full battle armor, but it was too heavy for me, especially since I still lacked the full strength I'd had before my time in Vargan's camp. Besides that, I was neither the biggest nor the strongest in this battle. My only hope was to be the quickest, and for that, I needed light armor. In better news, Mott informed me that my horse, Mystic, had been sent to the camp in anticipation of my arrival. I was thrilled for that. Mystic knew me well and would cooperate better with my plans than another, less fierce horse. I dismissed Mott to prepare Mystic for the ride while I finished getting ready. All that remained was to strap on my sword and whisper a request to the devils not to interfere with my plans.

Except this time, that didn't seem like enough, and my thoughts turned to the saints. When I was younger, the priests had always frowned and murmured to one another when I entered the chapel each week. Admittedly, that may have been because I rarely let pass the opportunity to make loud jokes to my brother about their tedious sermons. The priests said I wouldn't get any favors from the saints until I took their sermons seriously, but I tended to believe the saints were just as bored with their sermons as I was. Besides, I'd never considered myself the type of person the saints would be interested in helping anyway. As I thought about the coming day, I hoped I was wrong about that.

In the quiet of my tent, I reflected on what the priests had said about the afterlife. The idea that those who had passed on remained a part of our lives, eternally watching over us, appealed to me in a way it never had when I was younger. And if the priests were right, then Imogen must be a saint now, as well as my family. The saints would help me. Imogen would *make* them help me — I knew she would. So for the first time ever, I had no worries about the tricks of the devils. I would ride into battle on the wings of the saints.

As I strode from the tent, Mystic's reins were thrust into my hands. I climbed astride and immediately noticed Mott already on his own horse.

"What are you doing here?" I asked him.

"It's all very shameful," he said. "It turns out I'm one of your one hundred weakest men."

"You're not."

"I'm afraid it's true." Even as he spoke, Mott couldn't resist smiling. "It's a source of great embarrassment, Your Majesty, and I beg you not to question me about it any further."

I chuckled again, and then rode to where all the men could see me. "My friends, what we are about to do is not the battle of your forefathers, nor the time-tested strategies of the past. It has never been done, or to be fair, never been done successfully. But that is what will make us great. You will tell your children and your grandchildren of this moment. In your old age, the last smile on your lips will be the memory of what we are about to do. Your commanders undoubtedly told you that I wanted the weakest of our armies to ride with me here today. Be grateful that you were chosen, because it is through the weakest that the strong arm of Carthya will wield its strength. My friends, we ride as the weak always will: quietly and without drawing even the attention of the sleeping bird to our path. Follow me."

Only a few dim lanterns highlighted the grave expressions of the soldiers, but I saw Mott's face well enough. He smiled at me with a look I'd seen before: He thought me the biggest fool he had ever known, and hoped that very quality might save us all. I hoped so too.

I led the way along a trail I had studied earlier that day. It would take us from our camp overlooking the valley down to the floor through a narrow pathway largely obscured by thick trees and tall shrubbery. It would eventually empty out not far from where I intended to lie in wait for Mendenwal.

Our group traveled in complete silence. Of course, the horses made plenty of noise, but as was common in the nights here, wind swirled throughout the valley. As long as we were careful, our sounds wouldn't carry all the way to Mendenwal's camp.

By dawn, I sat upon Mystic's back at the far end of the valley floor, easily within Mendenwal's grasp. Mott was at my side and one hundred of Carthya's least impressive soldiers sat on horses behind me. What they lacked in skill, they made up for with confident postures and calm stillness.

The scouts of Mendenwal saw us at first light and quickly rode back to their camp with shouts of alarm.

"They'll gather their armies now," I announced. "Everyone stay ready and wait here."

Once the first group from Mendenwal entered the valley floor, I rode forward, flanked by Mott and my standard bearer, who held the flag of Carthya aloft in the morning breeze. It was emblazoned with my family's coat of arms over the blue and gold colors that had always symbolized the compassion and courage of my country. We stopped within calling distance of each other, no closer than necessary.

Their commander had brought ten men ahead with him. Since I had only Mott and a poorly armed standard bearer, the ratio seemed about right for our respective forces. I called to their commander, "What brings Mendenwal into war against Carthya? We have no quarrel with you."

"We ride on orders from King Humfrey. His reasons are his own."

"And are you certain those reasons are worth your deaths?" Mott cleared his throat as a warning to me, but I only smiled and raised my voice. "I don't wish to offend your king, of course, but it's clear his reasoning abilities have abandoned him. Perhaps you should take your armies and go home, while you can."

"You will not insult the king of Mendenwal!" the commander cried.

"It's not an insult. Only an observation of fact. The only reason King Humfrey would invade my country is because he was either threatened or else Avenia promised him something gold and shiny. Please believe me when I tell you that Avenia will not keep its promises. They are using you to destroy me, and they will turn on you next. For your own sake, Commander, I urge you to ride home as fast as your wobbly horse can carry you."

The commander's face tightened, which nearly made me laugh. I hadn't deliberately made anyone this angry since Master Graves had attempted to teach me my letters at Farthenwood so many months ago, and it felt good.

The commander gestured to the hundred men far behind me. "Is that your army, King Jaron? Or did you bring your country's fiercest kittens?"

I briefly turned back to them. "Be warned. Our kittens will scratch like lions. The men behind me are the ones who wanted the honor of crushing your army."

"I could send my nursemaids out here to fight those men."

"I'm sorry you have such little value for your nursemaids. We invite them to become Carthyan citizens. You are warned,

Commander. We will defeat all of your army camped here this day. I meant what I said before. Most of your men will not survive. Including you."

The commander laughed. "Surrender to me now, Jaron."

"No, you surrender to me!" I yelled. "I'm bored of this conversation. Either promise to leave Carthya this instant and you will live, or go and fetch your armies. I will take out the first thousand myself. Maybe more if they're no sharper than you seem to be."

The commander looked to his companions, who snorted their disdain for me, and then he said, "Very well, King Jaron. You have sealed your doom."

"So said the last man I defeated. Off you go, then! Bring me your worst, and hurry! I was awake early and am hoping for a nap this afternoon."

As the Mendenwal group rode away, Mott turned to me and said, "Are you insane?" I smiled back at him and he said, "Of course you are. Please tell me you have a plan."

"Here's my plan," I replied. "We stay right here. Do you know any tunes to whistle while we wait?"

Apparently, Mott did not know any tunes for whistling, but he did work in a nice chorus of grunts and sighs.

The Mendenwal armies must have been ready to march, because it wasn't long before I saw them. Mendenwal soldiers were swordsmen, well trained and well disciplined. There were far too many of them to travel by horse, so nearly all of them entered the valley on foot. I saw the commander and his leaders on their horses, but they led from behind, which I had expected. They wanted the least valuable of their men, the ones in front, to take the worst of whatever my armies would bring.

"How many men are coming?" I asked Mott.

He squinted. "I estimate at least a thousand already on the march, but I can't see the end of their lines. You can't expect to fight them all."

"No," I said. "I don't expect to fight any of them."

Once they were close enough to begin the battle, the order was given for the soldiers to run for the three of us. I made a loud comment about the unfortunate tendency of Mendenwal women to sprout warts on their faces, then turned and began riding away. Not too quickly. Just a bit faster than they could run.

"Our one hundred can't handle them," Mott said. "Some are very poor fighters."

"That's why they're here, and not with the others."

Mott quickened his horse to keep pace with mine. "I cannot believe that you would sacrifice these men for any reason. It's not like you."

I only smiled. "How many men are behind us now?"

He glanced back and said, "Their lines are in disarray. But the valley is quickly filling."

By the time we reached my men, panic was clear on their faces. Most had drawn their swords, ready for a battle that was certain to end in devastating failure.

"Why do you all look so worried?" I asked, riding around them. "Have you seen the bright sun rising today? Is anyone else feeling warm?"

Judging by the sweat on their faces, they all were. Or maybe it had nothing to do with the heat. These men were terrified.

"Then let us ride," I said. "Not too fast. But stay ahead of their armies."

So we rode. With credit to the Mendenwal soldiers, some of them were excellent runners and seemingly tireless, so we moved faster than I would have liked. Behind us, the wide valley continued to fill, and their soldiers were becoming increasingly angry.

Finally, we were nearing the end of the valley. The Carthyan camp high above us was entirely empty now. We had no second chances, no support, and if things didn't go well, no place to go to save ourselves. With Mendenwal at our backs and impossibly steep climbs ahead of us, I could never get everyone to safety.

Except I had no intention of getting to the top. Only to get a little higher than where we were now.

I rode to the rear of my men and raised my sword. Then I yelled out to Mendenwal, "Lay down your weapons now and live." They only continued to run for me, which was unfortunate, but not unexpected. "Very well," I muttered. To whatever end, it was time to unleash a plan I had anticipated for months. In the next few minutes, we would face either great success or a certain slaughter.

# · THIRTY ·

With my one hundred men less than a minute from being literally trapped against a sheer cliff wall, I increased the speed of my horse. Mott matched my speed and together we returned to the front of the group and signaled to the three men who had climbed down the hill in the darkness. They had been hiding at the base of the wall, and were now in place. Upon my signal, a flaming torch was held high. They lit a rope that led inside the opened wood-and-iron trunk, and then ran for the hills.

"We should ride faster," I said to Mott.

"Is that what I think it is?" Following my lead, he said, "You told me the gunpowder at Vargan's camp was all you had."

"All I had with me," I corrected him. "Not all I had."

"You're going to blow up that wall?"

My focus remained on the growing fire ahead of us. "It's not a wall, Mott. It's a dam."

One of my first acts as king was to send every spare man to this area to dam up the Roving River. I had hoped for a barricade that would appear to be created by the natural flow of debris, and that vision had been executed to perfection. In fact, I'd heard that much of the dam was formed simply by sending large items down the river to clog the spillway.

Now, at full speed, I charged sideways for the hills with my men behind me. At first, the Mendenwal soldiers seemed more distracted by the fire at the base of the dam than the consequences of it. Once they realized what was happening, it was too late.

The explosion burst before my men reached the hills, and it shook the ground like violent thunder. Mystic panicked and tried to bolt, but in a battle of wills between us, I intended to win. It was the only way we'd survive. I dug my legs firmly into his side and urged him forward. My ears rang like chapel bells in my head from the noise while the disturbed air pressed in waves at my back.

The base of the dam burst with a fury I could not have imagined. Instantly, the walls above it collapsed, sending not only water, but also rocks and logs catapulting through the valley like a full-scale assault.

My men were drenched by the time we reached the hillside, but all of us were there. And the Mendenwal soldiers that had filled the valley like busy ants were swept away in the fierce waters. Falstan Lake was returning to its bed. Within a precious few seconds, more than half of their army was gone.

My men cheered, but the battle had only begun. Not all of Mendenwal had entered the valley, and they would be panicked now and need time to regroup and install new leaders. We would not allow any recovery. The remainder of my army had left camp and was already on their heels, advancing from the rear.

"The match is more even now," I said to Mott. "We can win this." Then I directed my attention to the men with me. "You have passed the test of courage, which is the hardest of all tests. Now is the time for battle, and I know you can do it. Stay on your horse to fight and keep moving. You hold swords in your hands, but remember that every part of you is a weapon. You have legs, and strong backs, and best of all, you have brains. Never stop thinking, never stop looking ahead and making your plans. As long as you think, you will survive."

Eager now to prove themselves in real battle, the men cheered again, and I led them back toward Mendenwal's camp. At the shores of the restored lake, the few soldiers who'd escaped the waters lay in the mud, both soaked and stunned. Maybe their retreat to the shore hadn't been slowed by the heavy weight of armor, or else they'd been strong enough to swim desperately for their lives. Unarmed and panicked, they ran toward their camp when they saw us riding for them. I let them run. It was better to have their armies collected all in one place once I arrived.

We rode into the Mendenwal camp amidst a chaotic battle with the rest of my armies, who had already entered from the opposite direction. The camp was situated in a small well of a valley with little vegetation and surrounded by tall walls of sharp gray rock. We entered at one end, and my army blocked the only other escape. Within this well, hundreds of soldiers fought one another on horse and on foot. Mendenwal was clearly unnerved, which gave my armies the advantage. I ordered my one hundred men to surround the camp as best as they could so that no one could escape, then located the narrow path I had seen on the maps the night before, the one that traveled up the cliff walls to the ledges high above the battlefield.

. I rode in that direction with my sword at the ready, and used it when necessary to clear the path ahead. With the bulk of their army gone, including most of their leaders, Mendenwal could not hope to win no matter how long they fought. But I didn't wish for this battle to last long either. Every lost soldier had someone at home who loved him. Most had wives or children or a mother who depended on them for survival. Each fallen Carthyan I passed caused a lurch within my gut. It was time for this battle to end.

Before starting up the steep path, I sheathed my sword and grabbed a torch instead. It was a slow, hard climb for Mystic, and the gravel-covered trail was more slippery than I liked. The sheer edges below me promised a straight fall to the valley floor, but Mystic was as surefooted as he was strong. Once I stood on top of the ridge, I surveyed the battle. My one hundred men had held their places to surround the camp. Nearly everyone was fighting, but we controlled the exits. Mendenwal still outnumbered my soldiers, but their numbers were also falling faster. Without leaders, they only continued fighting out of the desperate will to survive. All they needed was a reason to stop, and a chance to live. I would offer that.

First, I removed some rope from Mystic's saddlebag and tied one end to a tree. Next, I ran to a large rock nearby. It took all my strength to roll it to the very edge, then undoubtedly a nudge from the saints helped me tip it down the slope. The rock collected strength as it rolled and dislodged several others — a definite bonus. It created enough noise and threat that many of the closest men had to stop fighting and run to safety.

Finally, I had everyone's attention. With the torch back in one hand and the rope in my other, I raised both arms and yelled, "At the other end of this rope is more of the same explosives that just blew up the dam. If I light it, the same thing will happen to you, only your burial will be in rock, not water. You saw what happened to your brothers in the lake bed, how quickly your numbers were cut in half. Imagine what'll happen here. My men know how to survive that explosion. Do you?"

My soldiers smiled up at me. In truth, none of them knew how to survive an explosion of this rock, possibly because there was no way to survive it. And yet they trusted me to make it happen.

"You have two choices," I continued. "Lay down your swords and you'll be granted safe passage to return home in peace. Or try keeping your sword, and you'll get poked by the Carthyan closest to you. If I don't get everyone's cooperation, I'll light this rope and set off an explosion twice the size of what you just saw. None of you will ever see your homes and families again."

The soldiers of Mendenwal looked to one another, silently making their choices. I hoped they were the choices I wanted.

I let my arm holding the torch slack a little. "This is getting heavy, so I can't allow you much time to decide whether to live or die. How about if I count back from five?"

And my countdown began. At five, nearly half of Mendenwal instantly dropped their weapons and fell to their knees. By three, the clanging of swords to the ground was audible. But at the final count, I still saw far too many defiant men, preferring to die on their feet than surrender to a boy king.

I respected that — truly I did — but I could not tolerate it. This battle had to end.

So I stepped forward and, with the tip of the rope held out said, "We will meet again in the afterlife, then. You'll get there first, so be sure to save a nice place for me."

And I lit the end of the rope, which did the trick. Those who refused to kneel were forced to the ground by their own panicked peers. The rope only burned a few inches before I was looking down on the complete and total surrender of the Mendenwal army.

I snuffed out the flame beneath my boot, and then called down for my commanders to initiate an immediate evacuation for Mendenwal. "You will leave all weapons behind, but you may carry out your wounded and any supplies necessary for their care. And you will never come again to war against Carthya. Once you accept those terms, you are free to leave in peace."

Then I stowed the torch against the cliff's edge, and sat down to watch it happen. Their exodus would likely take a couple of hours, and I needed that time to determine our next move. I knew where I hoped to come against Avenia in battle; I just didn't know how to make it happen. Beyond that, I needed to rest. Weighed down and overheated by the chain mail and brigandine, I finally removed them so that I could recline more comfortably in a simple undershirt.

Below me, the evacuation was happening more quickly than I had anticipated. Thus, I learned the great secret to winning battles: Make the other side believe you are crazier than they are. Mendenwal wanted to get as far from me as possible before I went completely mad and relit the rope. Of course, there were no explosives left, never had been any up here, but I liked the idea of them leaving Carthya as quickly as their retreating legs could run.

Eventually, a shout came from below that the last of Mendenwal had gone. I had stayed at this perch too long and too selfishly. It was time to meet again with my commanders and consider our next move.

# · THIRTY-ONE ·

With Mendenwal's armies in full retreat, I climbed to my feet again and loaded the chain mail into Mystic's saddlebag. I refastened the brigandine around my chest and sheathed my sword in preparation to ride back down the ridge. But somewhere in the fields far behind me, I heard a familiar voice calling my name. Looking for me.

"Fink?"

I grabbed my sword and ran toward his voice. He wasn't much taller than some of the grasses here, but he continued calling for me.

Finally I saw him, limping heavily and with his hands bound in front of him. He had a torn shirt and a dark bruise on one cheek, but otherwise, he seemed all right.

I started running toward him, but when he noticed me, he only started shaking his head and sobbing. "I'm sorry," he cried. "Jaron, I'm sorry."

"For what?" He already had my forgiveness, and always would have, but I needed to know what had happened.

"I told them about Falstan. That's why they weren't here before. They let Mendenwal get swallowed up in the lake and waited until it was over."

"Who did?"

"Vargan's army. I'm so sorry."

As he spoke those words, I heard a sound growing from the base of the hill upon which Fink and I stood. Horses snorted while their hoofbeats pounded against stone and earth. We were not alone, and I figured it was a safe guess that whoever was coming was no friend of mine.

In the distance, a mass of mounted soldiers was approaching. Even from here I could see their black livery coats crossed in red. Having been surrounded by them for so long, the uniform of Avenia was painfully familiar to me. Far ahead of them was an advance group on horseback, and I knew nearly all of them. At the lead, King Vargan was accompanied by Commander Kippenger and Avenia's standard bearers. Another man rode with them, not in Avenia's colors, but dressed instead in the fine robes of a nobleman. I squinted to see him better. It couldn't be. . . .

But it was. Bevin Conner was riding directly beside the king of Avenia. Conner pointed me out first, and Vargan turned course straight for me. I told Fink to get behind me, and then withdrew my sword, eager to test its sharpness. For all of Conner's arrogant claims that everything he had done was for the benefit of our country, this was a complete betrayal of

Carthya. Whatever bargain he had made to ride beside Vargan now, he could never justify this treason, even to himself.

"Let's just run," Fink said.

"There's nowhere to go," I muttered back to him. For as far as I could see ahead, there was nothing but red and black uniforms growing on the horizon. And there was nothing behind us but a sheer cliff and a long fall.

My sword was ready when they stopped in front of us. I hadn't yet decided which of them to attack, since I'd likely only get one target before the rest of them stopped me. It would've been satisfying to get Conner, but the sneer on Vargan's face made me furious, and Kippenger had actively participated in the abuse I'd suffered in Vargan's camp. I owed each of them a response.

Vargan greeted me first. "King Jaron, how nice it is to see you again. My apologies for being late to all your fun with Mendenwal."

"I wish you'd have come. I would've loved for you to meet their fate. Preferred it, actually."

Vargan arched an eyebrow. "Is there no one left?"

"Not unless they have some excellent swimmers. Either way, you won't have their services any longer."

"Other soldiers from Mendenwal are here in your country," he said. "You haven't defeated them all."

"No," I said. "Not yet. But my captain and I have a bet. Whoever wins the most battles gets to melt your crown for the gold. I'm planning to win, since we have business to settle — I made a promise to that effect."

Vargan laughed, echoed by the men who flanked him. He said, "I am eager to see you try to destroy my great armies, boy king."

If it were only me on this hill, my decision would've been made. I would've rushed at Vargan with my sword held high, letting the consequences fall where they would. But Fink was still behind me, and I couldn't abandon him.

"You have a difficult decision now," Kippenger said. "Do you attack us and lose that boy behind you? Or try to escape, in which case you will also lose that boy."

"All we want is you," Vargan told me. "Lower your sword and we'll let the boy go."

"Is nothing beneath you?" I asked. "He's just a boy, not a pawn in our talks."

"A boy who I've heard means a great deal to you." Vargan glanced down at Fink, eager for any depth of cruelty if it could touch me. "What will you give me to save his life?"

"A deep cut with my sword," I responded. "Carthya will never bow to you, Vargan."

"Carthya already bows to me! Did you think my offer to let you keep your throne would last forever? No, Jaron, you had your opportunity. Things have changed. Now, Lord Conner will be the king of Carthya, subject to my Avenian empire. Our agreement is made."

Conner arched his neck and stared down at me. So he would have his throne after all.

"He's no king," I said. "Rulers aren't made just because they sit on the throne. A true king serves his people, protects them, and sees to their happiness if he can."

Conner's lip curled when he asked, "What about dying for his people?"

My eyes darted sideways a moment. "Yes, he would die, if necessary. Though I hope we're speaking about your death, and not mine."

"King Vargan and I have made some agreements," Conner said in his mocking tone. "They will ensure one of us a long and prosperous life. Can you guess which of us that is?"

I turned to Vargan. "You might be a horrible king and, for that matter, a horrible person. But Conner is worse. He's a traitor and a murderer. Be careful in your bargains."

"If I'm accused of being a traitor, I may as well act that way," Conner replied. "And as to your other accusation, I intend to be the cause of only one more death, one I've been anticipating for months."

Mine.

Vargan's smile revealed his hunger for just that. "You're trapped here, Jaron, with a cliff at your back and thousands of my men in every other direction. There's no escape this time."

A quick scan of the hills revealed the full size of his massive army, beyond anything I could hope to defeat. Most of them were still moving toward the valley, to where my army was stationed with no idea of what was coming their way. Just as we had blocked Mendenwal's escape, they would soon block ours.

"You will come with Lord Conner and myself to Farthenwood," Vargan said.

"Absolutely not." I shook my head to emphasize my refusal. "Conner's already taken me to Farthenwood once. Trust me, he isn't nearly as good a host as he pretends to be."

Conner laughed darkly. "I'd have thought you'd be happy at the news. To see your reign end where it began."

"Farthenwood is where you met your downfall, Conner. It is not where I will meet mine." My eyes settled on Vargan's puckered face. "If we must talk, then let's do it at Drylliad. There's no reason for us to go to Farthenwood."

"Of course there is." Vargan chuckled now, as if he and Conner knew a joke they had yet to share with me. "You chose Farthenwood yourself. Do you remember when?"

The message I had sent with the Avenian thief. He took it to Vargan instead of keeping his promise to me. That was their joke.

Conner seemed almost disappointed. "I expected more from you, Jaron."

"And I expected less from you." I grinned. "Though I suppose if you and Vargan combined your brainpower, you might have enough wits for me. Almost."

Vargan stiffened at the insult. "I will see you hanged this very week, and kill everyone who stands with you, just as I did to Imogen."

My heart pounded at the mention of her name, but I finally saw a purpose in her death. No matter what else happened in this war, I could not allow anyone else I loved to die. I had to find a way to see this through.

With that thought, my eyes shifted from Conner to Vargan. "I understand your interest in hanging me," I said. "But first I must carry out my promise to destroy you. And I might need a little more time for that, now that I have to add Conner to my list." I gestured to Commander Kippenger. "Probably you too, by the way."

"Take him," Vargan ordered.

Kippenger rode for me, but I grabbed a knife from my belt and hurled it at Conner. The flat edge struck his horse, who bucked hard and startled Kippenger's horse. Both Kippenger and Conner fell to the ground, which created even greater confusion amongst the animals. I turned and pushed Fink forward with me. Somewhere behind us, Vargan screamed orders to chase us as we raced toward the cliff.

"They're coming!" Fink cried.

I couldn't go down the steep trail I had come up before. The risk of someone catching up to us there was too great. But as we got to the ledge, I knew only one option remained, and it wasn't good.

"How tight are your hands tied?" I asked him.

He pulled at them, but there was no give. "Very."

"Put them over my shoulders." I ducked low enough for him to comply while I grabbed the rope that I'd partially burned for Mendenwal's army. I knotted it, then wrapped it two or three times around my waist. There was no time to do this properly.

Fink tried to wiggle off me. "No, Jaron. Please don't."

"Yes, Fink. Close your eyes if you must."

Kippenger entered the ridge first and swiped at me with his sword. It stung my arm but I was already running. With Fink on my back and screaming in my ear, I ran off the side of the ledge and into thin air.

# · THIRTY-TWO ·

Over the history of my life, the stupidest thing I had ever attempted was at age seven, when I tested the power of an old trebuchet against a standing target on castle grounds. Darius and I had just had a lesson on how catapults work, and I was curious. However, my aim was off and instead of hitting the target, the boulder put a hole through the roof of my father's private apartments. Fortunately, the rooms were empty at the time apart from one unlucky servant who saved his life by diving through a latrine into the fetid waters below.

It *had* been the stupidest thing I'd ever done, that is, until I ran off a cliff with Fink's arms around my neck and a rope knotted around my waist. In the last second before I jumped, it occurred to me that I hadn't verified if the knot binding the rope to the tree was tied tightly enough, or how long the rope even was. Would Fink and I crash into the floor of the valley before the rope pulled tight?

However, I had Vargan's men chasing me, so my fate was certain if we didn't jump. I only hoped if this failed that my death would be quick. I hated pain.

As it turned out, the saints may have listened when I begged for their help before. Or at least, we didn't crash to the valley floor. But the devils certainly had their fun with me when we met the length of the rope.

The first thing I felt was the rope pulling tight against my waist and then cinching like a noose against my rib cage. The next sensation was Fink's arms locked against my throat. It was the only way he could hold on when I jumped, but he was choking me nonetheless. From there, we collided into the side of the cliff wall. I took the brunt of it with my shoulder, which was hardly helpful in keeping hold of the rope — the one thing still keeping us from falling any farther. The rope had been wrapped two or three times around my waist, but no longer. Once we hit the cliff wall, only then did I realize my palms were stinging with rope burn.

We were alive, but our troubles were far from over. We were about halfway down the cliff wall — too high to jump down and too dangerous to climb up. Several of my men had seen what we did and were shouting cries of alarm from below. Overhead, Vargan realized he had been spotted. But I felt vibrations on the rope from above and knew they wouldn't leave until they had done their best to ruin my escape, such as it was.

"Grab on to the wall!" I yelled to Fink. "They're cutting the rope!"

I rotated his body in front of mine, then braced against the wall while he transferred his weight from me to the rock. Once he did, I got myself in a better position, but as I moved, the rope from above us fell. I would've gone with it if Fink didn't have his foot tucked around my weaker right leg.

Vargan peered over the edge. "I'm told you haven't climbed since returning from the pirates. You'll fall from there."

I didn't answer. It took enough of my concentration not to make any move that proved him right.

Vargan growled at me, but by then my archers were taking aim at him and he had no choice but to run. I yelled down that Carthya needed to gather for a quick retreat. I had seen Vargan's army. We were no match for their numbers.

Orders were shouted in all directions below me, but one voice rose higher than the others. Mott.

"We'll get you both down from there. Hold on!" he yelled.

"Their army is coming," I cried. "Go!"

But Mott ignored me and instead called out for help from climbers who could get up to me. It was humiliating. Before Roden had broken my leg, I could've scaled this wall in minutes. Now, I was frozen upon it.

I twisted enough to reach a second, smaller knife attached to my boot, and then used it on the rope tying Fink's hands. Once they were free, he was able to get a stronger grip on the wall, though his knuckles were white and his face was showing the strain on his muscles.

"Listen to me," I said to Fink. "Climbing up is one thing, but most falling happens on the way down. Every move you make is important. You don't get to be stupid when stepping down, not even once."

"Stupid?" Fink cried. "Like jumping off a cliff? Because that's a really, really big step down, Jaron!"

He was still too panicked to make safe choices. The wall directly below us was too smooth for us to scale down, and the climbers could never get up to rescue us. Far to our right was a tree rooted into the cliff. It wasn't thick, but it would handle our weight. I still had my end of the rope that I'd used to jump. If I tied it to the tree trunk, it'd get us pretty close to the floor.

I cocked my head at the tree. "That's where we're going." Then I called down to Mott. "I am ordering your retreat! Vargan is bringing his army right into this valley. We'll be trapped if you don't get out!"

"Nobody is leaving you!" Mott yelled back.

It put a terrible strain on my shoulders, but I swung around as far as I dared. Although we were at some distance from each other, I tried to make Mott see the earnestness in my face. "Leave," I told him. "Mott, these are my orders. Make everyone go or they will die. I'll find a way down."

This time, Mott nodded. He joined the others who were issuing orders and directed the commanders to move our men out of the valley and away from the lake. Once he had them in motion, he returned to the base of the cliff and called back, "Now you have your way. But I will not leave until you're with me."

It was my turn to nod back to him. I handed the rope to Fink and told him what to do if I fell. I hoped my arms and my left leg could keep me on the cliff to move horizontally, but that wasn't certain. My muscles were significantly weakened from the old injury to my leg and my imprisonment in Vargan's camp. My hands stung from the jump just now and my shoulder throbbed worse than it should have. I truly didn't know if I could keep myself up here.

So we took each move slowly. I avoided putting any weight on my right leg, and chose my holds carefully. Then I gave Fink specific instructions for each hold he must make. That was the harder part since he was smaller and didn't have my reach. We were unimpressive in our speed, but at least we were moving. With a little patience and a great deal of endurance, we would reach the tree. And once there, it would be a simple matter to tie off the rope and slide down to the floor.

But nothing in my life was ever simple. And this time, it wasn't only me who would suffer. Beyond the well of this valley, exactly where my retreating army would be, the sounds of a great battle had begun. Vargan's army had met them. We had failed to retreat in time.

Mott was aware of it too, and urged us to get off the cliff as quickly as possible. I pushed Fink to move a little faster, but his muscles were already shaking against the strain. I tried to distract him, asking how he had come to be captured by Vargan.

"After I left Bymar, I thought it'd be no trouble to come through Avenia again," Fink said. "Nobody bothered me before. But Vargan recruited nearly all of Erick's thieves into his army, and when I tried to pass through the border into Carthya, one of them recognized me. They knew I was with you now, so they sent me directly to Vargan for questioning."

I showed Fink his next hold on the wall, then asked, "Other than my plans for Falstan Lake, did you tell Vargan anything else?"

"Yes." Fink smiled. "I told him he didn't have a chance of winning this war against you. That's when he got angry."

We continued making our way toward the tree. I found it impossible to ignore the sounds of the battle and feared what must be happening. It was torture to hear the cries of injured men, listen to orders being called, and cringe at the clang of sword against sword, all while I remained trapped on this wall. At best, I was useless, and at worst, a deadly distraction.

Below us, Mott called that Mystic had come down from the ledge on his own. I squinted down long enough to see my horse below, and then scowled at him. Maybe it would've been better to take Fink down the trail. Probably not — Vargan undoubtedly would've followed. But Mystic didn't seem any worse for his journey, while Fink and I were bruised, exhausted, and still inching sideways for our lives.

"I can't go any farther," Fink finally said.

I looked back at him. We were getting close to the tree now, just four or five careful holds away.

"You can do this," I told him.

"I can't! I'm telling you, Jaron, if you make me keep going, I'll fall!"

"Listen to me," I said firmly. "If you fall from here, it'll hurt a lot more than you're hurting now, and you will die. Once you're dead, I'll tell the saints to refuse you entrance into the afterlife. You'll wander forever as a spirit, never getting a moment's rest."

My threat worked. "You wouldn't dare," he said.

"You know I'll do it. So you'll hold on, or else." Then I gritted my teeth and moved faster. With a good leg, I could've been there in less than a minute, and Fink's muscles were shaking uncontrollably now. As a test, I put enough weight on my right leg to help me skirt a little higher toward the tree, but it collapsed beneath me. I lost all my footing and the grip of my right hand. All that kept me on the cliff was the knuckle of my left forefinger, which I had wormed through the curve of a small root that arched away from the earth.

Fink cried out when I slipped, and somewhere far below, Mott ran to stand beneath me. But I only cursed and pulled myself back into place.

"Don't do that again!" Fink yelled.

"Hush!"

Angry with myself now for a weakness I still couldn't conquer, I climbed more deliberately, and made it to the tree. I tossed the rope around the trunk, knotted it tightly, and then wound it beneath my arms. I swung over to Fink and grabbed on to him, then literally peeled him off the cliff and back to the tree.

Once there, I detached myself from the rope, then wound it around him and carefully lowered him down the side of the cliff. When he reached the bottom, Mott pressed him against the side of the cliff where he was safest. The battle continued to rage outside the valley well, and if it moved toward us, it would quickly absorb us into the fighting. I needed to join them — but I felt my strength lagging. It really had been too long since I'd climbed, and I hadn't appreciated the demands it placed on muscles I rarely used otherwise.

"Get on the rope, Jaron!" Mott ordered.

This time, I felt no resentment for his attempt to order me and took hold of the rope again. But I was dropping faster than I wanted, mostly because with my tired arms it was hard to keep control of the fall. And when I was farther up than I ought to have been, my hold failed completely and I simply fell. I half landed on Mott, who had been anticipating my crash. It saved me from a major injury, though I still collapsed on my weaker leg. It sent a wave of pain up my spine and I grabbed on to the leg to quiet the tremors. But I said nothing.

"Can you walk?" Mott asked, coming to his feet.

I wasn't entirely sure if I could. Fink ran over to me and put his shoulders under my arm. With his help and Mott's, I stood and found my balance. Mott helped me into Mystic's saddle, then I rode far enough into the valley to see the outer edges of the brawl. The bulk of the fighting had already moved away from us, but too many of my men had already fallen here. We weren't fighting a battle; we were targets for slaughter.

When Mott and Fink rode up beside me, I asked, "Where is the fighting moving?"

Mott scanned the horizon. "Back to higher ground. Away from the lake."

"Toward our camp?" My eyes widened in horror. "Tobias and Amarinda are still up there!"

"We can't make it past the battle to warn them," Mott said.

I steered Mystic around. "We'll climb up where the dam used to be."

"You exploded most of that hillside," Mott said. "Are you sure anything is there to be climbed?"

"If it isn't, we'll build a way to the top," I said. "We've got to warn them before Vargan arrives."

# · THIRTY-THREE ·

**M**ott had been right about the shortcut trail up to our camp — the little that still existed was in terrible condition, and it certainly wasn't safe to attempt a climb on horseback. But the fighting between my army and Avenia was moving through the valley and toward us. To avoid it, this had to be our route.

We left the horses at the base of the hill. I hated to leave Mystic behind, but much of our climb would involve scrambling over rocks and across thin remnants of steep trails. We had no other choice.

My leg still throbbed from the fall off the cliff, but I didn't say anything about it to Mott. Besides, he probably already knew, based on the way I favored it. At least, he stayed right behind me to offer a boost whenever I needed to use it.

When we were nearly to the top, we came to an edge of the trail where it was possible to look down on the battle below. My heart stopped as I realized it was going far worse than I had feared. The hills were stained with blood and littered with the bodies of the dead and wounded, who writhed in pain, crying for help. Hundreds of Avenians had fallen, but at least that many of my own men were lost as well, and the survivors on my side were fighting with ever-increasing odds against them. We were going to lose.

Beside me, Mott and Fink were absorbing the same horrifying scene. Finally, Mott tapped my shoulder and said, "It's moving this way, Jaron. We must get to the top."

We finished the climb as if a fire was at our heels, and what I found once we reached the camp surprised me. The men who had remained here were rapidly organizing the linens, tables, and beds to receive the wounded from battle.

A few wounded had already arrived and Tobias was rushing from one man to the other, attempting to care for their injuries. When Tobias had mentioned that he was studying to become a physician, I'd had no idea of the extent of his learning. He was doing far more than binding wounds or applying medicines. He was sewing them up, stopping the bleeding, and even appeared to have performed more complicated surgeries. Amidst all the chaos and cries, he was at his best, working fast and hard. Amarinda stood at his side, working as his assistant and comforting each man as best as she could.

I slowed just long enough to watch the two of them. They operated as a team, each one the half of the other. They belonged together.

Amarinda saw us first. She grabbed a bucket of water and rushed toward us. She offered me the ladle, and while I drank, she inspected the cut on my arm from Kippenger. When

I finished, I handed the ladle to Mott and Fink, then Amarinda and I walked over to Tobias.

His eyes were wide but calm when he saw me. Tobias gestured to the wounded man before him and said, "I've only read about this, but I'm doing what I can."

"You'll do this somewhere else," I said. "The battle is coming this way. You must leave."

"No!" Tobias continued to sew the wound of the man between us. "I can't fight, I'm useless for battle strategy, and I'll only get in the way here as a regent. But I can help save these men."

Amarinda touched my arm. "We want to do this, Jaron."

Every life they might save up here mattered to Carthya. But I gestured across this camp and said, "Within minutes, this whole hillside will be a battlefield. You and Fink must all leave now, or they will take the princess. Amarinda is in danger."

Without another passing second, Tobias finished the knot for the wound and set his tools down. He took Amarinda by the hand as she called for help to load the injured men into wagons for immediate departure.

Meanwhile, Mott gathered several soldiers who had remained in the camp and then located new horses for the two of us. He helped me onto mine, and then climbed onto his. "Your orders, my king?"

When he and I were alone, Mott rarely addressed me with any title, and it startled me until I realized he had intended to speak to me that way. I briefly glanced back to see Fink helping

Tobias and Amarinda. They would leave soon, but the best thing we could do was to hold off any early arrivals.

I turned back to Mott and withdrew my sword. "We ride."

Mott grinned and withdrew his own sword, followed by the other soldiers behind us. Together, we urged the horses forward and rode toward the battle.

We quickly met a small advance group on horseback, too close to camp for my comfort. However, they were tired from having battled this far forward, and I was eager to take part in this fight. We dispensed with the group easily enough, and then charged onward.

There was only one soldier behind them, but he was as large as a pirate and looked equally as mean. Our swords met, but he struck hard enough to push me off my horse. I fell to the ground and rolled to avoid being crushed by either of our animals. He started to move on, then realized who I was and came around again. This time when he did, Mott crashed into him as if he'd become my own personal battering ram. The man hit the ground with a solid thud.

I swung back into my horse's saddle, but only had time for a quick nod of thanks before we were met with another group. The first few were big, arrogant, and had clearly underestimated how much better I fought when angry. This was my country, a land my forefathers had protected for generations. Until everything else had been taken from me, I would *not* let it go.

"To your right, Jaron!"

The warning came from Mott, who was locked in battle with a soldier who had brought a mace, which he swung skillfully over his head. I charged for the man at my right. He had a quiver on his back and carried a bow in the same hand with which he held the reins to his horse. Dangling from his waist was an unfriendly looking battle-ax.

He saw me coming and reached for an arrow, but by then I was close enough to give him a deep cut that also severed the cord attached to his battle-ax. As he started to fall from his horse, I grabbed on to his bow and the arrow he had drawn. Once they were in my hands, I notched the arrow, twisted around, and shot for the man with the mace. I actually would've missed him, but at the last moment, his horse darted to the left and my arrow hit the man's stomach. His mace was still in motion, and when the man lurched forward, his mace swung onto his own head.

More of my soldiers were joining us now, both from behind and up ahead, but more Avenians were here too. Many more. We may have bought Tobias and Amarinda an extra fifteen minutes to escape, but that wasn't nearly enough time. The road ahead of them was better suited to horses than to carriages. If Tobias chose to stay with the wounded in their wagons, he and Amarinda wouldn't have a chance. They needed every minute I could give them.

So I pushed down the hillside. Mott was a little ahead of me, fighting with a small group riding toward us. I joined him and locked swords with a man I remembered from my time at Vargan's camp. He was a fine swordsman, likely better than me, and certain of his win in our duel. Nevertheless, I laughed and told him that he fought like an old woman. A blind old woman with advanced dysentery, to be more specific.

"You have your spirit back," the man replied. I grinned at that until he added, "Luckily, you recovered better than that girl I shot with the arrow. It should've been you."

Every muscle in my body tensed, and time seemed to slow. As if every second of my life became focused into that one moment, I arced my sword away and then back again, piercing him exactly where he had shot Imogen. His entire face became a series of Os, and then his horse charged away from beneath him.

I moved on to battle with the next man and was engaged with him while, out of the corner of my eye, I saw Mott riding into another group.

Mott was a skilled sword fighter, well trained and confident in his swings. But he rode directly into the center of a large group, hoping to draw their attention his way and allow my tired army to cut them down from behind. It was a grave error. No single man could fight off so many others.

I finally got in a jab at the nearest Avenian, felling him from his horse, and rode down to help Mott. So far, his strategy was working — Carthya was making good progress on this hill. But it couldn't last long.

I charged my horse into the center of the group, but this mare wasn't as strong as Mystic and wasn't powerful enough to force the circle apart. So I fought my way in, hitting hard and swinging at every red symbol on the Avenian livery.

I was nearly to Mott when I spotted another man charging in from behind. I recognized him immediately as Fendon, the scarred thief I had wounded in the wild on the night I left for the pirates. He had vowed that we would fight the next time he saw me. I had told him he would not see me again.

Clearly, I was wrong.

His sword was ready and he was screaming at the others to get out of his way. I raised my own sword and started toward him, but my path was blocked. I hit at the Avenians and yelled at Mott to watch out. Mott turned and saw Fendon coming, but couldn't get his sword at a proper angle.

Fendon's sword stabbed Mott in his side, and it went in deep. Blood poured from him and he fell from his horse.

Almost blind with anger, I struck at the Avenians still surrounding me as I made my way toward Fendon. He saw me coming and backed up his horse, readying himself for whatever fight was still left in me. Once I left the crowd behind, I charged at him so fiercely that he barely had time to register the danger he was now in.

I struck only once and I struck hard. My sword pierced his chest and he fell, dead in an instant.

My own chest felt as if it were clutched in a vise as I leapt from my horse and made my way toward Mott, who had managed to crawl away from the crowd. His breaths were shallow and his face was losing its life. Mott was dying.

Blood was everywhere, so much that I couldn't tell exactly where it was coming from now. Mott grimaced with pain, but

I was already tearing off a length of his undershirt to create a bandage. Once I found the wound, I pressed the cloth against his side, but couldn't make him roll over to tie the knot.

"If you were tired of fighting, there were easier ways to get out of this battle," I said.

The sweat on his face mingled with his tears. "I wanted to be there when you finished this."

"You will be there." Now I felt the sting in my own eyes, but I refused to let him see my despair. "You'll get better, and then you and I will fight again, side by side."

Mott smiled. "You're not as good a liar as you think you are."

The nails of my fingers dug into my palm. "I don't lie nearly as often as people think. And you are going to live. You must!"

"Promise me that you will find happiness in life, Jaron. Don't give in to bitterness."

Now the tears spilled from my eyes. "The crown has taken everything else from me. Not you too."

He grabbed my arm, though his grip was weak and fading fast. "Your test has always been the same. Be stronger than whatever life brings at you. You will rise from this."

"Not without you, Mott. You have to stay with me."

He only smiled and closed his eyes.

I stood and searched for any Carthyans around me. "Help me!" I yelled. "This man needs help!"

# · THIRTY-FOUR ·

There was no immediate response, but I kept yelling, desperate for help. I tried again to move Mott and successfully dragged him a little ways, but that was surely making his wounds worse. I'd never be able to do this alone.

I placed my hands under his arms to try pulling him again, but this time I felt a change in his weight. It took me a minute to recognize the person who was lifting his legs, but then I caught a glimpse of bright red hair beneath an Avenian helmet and remembered. It was Mavis, who had fallen into the hunter's trap.

There were no words between us. All I cared about then was that Mott was dying before my eyes and my armies were falling around me. This was Avenia's fault, and whether Mavis had chosen to fight or not, he was with them. He was hardly my friend. But I looked at him as we struggled to carry Mott to his horse. His mouth was turned in a grim smile and his eyes were full of sympathy. Mavis wasn't my enemy either.

Finally, we managed to hoist Mott into his saddle. I gave Mavis a quick nod of thanks, then got onto my horse and steered Mott around the fighting to return to the camp. Tobias had probably left, but if there was still a wagon, Mott could be taken to wherever he was going.

So it was a surprise to see that the wagon Tobias and Amarinda should have taken was still in its place. A part of me hoped they had used horses instead and were far from this camp by now. But if they did, then there was no chance left for Mott.

With almost the same speed of Falstan Lake returning to its bed, the camp was filling with both Carthyan and Avenian soldiers. Staying just ahead of the fighting, I led Mott to the wagon and this time it took the help of two of my soldiers to get him safely inside. One of them commented that Mott's body was total deadweight, and with a nasty glare I told him to hush. Mott was still alive and I didn't want him to hear any such talk. Even so, it was probably already too late. I asked one man to stay inside the wagon with Mott and do whatever was necessary to keep him alive until I could find help. Then I directed the other soldier to drive the wagon past a wide field on the outskirts of the camp and into the dense forest. I didn't think Avenia would follow them there. Night was falling and they would want to regroup.

Once I saw him safely away from the worst of it, I returned to the battle, fighting where I could while trying to absorb the magnitude of the destruction we faced. For every Carthyan still holding a weapon, I saw ten Avenians equally armed. The air was filled with cries of pain and shouts of anger. And everywhere there was death and suffering, all of it beyond my control. I had never wanted war, and now that I was a part of it, what I saw was worse than anything I could have imagined. I was forced to ask myself whether the freedom of Carthya was worth all of this.

A lieutenant found me there and said he had just received a small group of our men who had escaped from a battle farther north.

"What do you mean 'escaped'?" I asked.

His eyes darted, and I wondered if they had deserted their countrymen. The punishment for that was severe and I didn't have the heart to enforce it now. But as it turned out, his news was worse.

"My king, the battle did not go well. They are the few who survived."

I hardly dared ask. "Roden?"

"He was taken prisoner. My lord, we will fight as long as you command it, but things are not good."

I scuffed my boot against the dirt, and then looked back at him. "Lieutenant, you will order the immediate retreat of our men into the forest. Get them as deep as they must go to be safe."

He bowed. "Yes, my king."

As he began rounding up our men to pull them away, I continued looking for any signs of Tobias and Amarinda.

Then, with more horror than I could absorb, I realized where they must be: behind a woodpile at the edge of camp. I couldn't see them, but Fink was standing in front of the pile, his sword so heavy that he could barely hold it with both hands. Fink was trying to protect them.

I kicked at the horse beneath me, urging him toward the woodpile. Several of the Avenians followed, swarming me like rabid dogs. But I had no time for them, and dispatched them as fiercely and quickly as possible.

However, another Avenian on a courser horse near the woodpile had spotted Fink, who yelled in terror. From behind the woodpile, Tobias leapt forward. He grabbed the sword from Fink's hands and pushed him aside.

Tobias swung wildly at the soldier, who quickly knocked him to the ground. The Avenian then turned his sights on Amarinda, who had also emerged. She started to run and the soldier kicked at his horse to follow, but Fink crossed between her and the horse, the sword in his hands again. He was so short that his sword came at the soldier at a sharp angle. It pierced the man's armor beneath his knee and the man cried as loudly as Fink had just yelled. He collapsed forward, blood spilling from the wound.

When Fink saw me coming, he said, "I did that! Me!"

"You acted as a knight should," I said. When Tobias and Amarinda were closer, I turned to them. "You were supposed to leave."

"We tried," Tobias said. "But they came too fast."

I slid to the ground and gave Tobias the reins for my horse and the fallen soldier's as well. "Get into the forest. We'll gather there."

"But I already sent the wounded on ahead."

"There is nothing ahead, Tobias! Look around us!" Then I lowered my voice. "There will be more wounded in the forest. Mott is amongst them."

That was all Tobias needed to hear. Once they were mounted on horses, Fink led the way. Tobias and Amarinda pushed him from behind, hurrying him into the cover of the woods.

By that time, the battlefield had mostly emptied of Carthyans. I wanted to stay and fight, but nothing I did at that point would end in any way other than with my death.

I never run.

That was what I had said once to Gregor, the former captain of my guard. And now, I had not only ordered the retreat of my army, but I was forced to retreat with them as well.

What was left of the Carthyan camp belonged to Avenia now. The land was littered with our wounded and dead, and if I didn't find a way out, the rest of us would be dead by tomorrow.

I didn't look back as I escaped into the forest.

# · THIRTY-FIVE ·

Of the thousand men who had been stationed at Falstan Lake, fewer than a couple hundred had made it into the forest. We took refuge deep within the thickest part of the woods where little light from the stars broke through. A few fires were already built, and my soldiers huddled around them, exhausted, broken, and without hope. Tobias and Amarinda were busy treating the mildly wounded, but the more seriously injured remained in the wagons. Nothing could save them.

And then there was Mott, his life teetering at the edge of death. I stood beside the wagon that had carried him here, feeling more helpless than I ever had before. Tobias had already bound the stab wound, but Mott was still struggling for breath and falling in and out of consciousness.

"What can be done to save him?" I asked Tobias quietly.

Tobias only shrugged. "Everything was left behind in our camp. All the bandages, and medicines, and tools. I found an aravac plant to help with his pain. But I can't save him. Not here."

Until his last drawn breath, I would never give up on Mott. How many times had he expressed his willingness to follow me into the devils' lair and back again? War had come, and he had indeed followed me down the darkest of paths. He remained there now, hovering in the shadows between life and death. I had to lead him back out again. But it would cost me dearly.

I bit on my lip as I considered my options. Or, if I was being honest, there was only one terrible choice left. It had always been in the back of my mind, as if I knew from the beginning that something like this would be inevitable. Once the decision was made, every other random possibility I'd ever considered came together in my mind like a completed puzzle. To Tobias, I said, "If you had those supplies, could you save him?"

"I could probably save many of these men. But —" Tobias's eyes narrowed. "No, Jaron. Whatever you're thinking —"

"I'm thinking that Mott is going to die!" I hissed. "I already lost Imogen and it nearly destroyed me. We're going to lose this war too. I will *not* lose any more lives."

"What about your life? That camp is crawling with Avenians. You cannot sneak back there!"

"No," I mumbled, "I can't sneak in. But I will get those supplies." He called after me when I strode away, but I refused to acknowledge him. The last thing I needed was rational advice.

Amarinda found me several minutes later as I was at the edge of our refuge, saddling a horse. Her fists were clenched and her shoulders thrown back. I recognized that posture from the many times Imogen had been angry with me. Now Amarinda said, "I know where you're going. Jaron, I am begging you not to do this!"

I had no interest in quarreling with her. For better or worse, nothing could change my mind at this point. "Tobias must be desperate if he sent you to stop me."

"He sent me too." Fink appeared from behind her. "Please don't go."

I didn't look at him. I couldn't. With my eyes still on the saddle, I said, "This has to be done, Fink. Even if you don't understand that yet."

"I understand it plenty. They're going to kill you!"

Did he think my fate was any better if I stayed in the woods? Even if none of us wanted to say it, we all knew there would be another battle tomorrow, far worse than today's disaster. No matter how hard we fought, or how cleverly I planned, by sunset tomorrow, several hundred more would be dead. I would be one of them.

"What would Imogen want you to do?" Amarinda asked. "If she asked you to stay here, would you run so openly toward your own death?"

My voice was gentle when I spoke to her. "It's never been a secret that I've had no desire to be king. Why did people think that was? I always knew how this might end." Then I turned back to the saddle to tighten the straps. "But it's all right. I understand now what Imogen did for me, and that's what I've got to do for Carthya."

"Imogen would —"

"She would hate me for this." I released the saddle straps and took Amarinda by the hand instead. "But that doesn't mean I'm wrong. I'm going to try my best, and I still have some options. But if things go badly, and they might, then don't be sad for me." She looked away, but she needed to understand that I intended to bring this war to an end. One way or another, I would soon be at peace, which was all I had ever wanted. "Imogen will meet me in the afterlife. My family will be there too, and Mott if I don't get him those medicines."

When he spoke, the muscles on Fink's face became pinched and knotted. "What about me? You're the only family I've got." His tone nearly stopped me then. He'd already gone through believing me to be dead once. I hated to make him endure that again.

I released Amarinda, and then reached for my sword, which I had left propped against a tree. I told Fink to hold out his hands, and into them I placed my sword.

"Take care of this," I said. "You're a knight of Carthya, remember? This sword belongs to you now."

"Only until you come back." He lowered the sword to his side, then said, "Come back, please. I don't want to be alone again."

"I promise to try. But even if I don't, you'll always have Amarinda and Tobias."

"Tobias lectures too much." Fink closed his eyes tight and shook his head. "Besides, I need you."

"All of Carthya needs you," Amarinda added.

"Then let me do what I must to save it." I finished preparing the horse, but before I could climb on, Amarinda put a hand on my arm.

"Your family would be proud of who you've become," she whispered. "They would've given everything to see what a great leader you are."

"They did give everything." I sighed as their faces passed through my mind. "Whatever happens next, never let it be said that I failed my father. Tell the people I did everything I could."

"They already know it. Come back to us, Jaron."

"If you die, I'll tell the saints not to let you in," Fink said irritably. It was nearly what I had told him while we were stranded on the cliff.

I answered that he'd better hope the saints did let me in, or who else would take care of him in the afterlife one day? I smiled when I said it, but Fink only stuck his jaw forward, similar to the way I did when I was being stubborn. Then I kissed Amarinda's cheek and climbed onto the horse. Before I left, I turned back to them and said, "If Tobias becomes king of this land, then don't let him touch my sword. He'll hurt somebody with it, and not in the good way either."

I rode off without looking back, and paused only once, at the edge of the forest. The camp that had been mine only hours ago now displayed Avenian colors, and was alive with crackling fires and the smell of stew. The shadows of soldiers at vigil duty frequently crossed in front of the fires, and orders were being shouted to situate everyone within the camp for the night. I got a distant look at my tent, lit from within by lanterns. Perhaps Vargan was in there, maybe Conner as well.

Amarinda's question echoed in my head, of what Imogen would say if she were here. She'd be furious, no doubt. And then I'd remind her that it wasn't much different from what she had done for me. Sacrificing oneself so that others might live was the ultimate act of love.

That was what Mott had wanted me to understand, and now I did. Of all emotions, none were more powerful than love. The irony was that if he knew my plans, Mott would rise from his bed and crawl here to stop me. If he knew what I was about to do, not the devils nor death itself could keep him away.

Reminded of him now, and the urgency of time, I pressed forward. But the memories of how Vargan's men had treated me before were still fresh in my mind, like tender scars that would soon be torn apart into new wounds. It would be worse this time, and the thought of it made my hands shake so hard that it was difficult to keep hold of the reins. I cursed at my cowardice and told myself this was the last hope we had. Even knowing that, I still had to force my legs to prod the horse onward.

The vigils saw me coming from some distance and a dozen or more of them rode out to meet me. Terrowic, the man who had been so cruel when I was a prisoner before, reached me first. I was unarmed and told him so before they arrived, but they still surrounded me as if I were packed with gunpowder. Even though I was offering no threat, when Commander Kippenger arrived, he yanked me off the horse and threw me to the ground. His men carefully checked me for any weapons, then at last he pulled me to my feet and demanded to know why I had come.

"Take me to King Vargan," I said. "If he can hear you calling him above the sound of his snores."

"The king and Lord Conner have left for elsewhere in Carthya. There are other battles besides this one, you know."

"But this is the only one that matters." I studied Kippenger's eyes. He looked as tired as I felt, and certainly as battle weary. "We both lost a lot of men here today. There's one in particular, a very good friend of mine, who will die if I don't get your help."

Kippenger folded his arms, but didn't display any of the cold arrogance I would have expected. He only said, "Why should I help you?"

"Because it benefits you too. If you wish to gain favor with your king, then help me. If you will, then I'll give you what he wants most."

"What's that?"

I rolled my eyes. "Well, me." Obviously.

"You dare to set terms? I have you right now."

"You have the cooperative me right now. Try to take me by force and I promise that one of us will not make it to Vargan alive. My terms are simple, Kippenger."

His patience with me was already wearing thin. "What is it you want, then?" he asked.

"An end to the fighting. Take your men and leave this place. And I want the immediate delivery of all medical supplies in this camp to my soldiers who are in the forest."

"Ah. And for that, I get to take you to my king?"

For the first time that evening, my breath relaxed. "Better than that. In exchange for my demands, I will surrender Carthya."

# · THIRTY-SIX ·

Despite his suspicions that I was attempting some sort of trick, Commander Kippenger quickly agreed to my terms. He demanded I remove my brigandine, since it was filthy from the day's battle. I agreed, on the terms that he find me something suitable to replace it with and nothing in Avenia's colors. Then Kippenger ordered the medical supplies be taken immediately to the forest. Once that was under way, he announced to his men that all of Avenia would leave camp as soon as possible, with me in their company.

"King Vargan left specific orders if you were captured," he said.

"But you didn't capture me. I gave myself up. So unless the orders were to provide me with a supper of roasted goose, you shouldn't feel any need to obey them."

"His orders were to deliver you for execution." Kippenger paused, and then added, "At Farthenwood."

I breathed out a curse that likely caused my mother to curl in her grave. "No, that's unacceptable. My kingdom begins in Drylliad and that is the only place this war must end."

I made a move to back away, but was blocked by Terrowic, immediately behind me. He said, "Conner thought you'd resist a return to his estate. Why is that?" I tried to ignore him, but he poked at the center of my back. "Don't you have scars that came from Farthenwood? Wasn't it there you also found out your entire family had been killed? And whatever happened to that servant girl you made friends with there? She was a pretty thing, I thought."

My jaw tightened, and I considered the risks of taking just one swing at him. Fortunately for us both, Kippenger came between us. To me, he said, "Farthenwood is our destination, and there's no one to blame for that but yourself. You sent a message with an Avenian thief several days ago. It was intended to reach your commanders in Drylliad, but the thief brought it to our king instead."

I had suspected as much, but only muttered, "I should've paid him better."

"You needn't worry about that. King Vargan rewarded him very well. In that message, you ordered every spare man to gather in Drylliad. Why do you think we let Mendenwal fight that battle? If you had so many men, it wouldn't be Avenia who suffered there. You also ordered your gold to be taken to Farthenwood. There's obviously a trap waiting for us if we go to your castle. But the spoils are at Farthenwood."

"The message was a lie." The waver in my voice sounded worried and uncertain. "Do you think I gave it to an Avenian thief truly expecting it would reach my castle? My armies in Drylliad are few and weak, and there is no gold at Farthenwood."

Kippenger laughed. "Oh, but that message did reach your castle. King Vargan was kind enough to send it on to your regents, after he read it. Whether you intended the order or not, your men are obeying it. Lord Conner verified that your men are collecting in Drylliad and the wealth of your country was moved to his estate, all as your message instructed. I believe you've been sunk by your own cleverness."

"It wouldn't be the first time for that."

"You're reasonably intelligent, and braver than most people I've known," Kippenger said. "But you're still just a boy. You never did have a chance against us."

Now wasn't the best time to argue, but I felt like it. Instead, I kept my mind fixed on what I had to do and glared up at him. "You must allow me some terms in exchange for my surrender. I demand to end this war at my castle and nowhere else."

"We've already met enough of your demands!" Then Kippenger's voice softened. "Don't despair, Jaron. There is good news too. My king orders that you not be harmed — not yet anyway. He intends a large audience for your hanging and doesn't want you to appear injured — he doesn't want to make you into a martyr."

That was a great relief, although considering Vargan's orders ended with my execution, the news could have been better. Still, I promised Kippenger if he gave me a bed to sleep in that night, he would find me there in the morning. The commander agreed to the deal, but insisted I wear a chain at my ankle and have vigils in my tent. It wasn't a great show of trust, but then again, I wasn't the most trustworthy prisoner. Once I was given the bed, I almost immediately fell asleep.

The following morning, I was told Avenia would keep the camp for another day to give their men some rest. That allowed me another day before my execution, so I made no objection. I was also offered another livery in the red and black of Avenia, and told it was all they had. I pointed out that it was in poor condition and smelly, and Terrowic countered that so was I, which probably was pretty accurate. When I refused it, he called in enough men to ensure I put it on. I didn't put up nearly as much of a fuss as I should have. I figured it was more important to save my energy for later, when I'd undoubtedly need it.

Other than a few heavily guarded allowances for me to leave the tent, I was kept chained to the bed, and for the most part, I made no protest. At least it was a bed, and Kippenger was strictly enforcing the orders for nobody to harm me. Admittedly, I took advantage of that and offered more insults than I'd otherwise have dared. The worst anyone gave me in response was a hard kick to my shin, which the soldier claimed was an accident. I couldn't complain to Kippenger, though, mostly because Kippenger's mother had been included as part of the insult. Otherwise, I ate every bite of what little they offered me and slept as much as I could. At least when I was asleep, I didn't have to worry about Mott or Fink or how my soldiers who remained in the woods were faring.

On the morning of Avenia's exodus from camp, the soldiers left in an orderly fashion. Nearly all of them were on horseback and I wondered what had happened to their wounded, who were clearly not amongst them. Kippenger had given me nothing to eat before we left, even though I smelled food from the fires and knew even the lowliest soldier there had eaten. And he had the chains on my wrists tethered to another chain behind Terrowic's horse. While the officers and most of the soldiers were riding from here, I'd be walking. Or be dragged if I couldn't keep up.

"I can't follow behind Terrowic's horse," I protested. "The smell will be unbearable."

"All horses smell the same," Kippenger replied.

But I eyed Terrowic. "I wasn't talking about the horse."

Kippenger only chuckled and strode away. Terrowic quietly promised that he'd lead me through paths with the sharpest rocks he could find. He probably meant what he said, but then, so had I.

Several times along the way, I asked if our destination was still Farthenwood, to which I only received impolite smirks from whoever heard my complaints. We were moving northeast, steadily toward Farthenwood. Vargan and Conner were probably there already, plotting the next phase in this war. A messenger had been sent ahead. Soon they would learn that I was coming to surrender. Conner was probably ecstatic at the prospect of watching me accept defeat at his former home. That sort of justice would appeal to his twisted nature.

My right leg began bothering me fairly early in the trek. I'd hardly given it the gentle care the castle physicians had insisted upon when they'd removed the brace, and my recent fall from the cliff had deeply bruised the flesh. But despite the pain, I hoped this trek would strengthen my muscles. I didn't intend to fall from a climb again.

Several miles into the journey, I became bored. We passed a fallen tree along the way that was littered with small rocks. I casually scooped a couple into my hands. When the two men on horses behind me became engaged in conversation, I hurled one of the rocks at the back of Terrowic's head. It hit him, hard.

He stopped and turned around, but my eyes were already wandering to the views along the trail. When he caught my attention, I shrugged innocently, and then cocked my head at the man behind me, blaming him for the incident.

Terrowic frowned at me, then turned around and continued riding. I waited a few more minutes, and then threw the second rock, hitting him again.

He was ready for me this time and leapt to the ground. He shoved me down, and then raised the whip he had used for his horse.

"Get off me," I snarled. "Or else after I win this war, I will find you and return tenfold everything you've done to me. I want to talk to Commander Kippenger. Now!"

He glared at the men who were still on their horses behind me, then stomped away. A few minutes later he returned with Kippenger, who was clearly displeased at our trek coming to a halt.

"Get on your feet," he ordered me. "We're expected by nightfall."

"At which point I'll be killed. I'm in no hurry."

"I should kill you now."

"I wish you would. Because then I can die with a smile on my face."

"Why's that?"

"What punishment will you get if you fail to arrive with me? They'll beat you harder than you could ever beat me here."

"You are more obstinate than your worst reputation." He tried again. "Now, get on your feet."

"You can knock me unconscious or drag me to my death, but I will not walk any farther. Get me a horse."

"That's ridiculous. You're a prisoner."

"I'm a king. And I demand to be treated as such. Get me a horse."

Kippenger licked his lips, and then turned to Terrowic. "He'll use your horse. Help him up, then see that it's tethered to mine."

Terrowic's eyes darkened, but the order had been given and the commander was already marching away. He grabbed me from the ground and all but threw me onto his horse.

In his anger, Terrowic had neglected to remove his pack from the horse's saddle. Once we were under way again, I took advantage of that. He had a container of water, some dried meat and biscuits, and a few apples. When I finished the first apple, I made sure to toss the core over my shoulder and hoped it hit him on the head too.

Other than what was necessary for the care of the horses, we took very few breaks throughout the journey. Still, it was dark when I first saw the lights of Farthenwood in the distance. Once we got closer, I saw that a gallows was being constructed at the front of the home. Two nooses were already in place. One was for me. I didn't know who the other was for.

At the far end of the property were several Carthyan wagons, under heavy guard. Most of them were covered, but the corner of one had come undone and flapped in the breeze. The moonlight lit the gold inside the wagon. As Kippenger had said, the wealth of Carthya was here indeed.

Kippenger personally verified the chains were still firm around my wrists, which I thought should've been obvious by the way the metal had worn sores into my flesh. When he was satisfied, they pulled me off the horse and made me wait while someone informed their king I had arrived.

I was once again amazed by how little Farthenwood had changed since my last visit here. Certainly to attend Vargan, the grand estate was filling with people, but they couldn't have been here long. Other than the gallows and the gold-filled wagons, the home itself seemed no different.

Eventually I was led inside. On my first trip here, I had also been a prisoner. Escorted in with more courtesy and fewer chains, but a prisoner nonetheless. I hated the thought of having to face Vargan here. Vargan would gloat over his victory, humiliating me as I signed papers that preserved the lives of my countrymen, giving us peace, but at the very highest price. And Vargan would be sure I knew every detail of what would happen tomorrow, the day of my execution. That was intolerable, but it infuriated me to know that Conner would be here too. He had wanted the throne from the moment he became a regent. He had murdered my family and expressed his regrets that I hadn't been amongst his victims. And he was willing to turn Carthya into a feeding gallery for the Avenian vultures, just so he could wear a crown and pretend that made him any sort of a royal.

I was taken to Conner's office, or perhaps it was considered Vargan's office now. Conner's wide desk was gone, as were his books and other decorations. Over the past several months, nearly everything of value had been stripped from this place. Vargan rose from a simple wooden chair that must have been intended as a temporary throne. Conner was already standing behind him, arms folded and dressed in all his former finery. He appeared to have aged considerably in the prison, but now, with his hair washed and combed neatly back, he looked rather distinguished, a weak facade for his rotting soul inside.

Vargan immediately spoke. "You gave yourself up, Jaron. Why?"

"I needed medical supplies for my men."

"Are you surrendering?"

My jaw tightened. "Call it that if you'd like."

"Then you will kneel."

I had known this was coming, but my muscles instinctively locked against his command. It was not in me to kneel to another ruler.

Behind me, Commander Kippenger took exception to my hesitation. He kicked behind the knee of my right leg, which immediately buckled. I collapsed to the floor, and when I tried to rise, he pressed his foot down on my calf, ensuring I maintained a kneeling position.

"Very good," Vargan said. "The terms of your surrender are this. I will be the emperor of these lands. Carthya will become a tributary to Avenia. One half of everything Carthya produces will be sent to me. Carthya will be subject to my commands and my laws, but the people will be allowed to maintain their own customs under the leadership of King Bevin Conner."

"Then we have a problem," I muttered. "Carthya has no customs regarding enslavement, especially to a country of swine. That puppet who stands beside you will be overthrown before the year's end, and Carthya will rise against Avenia until we are free again."

"Perhaps they'll try," Vargan said. "But you won't be here to see it. The final term of surrender is that you must go to the gallows."

"Not here." I shook my head. "I am a king. If you will do this, it must be at my castle in Drylliad."

"Yes, Commander Kippenger told me of your objections. But I've already gone to the trouble of having the gallows built here. And besides, I know you intended Drylliad as a trap for me."

"Not for you specifically," I said. "Let me live until Conner is made king and tries to make his home there. I wish to see what my soldiers do to him upon his arrival."

"Your soldiers have been notified of the surrender and were summoned here to Farthenwood, unarmed, to witness your execution," Conner said. "A special command was sent to Lord Harlowe and his regents to attend. From the gallows you will order their loyalty to me, and they will agree, or follow you to their graves."

I closed my eyes and tried to imagine Harlowe's reaction when he heard of this. Harlowe would never agree to follow Conner. By the end of tomorrow, he would be dead too.

"The papers of surrender are being drawn up even as we speak," Vargan said. "You will sign them at first light and die immediately after."

"That doesn't give me much time, then," I said.

"For what?"

My glare began at Conner, then moved back to Vargan. "Not much time to win this war. You two had better spend tonight preparing your souls for the devils' lair. Because after tomorrow, that'll be your home."

Kippenger jerked on my chains, forcing me to my feet. Vargan raised a hand to strike my face, but slowly lowered it.

Conner said, "I've reserved a spot for him in the dungeons. Jaron will know the place well."

And as had happened months before, I was dragged from the room. But this time I did not go kicking and screaming. I was taken away without breaking my glare from Vargan's face. I might have been the one in chains, but he was the one who looked afraid.

## · THIRTY-SEVEN ·

I'd had the key to my chains folded in my palms since Terrowic first pulled me off his horse. I had expected him to protect it better since I'd already stolen his keys once before, but he was so angry when he grabbed me that he didn't even think to check his pockets. I had hoped they'd leave me alone in an upstairs room long enough to make an escape there, but they didn't. Besides, as far as I could tell, I was without friends anywhere at Farthenwood, so my escape would be brief and my recapture painful.

As they led me down the stairs toward the dungeon, I heard the sounds of another person already imprisoned there and tilted my head to see who it was. Roden was chained in the center of the room, the very spot where Mott had whipped me once. He still wore his captain's uniform, though it was torn and filthy. With his arms raised, I noted he was thinner than he had been before, but stronger too. He was also bruised along one side of his face, a mark of how poorly his last battle had gone. As bad as he looked, it was a blessing that he was still alive. Well, alive for now. I suspected his was the neck intended for the second noose.

When he saw me coming down the stairs he glanced to his right and mumbled something. He wasn't alone, then. I wondered who had been captured with him. Maybe the commander of Bymar, or one of the men I'd sent with him.

I didn't see who it was until we reached the bottom of the stairs and rounded the corner. Once I did, time itself paused. Everything but that single moment vanished, and I feared it was some horrible joke of the devils. For on the far wall, a girl with long brown hair and tea-colored eyes was slowly rising to her feet.

Imogen.

She was in a simple bleached-muslin dress, with no hint of decoration. It was wide at the neck, and I could see bandages wrapped over her left shoulder. Her hair was matted on one side, and her thin face looked dangerously pale.

But she was alive.

How was that possible? I had seen the arrow pierce her shoulder, seen her fall, and every conversation since that moment had confirmed the worst of my fears. Yet here she was, standing before me.

The vigils holding my arms had relaxed their grip while Terrowic unlocked the cell door. The second he opened the door, I twisted around and snatched the keys from his hand. Before any of them could react, I darted into the cell, slammed the door shut behind me, and dropped the keys somewhere on the floor. I was vaguely aware of their curses and threats, but barely took notice of them. My only care at the moment stood directly in front of me.

I had seen her every time I closed my eyes, heard her voice in my dreams, and had replayed that moment with the arrow in nightmares that consumed my thoughts like deadly parasites. Could it be that she wasn't truly here? That what I saw in front of me was the ultimate joke of the devils — their final gouge for all the crimes of my life? If they wanted one last laugh at my expense, this would be their cruelest trick.

I crossed the room and studied Imogen's face. I knew every curve, every line. It was her, and yet I could not fathom how she could actually be standing there.

In only a whisper, I said, "If this is a trick, please tell me now. Are you real?" It was a fool's question, perhaps, but I had to be sure. When she nodded, with my hands still bound in chains, I cupped her face, holding her as delicately as a teacup. Just to touch her sent a flood of emotions through me. My eyes filled with tears, but I didn't care if anyone saw.

Imogen's hands were chained separately, connecting her to the wall. But her left hand pressed against my chest, where my heart pounded just to get closer to her touch. Her eyes revealed some mixture of joy and sadness to see me, but within me there was only one emotion. I kissed her lightly at first, then again and again, as if nothing in the world existed but us. Her hand slid over my shoulder until the chain pulled tight, drawing me against her. She wanted me as close as I needed to be to her, and I became lost in the moment, with no intention of breaking away ever again.

The vigils outside of the cell were yelling now, and Terrowic ordered the others to go back upstairs and locate more keys. They'd be angry once they finally got in here. But they weren't inside yet.

My fingers caressed the curve of her jaw, then her hand folded into mine. She glanced down at our intertwined hands only momentarily, then, when she looked back up, the corners of her eyes creased.

"Tell me that you love me," I whispered.

"But what if —"

"There are no what ifs, only us. Just say the words, Imogen. And mean them."

Imogen's eyes filled with tears, and I worried that perhaps, once again, I had asked for more than she could give me. She bit into her lip and finally said, "Jaron, I can't —"

She stopped there, and my heart sank. That she was alive gave me an immeasurable happiness, but it wasn't enough. I loved her, and needed her like I needed the beat of my heart. But none of it was complete unless I knew she could feel even the smallest part of that for me.

I began to say something, but she wasn't finished. "I can't remember a minute since we met when I haven't been in love with you."

A smile spread across my face, and I moved in to kiss her again, but by then, the vigils had gotten into the cell. One grabbed my shoulders and threw me to the far side of the dungeons. I hit the floor not far from the bandages Mott had used months ago to wrap the injury from my whipping here. Another vigil yanked me back to my feet while Terrowic raised an arm to take a swing at me.

"You leave so much as the smell of dirt on me and Vargan will hear about it," I snarled. "No marks, remember?"

His expression turned murderous, but I was equally angry. His timing couldn't possibly have been worse, and I wouldn't forgive him for that.

They chained me to the wall, much as they had kept me in Vargan's camp. Terrowic surveyed me as though he wanted a way to get in a hit without Vargan noticing. Before he chose a spot, I sat on the ground. I didn't want a fight and certainly didn't need another injury. I only wanted him to leave so that I could speak with Roden and Imogen alone.

Against all odds, Roden had survived the latest battle with Mendenwal. And against even greater odds, Imogen was also alive. I had never been one to believe the saints still granted miracles to the living, but maybe they did. There was no other explanation for either of them being here.

"You enjoy this moment all you want," Terrowic said. "Tomorrow morning they'll hang you like a common thief."

"I'm counting on that," I retorted. Terrowic started to leave, but I called after him and added, "She was about to kiss me when you dragged me away. That alone is good enough reason for the revenge I'm bringing you."

He only laughed and followed the other vigils up the stairs. But he shouldn't have ignored my threat. I had been perfectly sincere.

Once we were alone, Imogen unfolded her hand. In it, she held the key to the chains. I had passed it to her while we were in the embrace.

Roden noticed it and scowled. "You gave her the key and not me? I could be free already."

I smiled at him. "Yes, but I wasn't going to kiss you."

"Fair enough," he said with a laugh.

Then my attention returned to Imogen. "Tell me how you can possibly be alive. I saw you fall."

"They thought I was dead at first, even loaded me onto the wagon meant to collect the bodies." I closed my eyes to picture her words. That's the part Mott would have seen. She continued, "We didn't drive very far before someone heard my cries. This man, a commander —"

"Kippenger."

"Yes. He told me that once I was strong enough, they'd bring me back and force you to do everything they wanted. I knew what that would involve, how I'd forever be the cause of Carthya's downfall. I couldn't do that, couldn't let them use me against you. So I decided not to get well."

"You tried to die," I whispered. "Imogen, no."

"I knew you were in the camp with me. I heard the soldiers pass by, discussing the things they'd done to you that day, or bragging of how they'd finally broken you. If I survived, I knew it would only get more horrible for both of us. So every day, no matter how hard they tried to heal me, I only got worse."

I thought about how I'd have felt if our situations were reversed. If I'd had to hear them boasting about her mistreatment, and knowing full well it would only get worse if I survived. I couldn't imagine how Imogen bore all that.

Tears welled in her eyes. "Then I heard all the commotion on the night you escaped from that camp — I think you probably rode right past my tent and never knew. After that, I knew you would survive, and that if I did too, I'd see you again. So from that moment, I fought to get better."

"This is all very sweet," Roden said bitterly. "But you see where we are. With worse odds for survival than any of us have faced before. Jaron, I want to hear your plan for escape."

"I gave Imogen the key to her chains. That's a start."

"When Conner told me you were coming here, I hoped he'd let me stay in the bed," Imogen said. "I could've escaped from there to help you. Maybe he knew that too, because he sent me here. Either way, I'm not strong enough yet to help you fight."

"Your only duty is to get well," I said, and then gave her a mischievous smile. "There is unfinished business between us."

"I'm going to be ill if they leave me in here with you two," Roden groaned. "Jaron, even with Imogen's key, we can't get through the bars. And even if we did, the estate is full of Avenian soldiers. You and I are going to be executed at first light. Please tell me you can stop this."

"Of course I can," I said. "We're going to win."

# · THIRTY-EIGHT ·

As the night wore on, I told Imogen and Roden about Mott's uncertain condition, about Tobias and Amarinda, and about our progress in the war. In turn, Roden told me everything from the time I left him near Drylliad.

"We were on the march when Mendenwal attacked. They came so quickly, we had no time to do anything but react." Roden tilted his head so that I might better see his injury. "Unfortunately, I got this rather early in the battle, when a horse reared up and then landed on me."

"You're lucky it wasn't worse."

"It *was* worse, for most of my men. I awoke on a battlefield blanketed with the dead. I've never seen anything more awful. Soldiers from Mendenwal were searching for survivors, and when they found me, they recognized me as a captain. They said Avenia had demanded I be brought here."

"Were you able to learn anything from their leaders about Mendenwal's involvement in this war?" It was a question that still bothered me.

He thought it over for a minute, and then said, "Now that you mention it, two of the men who escorted me were in an angry conversation about Avenia sending them to die while Vargan held his own armies back. They weren't leaders, but I'm sure there are others who feel the same way."

"Ah, good."

"It's not good, Jaron. I'm sorry. You made me captain, and I failed you."

"No one could've done more," I said optimistically. "Besides, I'll need your help tomorrow. Maybe our odds could be better — I admit that — but I believe we're positioned very well for success."

"Chained up in the dungeons of our enemy, on the verge of total defeat, and set for execution?"

I shrugged. "I already said that things could be better. But they could be worse too. Cheer up, Roden!"

"Do you remember our first morning here at Farthenwood? Tobias was still asleep, or we thought he was. You said it didn't matter if you died, because there was no one left who loved you and so your death wouldn't cause anyone pain."

I remembered that well, though it seemed so long ago now.

Roden's eyes shifted to Imogen. "That's not true for you now, obviously. But it still is for me. If you have to sacrifice me to win this war, and to save your own life, I will be honored to go that way."

"You're being ridiculous," I said. "Either my head will be

in the noose next to yours, or I'll figure out some way to save us both. Personally, I prefer the latter."

Roden mumbled in agreement, then turned his attention to Imogen. "If they do take us, then without Jaron, they'll have no reason to keep you here. So once you're free, will you do me a favor?"

"Of course."

"I have only the one name for my gravestone, like a servant or an orphan would. But I'm more than that now, and I don't want to be remembered only as Roden."

"You may have any name you wish," I offered. "Including that of my own house."

Roden gave his thanks, but he already seemed to have another name in mind. He said, "When I was a baby, an old Avenian woman was my caretaker. But it was a brutal winter and she became sick. Before she died, she left me with a midwife and told her my mother had been named Havanila. She mentioned no other family, and the midwife eventually gave me to an orphanage. I'd like to use my mother's name on my gravestone, Roden of the house of Havanila."

Havanila. The name echoed in my ears.

"Why have you never told me this story?" I breathed out the words, barely able to use my voice.

He shrugged as if none of that mattered. "There was nothing to tell. Obviously my parents were dead, which is how I came into that old woman's care. Why?"

I closed my eyes and shook my head. Roden's mother had a name I'd never heard anywhere before, except from one other man. Roden was Harlowe's younger son, the infant who had been taken in an attempt to extract a ransom from Harlowe. But before the exchange could be made, the Avenian woman who had taken him died. Unaware of his noble birth, the midwife sent Roden to an orphanage, where he remained until Conner brought him to Farthenwood. Roden was chosen because he looked a little like me, and I'd often been told that I looked somewhat like Harlowe's other son and Roden's brother, Mathis.

Except they were family, and I was not.

Roden had a father. Who would be in attendance tomorrow as Roden and I were hanged at the gallows. Roden deserved to know that, to look Harlowe directly in the eyes for a final farewell.

And yet I couldn't force the words out. From the moment of our meeting, Harlowe had been as a father to me. Once Harlowe knew his son not only lived, but had been so close for all these weeks, his heart would naturally leave me and go to Roden. It may have been greedy on my part — I knew that it was — and yet I felt desperate for any sort of family. I did not want to give Roden this gift. Not yet anyway. I wanted a father.

With that, I scowled inwardly, berating myself for my unforgivable selfishness. I already had a father. Not alive, but I had his name and history, and memories I could hold on to. Some of them were better than others, but the failures were my fault as much as his. Once again, I recalled the image of having stood before him in the great hall as he accused me of being a thief. I should have explained then why I had taken the coins, and made him understand me. Or better yet, I should have tried to understand him. If I had, I knew now that my father would have helped that widow.

Whether we understood or agreed with each other, I had now come through enough war to accept that even if he and I would make different choices, he did have reasons for the choices he made. And wherever in the afterlife he wandered, I believed that my father was watching me, and knew I had my own reasons too.

I had to tell Roden.

And I started to say the words, because I knew he needed to be told. But I wondered if it would be cruel to give Roden the knowledge of his father before I knew whether we would survive. Perhaps it would only add to his pain as the noose was tightened around his neck, knowing he had come so close to the one thing he most desired.

"You do have a plan, right?"

Roden had continued in conversation with Imogen, though I had drifted into my own thoughts. I turned to him. "What?"

Roden rolled his eyes. "A plan for us to escape."

"Oh." I shrugged. "Not really."

His jaw fell open as I spoke, which I thought was rather bold. He might not have spent much time in chains and dungeons recently, but I certainly had. And Farthenwood was now filled with soldiers who'd consider it a personal honor to kill any of us in an escape attempt. Working through those challenges wasn't exactly as easy as, say, planning an evening menu. For now, my entire plan came down to four small words: try not to die.

"Not really?" Roden asked. "Jaron, night is passing quickly. In only a few short hours, they'll come for us. You must have something."

I closed my eyes, and then opened them to look at Imogen. "When Roden and I are taken away, we'll make a big fuss with the guards. Enough that any vigils nearby will have to come and get control of us. That will be your chance to escape. You know where to go until this is over, correct?"

"The hidden passages." She had been a servant here and probably knew the secret entrances as well as anyone could.

"Conner obviously knows about them too, but I doubt anyone will consider it worth the effort to look for you, even if they remember you're missing. Just stay in there, hidden as well as you can until you know it's safe to come out."

Roden wasn't convinced. "How big of a fuss will this require?"

I grinned. "Catastrophic levels of bad behavior. Trust me, it'll be fun."

"You have a sick idea of fun." Roden's cool expression seemed less than enthusiastic. "When we do this, will they hurt us?"

That made me sigh. "You're the captain of my guard, aren't you? Surely you can take a few hits by now. Besides, the pain will be forgotten once the ropes go around our necks."

"I don't want a rope going around my neck, Jaron! That's the part you need to figure out."

"Well, it probably will! You have to settle with that reality before we can figure anything out."

He calmed down and my attention went back to Imogen. With the wound in her shoulder, this night had been hard on her. But she was trying to stay strong and smiled back at me when our eyes met. I was overwhelmed with love for her. The warmth of it filled every vein of my body, consumed my fears and anger, and left in their place only a desire to be happy. It was what Mott had wished for me, to find happiness, to accept love as a far stronger force than any weapon. I ached to think of Mott, with no idea of whether he had survived.

"I promise to devise a plan," I said, "but until then, I think we should play a good joke, for when the vigils return for us."

Roden cocked an eyebrow, intrigued by the suggestion. Imogen muttered something about the foolishness of boys. She was probably right about that, so I couldn't argue her point. Also, I loved her, so I had no intention of arguing.

It took some straining against my chains and some creative footwork, but eventually I nudged the old bandages in the corner toward me. Once I had them in my hands, I unwound them to their full length.

"What are you going to do with those?" Roden asked. "You're not injured."

"The vigils are forbidden from harming me tonight. Vargan was very clear that I wasn't to come out tomorrow looking like a martyr." My grin widened. "But don't worry, Avenia already fell for this trick once before. They love it." I was remembering when I was with the thieves and had used bandages to make Vargan think I had the plague. Neither Imogen nor Roden were with me then, so they didn't understand the joke. But they would soon. I maneuvered my hands enough to wind the bandage around my ankle and calf, and then tucked the end back inside the wrapping. It was haphazardly done, but considering the limitations of my chains, I was actually impressed with the finished product.

"That's your trick?" Roden asked. "Can't you take this seriously?"

"If you understood what Vargan's men did to me, you'd know exactly how serious I am."

"Jaron, tomorrow we are —"

"Hush now," I said. "Imogen needs to sleep, I need to think, and you need to . . . let me think."

Roden made a face, but he did give me some silence. Imogen stared at me for several minutes before finally closing her eyes. And I turned away and set to the task of figuring out a way to survive the next day.

# · THIRTY-NINE ·

True to Vargan's word, the vigils came for me again at first light, Terrowic and Commander Kippenger amongst them. I asked if anyone had something to eat, but they only laughed at me. I actually would have liked some food and didn't appreciate their laughter.

Roden was unchained first and immediately balled his fists, as if eager for a fight. I wondered how he'd do against these vigils while unarmed. He probably wouldn't last as long as he thought he could.

They came for me next, and took great care in ensuring I never had a free hand. While they worked, I looked at Imogen and said, "I want you to marry me one day."

Now the tears spilled over her cheeks. "Look where we are."

I smiled back at her. "We won't marry here, of course. But in the great hall of my castle, in front of the entire kingdom."

Imogen bit her lip and nodded. "Yes, Jaron. I will marry you there."

"Then I'll find you soon. But if I don't — if I *can't* — then be happy and know I loved you."

More tears fell, but she said nothing.

The vigils pulled me forward, and saw me favoring the ankle wrapped in bandages. *Pretending* to favor it, actually.

Commander Kippenger asked, "What happened to your foot? It wasn't in bandages last night."

I winced as I limped forward another step. "Terrowic came in during the night and hurt me." It was a better-told lie than most I'd ever uttered, and one of the few for which I didn't feel the slightest shred of guilt. "He tried to wrap it and hoped you wouldn't notice."

"I — no, I — didn't!" Terrowic sputtered.

"We begged him to stop," Roden said, joining the fun. "But he wanted his revenge before Jaron's execution."

"They're lying!" Terrowic was completely flustered by now.

"I can't walk far enough to sign the surrender papers," I continued. "You should tell Vargan to delay the signing for another month while I heal."

"You'll sign even if we have to carry you there!" Without warning, Kippenger rounded on Terrowic and cracked a fist against his jaw. "How dare you defy the king's orders!" Then he ordered his other vigils, "Take him to my room and lock him in there. I will set a harsh discipline for him after the execution."

Kippenger's vigils gripped Terrowic's arms and started to lead him away, still protesting. With everyone watching Terrowic, I clicked my tongue to get his attention. I looked down at my ankle, wiggled it back and forth, then winked at him. He pointed at me and made an objection, but by then my expression had returned to one of appropriate pain and suffering, and he was quickly whisked back up the stairs for his punishment.

Kippenger turned back to me. "Can you walk?"

I shrugged. "I'll try. Just go easy on me."

He said, "I suggest *you* go easy, Jaron. If you don't, there's no end of things I can do to you that Vargan never has to know about."

I muttered an agreement I had no intention of honoring, then looked back at Imogen as he led us away. She still held one fist closed, hiding the key for her chains, and I motioned with my eyes that her chance for escape was coming soon. My final glance was to Roden, at my side. He didn't look entirely enthusiastic about what was about to happen, but he was ready.

Only halfway out of the dungeon, I grabbed the bars to the door and started screaming, "No, wait, I've changed my mind! Don't take me to Vargan!"

A vigil in front of me grabbed my legs to pull me away from the bars. The door swung wide open and still I held on. Now slightly ahead of me on the stairs, Roden started yelling as well, requiring the vigil behind him to scramble for his control.

Kippenger hit my arms with the broadside of his sword until my hold collapsed and I tumbled to the ground. Then two vigils interlocked arms with mine to drag me upstairs. A quick peek behind me revealed everything I needed to know — they had forgotten to close the dungeon door for Imogen. They probably had forgotten she was even in there.

We continued our rant until they dragged us upstairs, at which point Roden tried to make a run for the rear door.

I began cursing at him, accusing him of abandoning me in my darkest hour, or something equally silly and dramatic, and the commander shouted for more men to attend to us.

They ran at me first, lacking any grace in shoving me to the floor. I yelled at Kippenger not to let them leave any marks, but that clearly wasn't his concern at the moment. More men continued to come, and frankly, with the growing audience, I enjoyed screaming even louder. Unfortunately, nobody had been ordered to avoid leaving marks on Roden, so many of his cries might have been sincere.

Before it was over there were probably twenty men assigned to each of us. I felt slightly disappointed by that. I'd have preferred forty each, or a respectable number of thirty, at least. Most only stood around watching in horror and embarrassment for our childishness, but they all followed as we were carried to the office, and all were assigned to wait in the hallway in case they were needed.

I smiled over at Roden. A large bruise was already forming under his left eye and he had a bloody lip and possibly a broken nose. In my thrashing about, my head had collided with the corner of a wall and blood was running from that wound down the side of my face. Maybe some people would view that as my own fault, but I already had plans to put the blame elsewhere. To my delight, Roden smiled back. I wanted to remind him that I had been right before: In its own way, that had been fun. Beyond that, we'd accomplished our goal. Nobody would be watching the dungeon.

We calmed down once we arrived at the office, and after a few pointed threats if I misbehaved again, Commander Kippenger brought us inside.

Conner was alone in there this time, wearing different clothes from what he'd worn the previous evening. There was so much white on his silk shirt and vest, it was as if he had draped himself in the color of the saints to conceal the fact that he was the devils' worst. I wondered how he'd so suddenly acquired such a vast wardrobe.

Sometime in the night, a new desk had been located for the office. It wasn't as nice as Conner's original desk had been, but it was undoubtedly still expensive and likely had been forcibly taken from the closest nearby home.

Roden was shoved to his knees near the back wall and I was led to a chair in front of the desk. With Conner behind the desk, and Kippenger and another vigil standing on either side of me, I was reminded of a similar situation months ago. Back then, I had only suspected Conner of his crimes. Now I understood exactly who he was, and the depths to which he would sink to acquire power. Whatever my opinion had been of him then, it was nothing compared to the loathing I felt now.

"Was that your screaming I just heard?" Conner asked.

My expression was as innocent as ever. "I'm not sure what you're talking about. I heard no screaming."

"You have a nasty gash on your head."

"Oh, that." I gestured toward the commander. "He hit me. I begged him not to. He knew that Vargan didn't want any marks on me. But if there was any screaming, it was probably me pleading with him to stop."

Kippenger cursed at me, which gave me no small amount of pleasure.

"This boy can't be hanged in a coat with the Avenian colors," Conner said. "Remove his chains so I can get this off of him."

"We should ask the king's permission first," Kippenger offered.

"By the end of today I will be Carthya's king. This outfit offends me!"

"Carthya is honored to offend you," I said.

Kippenger lowered his voice. Maybe he didn't want me to hear, which was ridiculous. "Lord Conner, without the chains, this boy can be dangerous. Just before we came in here —"

"If he were any danger to me, I'd be dead long ago. Now, unchain him."

The chains were undone, leaving my arms feeling almost weightless when Kippenger pulled my livery off, and once again I was wearing only a plain undershirt. I said a farewell to Kippenger that included my wishes for him to develop boils in his armpits, and then told him to be more careful with me next time. Kippenger snarled and muttered something under his breath, but left. In his place, two other vigils entered the room. Maybe to protect me from Conner, or Conner from me. I wasn't sure which.

Conner sat on the edge of his desk. He pulled a handkerchief from his pocket and offered it to me for the gash on my head. When the bleeding was mostly stopped, he asked, "The night you were crowned, after you exposed my crimes to the court, why didn't you have me executed?"

"Obviously, that was a mistake on my part."

"Maybe so. But why didn't you?"

The heat in my glare could've boiled water. After a heavy sigh, I said, "I always felt you had more of a role to play for Carthya. Clearly you do, but it turned out to be somewhat less noble than I had hoped for. What you've done now, aligning yourself with Avenia, that's the ultimate betrayal of your country. You once told me that despite your crimes, you were still a patriot. I'm sure we can agree that's no longer true."

Conner's eyes narrowed. "Arrogant boy! Always so certain you have all the answers."

"Then answer me this. Imogen is still wounded — she needs food and a bed and a physician. I know how you treated her as a servant, but are you really so cruel as to let her die in the dungeons?"

"I sent her there so that you would know she still lives!" Conner crossed the room to stand directly in front of me. His eyes briefly flicked to the vigils behind us before he said, "You foiled plans I spent a lifetime creating. Took away everything I was, everything I had. I hate you for that. You know things about me I thought no one could, learned the secrets of Farthenwood, and you have crowded many more secrets within its walls. Jaron, you will not destroy this final plan of mine. Do you understand me?"

I stared back at him. "Yes, Sir Master Conner." I understood him perfectly now.

There was much more to say, but we both quieted when the doors opened behind us and Vargan slithered in with Kippenger and several other attendants on his heels. Conner left his post and bowed to Vargan, who acknowledged him with little more than an impolite grunt. Vargan held Conner in roughly the same respect as a spider admires its prey. Once he'd gotten everything he wanted from Conner, Vargan would hang him too.

Vargan's face wrinkled as he studied me. "That's a terrible cut on your head."

"Blame Commander Kippenger for that. I think it makes me look like a martyr, don't you?" I made a face of false regret. "You'll obviously have to delay this morning's activities until I'm healed."

"And disappoint your audience?" he countered. "I think not. Why is there a bandage around your ankle?"

In all the commotion, I'd actually forgotten it was there. "Oh, that? My foot got cold in the night."

"Only your foot?"

"It's always been extra sensitive. Like my feelings." I unwrapped it and let the bandages fall to the floor.

"You've been playing games with my men," Vargan said. "Therefore, I will feel no guilt in playing games with yours."

My eyes narrowed. "Playing games seems rather childish for someone so close to crumbling into dust."

Vargan chuckled. "I'm never too old to enjoy a good joke. And I know you'll like this as much as I will." He gestured to

Kippenger, who opened the door and exited. He returned only seconds later with another prisoner, his hands tied behind him and limping heavily. His head was down when he entered, and he raised it as if ashamed to be here. Only when he was forced to kneel beside Roden did his eyes meet mine.

"Tobias," I breathed. "Not you too."

"Here, at the end, the three orphan boys together?" Making no attempt to hide his pleasure, Conner clasped his hands and turned to Vargan. "Your Majesty, may I interpret this as your gift to me on the day of my coronation?"

"You may not," Vargan said tersely. Then to me, he added, "Not long after Kippenger began the exodus from your camp, this boy walked in unarmed and told my remaining men that in exchange for you, he would surrender himself and provide medical care to all of my wounded. It was stupid to think we'd ever consider trading a king for a young physician, but we do give him credit for his loyalty."

I snuck a glimpse at Tobias, who shrugged helplessly.

"Little did he know, you were already on your way here, and besides, we didn't need his help. Kippenger's orders were to kill all our wounded. They're a drain on our resources."

My eyes passed from Vargan to Kippenger, who was trying very hard not to betray his true feelings about having disposed of his own wounded men. Vargan may not have had much regard for his own armies, but that order seemed cruel even for him.

"Here is the game, then, Jaron." Vargan seemed so delighted with himself that he was practically bubbling over with wicked excitement. "I have three necks in here, all worthy of hanging, but only two nooses. I will give you the opportunity to save one of you three. Who will it be? The captain of your guard, perhaps? He is strong and courageous. With so many losses to your armies, he would be vital for Carthya's continued protection. Or will you save your scholar? He claimed to have saved many of your wounded the night before he surrendered, including a servant he says never leaves your side."

So Mott was safe, then. I had been desperate for news about him.

Vargan laughed again. "Or will you save yourself? Surely no one is more valuable to Carthya than its king. A very large crowd is already gathering in front of Farthenwood. Let them watch us come out together and announce a grand bargain for all our lands. Choose yourself to survive, and I'll allow you to serve me."

"Are those my only options?" I asked.

"Did you have another one in mind?"

"Two nooses. I'm looking at your neck, and Conner's."

His eyes darkened. "Choose now, or I will order them to string up a third rope."

"Let me die," Tobias said. "I did what I could for your wounded. Carthya doesn't need me any longer."

"We both know someone who needs you very much," I said. "You must live today."

"Then choose me to die," Roden said. "I'm honored to stand at your side, even at the gallows. Besides, there is nobody for me."

Except there was. A father who needed him.

"We'll both go," Tobias said. "Not you." Beside him, Roden nodded.

I appreciated their loyalty, but I still made a face. "Don't be ridiculous. The failure of this war lies solely with me." The weight of my attention shifted to Vargan. "This is my offer. I'll let you hang me twice. I won't even put up a fuss the second time."

Conner smirked back at me. "If you won't choose, then let's run the third rope."

"No." I cast my eyes downward, unwilling to look at either of my friends. "Take Tobias away from here. Roden and I will go to the gallows."

"No!" Tobias cried. "Save yourself, Jaron. Please!"

"Get him out of here," I said.

"Escort him to the crowd in front of Farthenwood," Vargan ordered. "Make sure he has a good view of his friends."

Tobias tried to remain in the room, and put up a better fight than I'd have expected. Once he was gone, I turned to Roden. "Forgive me."

"You made the right choice," Roden whispered. "Though you did choose his name rather quickly."

"He has a skinny neck. He'd have died faster."

"That's why you chose me? Because it'll take me longer to die?"

"Yes, Roden, that's exactly why."

"Enough bickering!" Vargan grabbed a quill from Conner, then shoved it at me. "Sign these papers, Jaron. With your signature, Conner becomes king and Carthya becomes mine. Sign them or else you'll —"

"No threats are necessary." I stood and dipped the quill in the ink. "I gave myself up to do this very thing." As I was writing, Roden, still kneeling in the back of the room, gasped. I knew he expected better from me, and certainly not my surrender. But I was doing the only thing I could, whether he understood that or not.

When I'd finished, I threw the quill against the back wall and told Vargan to get this next part over with. Conner inspected the document while Vargan called for my hands to be tied again. Conner asked for the honor of doing the task.

I held my hands out in front of me, but Conner ordered them at my back and wound the rope tightly against my wrists. With the sores already cut into the flesh, the rough cordage was far more painful than the chains had ever been. I suspected Conner must have known that, and likely took pleasure in it. Once we entered the great hall, I began working to untie the ropes, but Conner put one hand over the knots, preventing me from any movement there.

We stood at the doors of Farthenwood as an announcement was made that we were coming out. While we waited, Vargan leaned over to me and said, "Who did you think you were, to stand up to someone like me?"

I remained facing forward while I said, "I am Jaron, the Ascendant King of Carthya. You will regret ever bringing war against me."

And the doors opened.

## · FORTY ·

It was an unusually beautiful morning, warm and bright, with sapphire skies that were better suited to a picnic than a hanging. A light breeze stirred the two nooses hanging from the gallows in circles. The beams weren't tall, the kind that would snap a neck as soon as the floor collapsed, causing instant, relatively painless death. These were the shorter ones with a knot at the center of the neck. They'd cut off our air once the stools beneath our feet were kicked away, creating a slow and terrible death. That had been a deliberate choice, I suspected. They wanted me to suffer, and for everyone in the audience to have a long time to understand the consequences of defying King Vargan.

For there was indeed a large crowd gathered, many more than I had anticipated. Most of the audience was the soldiers of Avenia and Mendenwal. Tobias was now standing with my other regents near the front. Like those around him, his face registered dread for what was about to happen. But something more seemed etched into his expression — perhaps the conflicted feelings of guilt and relief that I had chosen him to escape the noose. I wished he wouldn't torture himself with that. The choice had been mine, and I'd made the correct one. If he would've looked directly at me, I'd have tried to communicate that to him, but his eyes were cast downward, ashamed.

The other regents were looking at me, and I gave them a respectful nod for having come. I suspected that immediately after our deaths, they'd be taken to Vargan and forced to give oaths of fealty to him and Conner. Kerwyn was missing from the group. Either he was still in Mendenwal, or else he had escaped Vargan's demands that he be in attendance. Standing beside Tobias was Harlowe. His eyes were filled with horror as he stared at me. Considering who walked beside me, it was wrong that he should care so much about my death.

I lowered my head and said to Roden, "There's something I should have told you last night."

Roden's voice wavered when he spoke. "Yes?"

"You have a father, Roden. He's alive, and he is here."

"What?" Roden jerked his whole body toward me. "Who?"

I cocked my head toward the center of the crowd. "Rulon Harlowe, the prime regent."

"How could you know that?"

"His wife was named Havanila. Harlowe is your father."

"But —" Roden paused and considered that a moment. "He lost a younger son as an infant. Didn't I hear that?"

"It was you. I'm sorry. I should've told you last night."

"Do you think so?" He cursed and craned his neck to look in the crowd. I knew by the slump in his shoulders when he located Harlowe. Then his tone softened. "Does he know?"

"No. I thought you should tell him."

"I wish I could." We took a few more steps, then he said, "I know you tried to save us, Jaron. I forgive you for failing."

With a coy smile, I glanced over at him. "What failure? Everything is exactly as it should be."

"I disagree," Roden said. "I can think of a thousand ways I'd rather spend my morning."

"Think of ways you'd like to spend your evening, then." With a smile, I added, "I intend to curl up in front of a warm fireplace, with Imogen beside me."

"That sounds nice. But if you're near any fires tonight, it might be that your soul landed in the devils' lair."

I chuckled. "That's more likely than either of us resting with the saints. But if we do, just imagine the trouble we could cause there."

He smiled back. "Good-bye, Jaron."

"No, Roden. Not yet."

At that, the commander pulled Roden onto the platform and directed him to stand on the stool. From my position, I could see the shaking of Roden's hands, so fierce it rattled the chains on his wrists. A man standing at the front of the platform announced that here was the captain of the Carthyan guard, guilty of war against Avenia, Gelyn, and Mendenwal. Roden stood tall as the noose was tightened around his neck. He was heaving deep breaths, as if that might somehow delay the suffocation.

Conner had left my side and turned his back on me to greet other dignitaries seated on the steps of Farthenwood. It allowed me to work at the ropes around my wrists, while the position of his body also blocked others from seeing what I was doing. I wasn't quite sure what I'd do once my hands were untied — I was still unarmed and surrounded by enemies. But it was a start.

Shortly before I was through the knots, Conner turned and grabbed my wrists again. Without calling attention to himself, he wound the loose rope back over my wrists. I couldn't tell whether he knotted anything again, but if he did, any hope I had was lost.

It was my turn now for the noose. Conner escorted me to the platform and told me to get on the stool, which I did. Then he pulled the noose around my neck and tightened it a little, though it would surely pull tighter to kill me. The coarse threads scratched like claws against my skin and I was already feeling the pinch for air.

From here, I could see the audience better. I recognized a few of the thieves amongst the Avenian soldiers. They were nearly expressionless as they stared up at me; it was impossible for me to tell whether they were regretting or celebrating my death. Probably the latter. And oddly, I saw Erick in the audience. Only Erick, none of the pirates. He acknowledged me with a grim smile and a slight nod. I returned the gesture, grateful beyond words that he had come.

"King Vargan will have you speak now," Conner said. "Remind our people of where their loyalties must be."

My eyes shifted from him back to the crowd. When those from Carthya saw me looking, they went to their knees. So did Erick, and a few others I didn't know. I swallowed hard to gain control of my emotions, and then said, "I am commanded by the king of Avenia to give you one last order and so I shall. Hear me now and always. Be loyal to the thing you know is right. Never bend to weakness, never yield to a false crown. Right will always triumph in the end, and you will want to be on that side when it does."

The ending I had intended would've been even better, if Conner had not cut me off by crashing his fist into my gut. A gasp spread through the audience, who went to their feet in my defense. Kippenger shouted to the crowd to ignore my last words or be hanged next. His soldiers left the platform and quieted a few of the more rowdy objectors with the hilt of their blades.

I had recovered from the punch, but my balance was threatened. I might've fallen then, but Conner put his hands on my arms to steady my weight. When he did, I felt something cold run up my sleeve and caught the end of it in my hand.

Conner had given me a knife.

It was small, but felt sharp enough, and I gripped it tightly to keep it hidden. He said nothing more, didn't even look at me as he left the platform.

The announcer on the platform said my name, gave my title as the king of Carthya, and then accused me of the crime of waging war against the kingdoms of Avenia, Mendenwal, and

Gelyn. Ridiculous charges, considering they were standing on my land.

When he finished, he walked off the platform too. King Vargan stood and spoke the simple words, "Do it."

And the two executioners kicked out the stools from beneath us.

# · FORTY-ONE ·

I jumped forward in the instant Vargan gave the order. It only gave me a little traction, but it was enough to keep me suspended in air for a precious second or two. I tore my hands free from the ropes and grabbed the noose to give myself some air. Vargan called out that I had a knife, but when I swung back, I kicked one executioner into the other and both toppled over the edge of the platform. Other soldiers were rushing forward though. I had to be fast.

I used my weight to swing toward Roden, who was quickly losing consciousness. I grabbed on to his rope and with the knife sliced through the cords. Roden fell to the platform, and listlessly rolled over the edge to the ground below. Harlowe and Tobias rushed forward to help him.

With one hand still holding the dangling portion of Roden's rope, I sliced through my own noose with my free hand, then jumped to the ground beside Roden. Harlowe had already loosened Roden's rope and Tobias was feeling for his pulse.

"Keep him alive." For Roden's protection, I pressed the knife into Harlowe's hands. "His life means everything to you."

The soldiers who had been slowed by the crowd were now advancing on me, but I ran the other way, beneath the gallows and back up Farthenwood's steps. I cupped my hands around my mouth and yelled, "Erick, call your men!"

Erick withdrew a horn from his side and blew on it, and the result was so instantaneous from within Farthenwood that the bulk of the pirates must have already left their place in the secret passages to wait for the signal. Back when we were alone in his office, Conner had confirmed that they were there — the many secrets I had crowded within his walls.

I'd never been sure exactly how this would come to be the final battle of the war. But I had always known this was where it must happen, and that it could not succeed without the pirates. I was certain it had been no small job to persuade them to fulfill their oaths. My gratitude to Erick was deeper than he could ever understand.

When Mott and I had visited the pirates, I had asked Erick to come here regardless of whether he was successful in bringing his men. But they were here, and they had clearly found the secret passages, as I had requested, though I couldn't imagine how long they'd had to hide in there, all the while completely silent. I hoped their anger for the endless wait would be exhausted on Vargan's armies.

At the sound of fighting, the bottoms of my wagons of gold collapsed — another use of the false floors designed by Tobias. Out poured one of my lieutenants, along with hundreds of weapons, enough for most of my soldiers who had been compelled to come here unarmed. Dozens more poured from the woods for a fight. It wasn't as many as I would have wanted, but Vargan had been a fool to believe every soldier I had was gathered in the audience. They stampeded from the woods outside Conner's estate, each heavily armed and ready to battle.

That was all wonderful to see, but in the present moment, it wasn't wise of me to stand and watch for long. Several Avenian soldiers chased me up Farthenwood's stairs, including Commander Kippenger, who was spending far more energy than he should have hurling threats my way. Once I reached the top, I leapt over the bronze railing to the ground. My landing on the grass below wasn't particularly graceful, but I thought my clumsiness here could easily be overlooked based on the art of my escape from the noose.

I ran across the back lawn with the Avenians in pursuit, and, due to my youth and lack of weighty armor, was getting a fair lead on them. But I stopped when I saw Mendenwal had rounded the far side of the estate and was coming at me from ahead.

There was nowhere to go but up.

I had not made a successful climb since the night I'd climbed the pirates' Tarblade cliffs, shortly after Roden broke my leg. I'd made many attempts since then, most which nobody else knew about, because it would've embarrassed me and made the castle surgeon furious. Also because they had all ended in failure.

This one could not.

I took hold of the square-cut rocks and reminded myself that while Conner had kept me here at Farthenwood, I'd made this climb several times. I might yet have a chance at winning, and I would *not* fail because of something as simple as a weakened right leg.

So I brushed my hands on my clothes to dry them, and climbed, just out of Kippenger's reach when he leapt for me. He cursed at me and kicked against the wall, then yelled, "If you go much higher, we won't need to hang you. Your fall should easily take care of your own death."

I wanted to retort — so many possibilities came to my mind that it was hard not to. But the climb needed my full attention. As easily as I had scaled these walls before my injury, now my hands seemed to grip smooth glass and my legs felt as if they were made of straw.

My right leg was the worst. It trembled beneath my weight and after one small slide I knew it could not be trusted.

"I'll be waiting here at the bottom when you fall," Kippenger yelled.

I would *not* fall. Never again. Gritting my teeth, I replayed Mott's voice in my mind, telling me that I was the Ascendant King. Meant to rise. And so I would.

From far below, Kippenger screamed at me, "You cannot win, Jaron! Those chains that held you in the dungeon aren't gone. I know you can feel them. All I must do is pull at the chains and you will fall."

By then, I had reached Conner's balcony. I paused just a moment before rolling over the balustrade. My hand dug deep into the pocket of my pants and withdrew a single garlin. I'd had it with me since the first night Kippenger placed it high on my prison walls in that camp. He had meant for it to be a lesson, that there was no point in me trying to win. But I had taken it as a challenge. Getting it had cost every ounce of strength I had, and I fell dozens of times in the attempt before figuring out how to maneuver my chains so that I could reach it. By the next day, Kippenger had forgotten his cruel game. I had not.

Now I held up the coin for him to see. "You were wrong, Commander. Whatever chains you try to place on me, I will always, *always* rise from them. I'm not buying my freedom because you never owned it. But I am taking it back, for me and for my country."

Then I set the coin on the edge of the balustrade and told him to reach for it, if he wished to purchase his own freedom. As I opened the door to Conner's old bedroom, Kippenger yelled at his men to get inside. I was only barely through the door when I heard his men pounding up the stairs.

I stepped forward but my tired legs turned to lead. So I braced my weight against the wall until I was all the way inside. At one time, a tapestry had masked the secret entrance to the passages. But even though the tapestry was missing now, the construction of the secret door remained impressive. If I had not already known where it was, I wouldn't have found it. Kippenger's men wouldn't find it now either.

Once the passage door clicked in place behind me, I took a single step forward and then my leg faltered, sending me to my knees. I wouldn't get another climb out of it today, and probably couldn't rely on it for fighting. Back in Conner's room, I heard the Commander ask, "Where did he go?"

It was time to leave. I got back on my feet and silently limped toward the main floor. Once I reached the bottom of the hidden stairs, I realized I wasn't alone. Imogen greeted me first, with a look that soured from loving to scolding once she noticed my limp and the dried blood from my head wound. There were others with her, and I whispered a promise not to betray them, unless they wished to reveal themselves. Then I left the passages and found myself alone in Conner's office. The door from his great hall was open, but I decided it would draw attention to this room if I shut it. Enough fighting was happening out in the main room; it was better if no one knew I was here.

The papers I'd signed were still laid out across the desk. I picked them up with the intent to burn them, but a creak on the floorboards behind me warned of someone else in the room. I turned around and saw Vargan poised with a dagger held over his head. With my leg in its current state, I couldn't outrun him, and no other weapons were nearby. There weren't many options if he decided to attack, and he clearly would be attacking.

"With my pirates in this battle, you're going to lose," I said. "But there is still time to save yourself. Surrender to me and you will live."

"Never."

Clearly, this man had no talent for negotiating. To be fair, I wasn't particularly good at it either.

"You intended for that thief to bring the message to me." Vargan's voice trembled with rage. "You wanted this to end at Farthenwood."

Of course I did. I knew this place as well as my own castle, and if one of these homes had to be destroyed, it wasn't going to be mine. At the time I arranged for the pirates to come here, there were still a few unresolved details in my mind. But I had known the pirates would be needed.

"It had to end here," I said. "Otherwise the pirates would've stayed hidden in the secret passages until they rotted. They'd have ended up smelling like you, and that would've been a shame."

Vargan cried out and rushed toward me. I started to duck, but he grabbed my shirt and shoved me onto the table, then pinned my legs with his weight.

He raised the dagger again, but was distracted by a loud cry. Conner was running toward us. I never saw him enter the room.

Vargan turned and with the dagger he had intended for me, slashed Conner across his chest. Everything froze in that moment, except for the fine white silks of Conner's vest that turned a horrible color of red. He patted at the blood and then raised his hand to look at it more closely, as if he couldn't quite believe what he was seeing. Once he accepted it, he lowered his hand and tumbled to the floor. By then, I had squirmed free and knelt beside Conner, who took my hand in his. With gasping words, he said, "I always was a patriot, Jaron.

I never lied when I said that you are my king. Forgive me."

He moved to kiss my fingers, but instead drew in a gurgled breath and slumped to the floor, dead.

"He was a traitor to us both," Vargan said.

Maybe he was, but he had also just saved my life. Conner had died much as he lived, in the grayest shadow between right and wrong.

By then, I had put some distance between Vargan's dagger and myself, but now Kippenger and several other soldiers from both Avenia and Mendenwal had heard Conner's cry and entered the office. I rolled my eyes and sighed, more irritated than afraid. Was it too much to hope for someone on my side to enter? Even one burly, angry pirate would've been nice.

I turned back to Vargan. "Why did Mendenwal join you? They've never been our enemy."

Vargan laughed. "When you disappeared four years ago, your father lied to all of us, a political game to keep us away from his borders. I thought it was a rather clever trick, but Mendenwal did not. So when you returned to the throne, it wasn't hard to stir up their anger. I reminded Humfrey of that time you challenged him as a child, how dangerous you could become if we allowed you to keep your crown. Then I promised him half of Carthya as his spoils of victory."

My eyes narrowed. "He can't possibly believe you'll allow that."

Vargan shrugged. "Humfrey is far too trusting. I alone am the emperor of Carthya now. That fool king sitting on

Mendenwal's throne doesn't realize I'm coming for him next."

"Avenia has no power over Mendenwal," a voice boomed. We all turned to the hidden passage door opening behind Conner's desk. The man who emerged was advanced in his years, but his voice betrayed nothing of his age. He was King Humfrey of Mendenwal, and Lord Kerwyn stood at his side.

# · FORTY-TWO ·

I turned to look back at Vargan, who had paled to the shade of new-fallen snow, but in the absence of Humfrey declaring any orders, Vargan said, "I have a treaty here signed by Jaron not one hour ago." He focused on me. "This was a clever trick, hiding the king in these walls. But none of it matters. If you had bothered to read the treaty, you'd know that it gives sole control of Carthya to Avenia. Mendenwal gets nothing. Jaron signed away everything to me."

I smiled back at him. "You require spectacles for reading, but don't want people to see you using them. Some might consider that vanity. I consider it foolish. *You* should have read my signature."

Vargan grabbed the treaty and squinted to read it. While he worked at it, I sat on the desk, crushing a corner of the papers beneath me and said, "I wouldn't sign so much as my toenail clippings over to you."

Kippenger pushed his way forward and scanned the treaty. "What did he write?" Vargan asked.

Kippenger suppressed a grin — I could've sworn he did. Without looking at anyone, he said, "Jaron wrote, 'You'll get nothing from me, ever, you dog-breath, rotted corpse of a king.'"

Vargan glowered at me. In return, I smiled and looked around the room, rather proud of myself for that.

King Humfrey addressed his soldiers in the room. "Send out word that Mendenwal has reunited with our longtime friends in the kingdom of Carthya. Any Avenian who continues to fight will now face Mendenwal's blades." Then he turned to Vargan. "Unless you wish to surrender."

"Never!"

"Your Majesty, it's over," Kippenger said. "Let's make our peace and save what lives we can."

Vargan shook his head. "I will lose every last man in my army if it means Jaron falls. Kill him!" Kippenger locked eyes with me but neither of us moved. He only studied me with a newfound respect.

Vargan noticed the exchange. With a snarl, he muttered, "I'll do it myself, then!"

He raised his dagger again and advanced on me, but Kippenger moved faster. His sword pierced the king from behind. Vargan fell to his knees, turned up his head with a face etched in pain, and then crumpled to the ground, dead by his own commander's hand.

It had happened so fast, none of us who remained in the room were sure of what to do next. Humfrey was looking at me, but my attention was locked on the commander.

Kippenger stared at his fallen king and slowly nodded his head, as if convincing himself that he had done the right thing. Then he knelt before me and placed his sword at my feet. "Avenia surrenders. Enough blood has been spilled."

"On all sides," I agreed. "So who rules Avenia now?"

Kippenger shrugged. "I do, I suppose."

"That won't work. You hate me."

"Less than I used to."

That was good enough. And I felt even better about him when he reached into his pocket and withdrew my father's ring — the king's ring — and held it out to me. He said, "I had thought by taking this that I would remove any traces of your nobility. But I could not take the royalty in your heart."

I couldn't help but grin. "For the record, I'm very glad you didn't try to take my heart." I took the ring from him and replaced it on my finger, grateful for the return of the now-familiar weight.

Then I looked back to Commander Kippenger — though, I supposed he was king now. "Your men will leave their weapons here. But I will allow you to collect your wounded men, and Tobias will provide you with any help we can offer in their care. Other than that, I want you and your soldiers out of my country immediately. Do not return again *ever* to make war against us."

Kippenger stood again, but his sword remained on the floor. "Yes, King Jaron. I'll see to it at once."

I tilted my head to excuse him, and he left the room. Next, the remaining soldiers deposited their swords at my feet, then heeded Kerwyn's order to remove Vargan's and Conner's bodies from the room.

Once they were gone, King Humfrey walked forward. "Lord Kerwyn convinced me to come here on the promise that I would have to see what became of the incorrigible boy who once challenged me to a duel. I believe that you are every bit as difficult now as you were then."

"You're wrong," I said. "I'm far worse now than I ever was."

He chuckled, and then with more seriousness said, "I was wrong about you. Forgive me."

Forgiveness would come in time. For now, it was enough to hear Humfrey's men in the great hall, shouting Mendenwal's new orders. Swords clanged to the floor and the grunts and cries of men at war were very quickly turning to silence, to peace.

I said to Kerwyn, "I'll return soon, but please watch over the retreat and help our wounded."

Kerwyn started to ask me where I was going, but as I opened the door to the passages, he only smiled and said, "Your lady is inside these walls, waiting for you."

# · FORTY·THREE ·

Imogen and I were married a little over a year later, in the great hall of my castle, as I had promised her. She wore my mother's wedding gown, carefully saved away all these years, and a wreath of miniature roses in her hair. The hall was filled to its capacity, and the courtyard outside was just as thickly packed, awaiting our first appearance as king and queen, husband and wife.

Tobias and Amarinda had married several months earlier and were happier than ever. They lived well here in the castle, and my friendship with them both had only strengthened since the war's end. He had become apprenticed to the castle physician, a profession that ensured he would continue finding ways to frustrate me, at least as often as I found ways to injure myself.

I would always be grateful to them for saving Mott's life. He moved slower than he used to, and I knew the wound he'd suffered still gave him pain. Although he would never fight again, I hoped to lead a kingdom where it would never again be necessary. He spent our entire first conversation after his recovery lecturing me for my usual failings of recklessness, but ended it by promising to serve me with even greater loyalty. I wasn't sure that was possible.

Fink held the ring for Imogen and gave it to me when the priest called for it. He winked at me, hoping for congratulations that he had managed not to lose it. That actually was a significant accomplishment and I gave him a wink back. Fink had become a younger brother to me. Every bit as annoying. Every bit as valuable.

Roden and Harlowe had spent most of the past year learning to know each other as father and son. Roden had been the one to tell him of their connection, though he'd waited several days after the war's end to find the right moment. I'd had little to do with their reunion, but Harlowe's gratitude to me was as warm as the day I'd saved Nila's life. Roden spent the bulk of his free time with his father, immersed in the education he should have had throughout his life. But he remained the captain of my guard and was growing continually more confident in his role. Under his command, Carthya would eventually rebuild an army strong enough to always keep us free.

My fears that Harlowe might abandon his attentions to me had turned out to be unfounded. Over the past several months I have come to understand that love can only expand and allow any number into its circle. Harlowe might have come to love me as a son, and yet I felt I had come to an understanding with my own father too. For the first time in my life, I was settled in my ways of thinking about him.

Immediately after the battle's end at Farthenwood, I had relinquished my title as king of the pirates and given the rule entirely to Erick. As far as I knew, he continued to lead them. Even still, their brand remained on my forearm, and a part of me would always belong to them. If ever they called for me in a time of need, I was bound by oath to answer.

It had been a difficult year in rebuilding Carthya. We had lost far too many men, and full recovery was at least a generation away. But each day was better, and nothing remained to threaten us.

Certainly not Avenia. Commander Kippenger had taken the throne and presided over a much diminished country. I had urged him to build schools, not weapons, and so far he seemed to have taken my advice. After tough negotiations, Gelyn and Carthya gradually reopened trading routes, though I kept a standing army on our northern border now. And the relationship was warming with Mendenwal. In fact, anticipating an eventual child for Imogen and me, King Humfrey had offered a treaty of betrothal with one of his grandchildren. Although his intentions were well meant, we kindly rejected his offer.

And on the night of my wedding, I held Imogen close in my arms with no thought of ever releasing her. Better still was that Imogen held me too. She was my family, my life, and the center of my world.

All that I knew was at peace.

# · ACKNOWLEDGMENTS ·

*With every released book of this series, my appreciation to others spreads wider and flows deeper. The Scholastic family has shown unwavering support and expertise in the various ways in which they have influenced this book. Thank you a thousand times over. Once each book has released into the world, I cannot adequately express my thanks to the bookstore geniuses, teachers, and librarians who have put a copy in a young person's hands, to bloggers who have spread the word, and to readers and fans from all over the world who have continued to read and share your enthusiasm with me and with others. You do make a difference, and if it were possible, I would thank you each by name.*

*There are a few who must be specifically listed here. First of all, my husband, Jeff, who is and always will be the love of my life. Without him, and the support of my* three children, I would not be where I am today. Thanks as well to my fabulous agent, Ammi-Joan Paquette, infinitely amazing, and among the best in this business. And final thanks to my editor, Lisa Sandell. Working with you is proof that the stars do align and still remain in their place today. As we turn the pages for the next chapter, I would want nobody else at my side, as editor, willing accomplice, and friend.

Toni Morrison said, "If there's a book you want to read, but it hasn't been written yet, then you must write it." And so I did. Thank you all for reading.

# · ABOUT THE AUTHOR ·

JENNIFER A. NIELSEN is the author of the *New York Times* best-selling *The False Prince* and *The Runaway King*, the first two books in The Ascendance Trilogy. She collects old books, loves good theater, and thinks that a quiet afternoon in the mountains is a nearly perfect moment.

A major influence in Jaron's story came from the music of Eddie Vedder and one of his greatest songs, "Guaranteed." From his line "I knew all the rules, but the rules did not know me," Jaron was born. Jaron's personality is his own, but Jennifer did borrow two of his traits from a couple of students she once taught in a high school debate class. One of them was popular, brilliant, and relentlessly mischievous. He could steal the watch off a person's wrist without their knowing and would return it to them later, usually to their embarrassment. The other student had a broad spectrum of impressive talents, not the least of which was his ability to roll a coin over his knuckles. If he had wanted to, he'd have made a fine pickpocket. As it was, he went on to become a lawyer. Go figure.

Jennifer lives in northern Utah with her husband, their three children, and a perpetually muddy dog.